MW01592837

CYNTHIA

CYNTHIA

Marilyn Bird

Northwest Publishing Inc.
Salt Lake City, Utah

Cynthia

All rights reserved.
Copyright © 1994 Marilyn Bird

Reproductions in any manner, in whole or in part,
in English or in other languages, or otherwise
without written permission of the publisher is prohibited.

For information address: Northwest Publishing, Inc.
6906 South 300 West, Salt Lake City, Utah 84047
JAC 5.19.94

First Printing 1994

ISBN: 1-880416-42-5

NPI books are published by Northwest Publishing, Incorporated,
6906 South 300 West, Salt Lake City, Utah 84047.
The name "NPI" and the "NPI" logo are trademarks belonging to
Northwest Publishing, Incorporated.

PRINTED IN THE UNITED STATES OF AMERICA.
10 9 8 7 6 5 4 3 2 1

To my wonderful husband Fred and our lovely daughters Nancy and Barbara.

To Iris Pavlik for making this book possible and to Ron Otto for his faith in me.

Finally, to my brilliant sister, Janet Kozlay, for her great job in editing this book.

Illustrations
starting on page 127:

Johnny Hale
Turk Prujansky
Rex Anderson
Rex Anderson
Bernie Sakosiac
Bill Neery

Chapter 1

On the night of April 14, 1912, the great ship Titanic lost her battle with the sea and slipped beneath the waves. At that same moment, Cynthia Ryan was slipping into the world from the body of her seventeen-year-old mother. It had been a difficult birth, and the doctor had been forced to use only recently invented instruments. He gave the baby the usual slap on the backside.

When he heard no cry from the infant, he tried putting ether on her chest. This also failed, and he carried the baby to the kitchen where the grandmother waited. He placed the baby on the kitchen table and regretfully said, "The baby is dead; I'll try to save the mother, but she's hemorrhaging badly."

The doctor hurriedly left the room, and the grandmother, without hesitation, picked the baby up and breathed into her mouth, slapping her repeatedly on the buttocks. She persisted even though there was no response, and at last the baby let out a loud cry of protest against the injustice of this treatment.

Perhaps this was her proclamation to the world, a portentous announcement that she would always be a survivor.

It certainly is evident in the pattern that her life took. She would face a childhood with relatives fighting over her as her parents' marriage disintegrated.

She would grow up and marry a man with bizarre sexual demands. She would have her second marriage broken up by Martha Raye—The Big Mouth.

She would subsequently marry three more times, with each marriage a disaster, ending in divorce.

She would have the excitement of knowing the famous and the infamous. She would meet Mickey Rooney, Roy Rogers, Ava Gardner, Warren Avis, Shelley Winters, Bugsy Siegel, the Purple Gang, and, of course, The Big Mouth.

She would learn about the grisly disposal of a body and would keep this secret for over twenty years.

She would comfort Clark Gable when his lovely wife's plane crashed behind Cynthia's home in Las Vegas.

She would become an informant for the F.B.I.

She would start businesses that would become very successful, but she would end up, at the age of 79, ill, with little money, living in a trailer park with her cats in an obscure town in Northern Michigan that has little to offer beyond providing an entrance and exit from the I-75 expressway.

Chapter 2

You will want to know something of Cynthia's background. Later in the story, you will understand her better if you know about her heritage.

The grandmother who brought her to life proudly asked whether the baby could be named after her. The grandmother's name was Sinthia, an old-time spelling. Considering her heroic efforts, it would seem appropriate to give this name to the baby, and the mother agreed. However, when the little girl became school-age, the teachers ridiculed the spelling and changed it.[1]

The baby Cynthia's mother did live. The baby's father, Norman, was a constable with the state police and was away

---

[1]To avoid confusion I have spelled it in the modern way from the beginning of this book.

from home as usual when Cynthia was born. His job required him to travel much of the time, and his young wife, Eunice, deeply resented this.

He was only seventeen at the time of his marriage, and his wife a mere fifteen. He installed her in the home of his parents and stuck by his job, despite her protests, knowing that jobs were hard to come by.

Norman's and Eunice's parents were close friends, and the two children, neither having any brothers or sisters, naturally played together as they were growing up. When Eunice's stepfather, a Civil War veteran, decided to move to Arkansas, the youngsters were terribly upset over the pending separation. Eunice's mother suggested that she leave Eunice with her friend Sinthia, Norman's mother, "until we get settled."

Sinthia, though willing to take the girl, said, "I won't have two of their age staying under my roof that aren't married."

So, rather than part with each other, Eunice and Norman did indeed get married.

Times were hard, and Norman was very young. He had few choices for employment in Northern Michigan. Of course there were the sawmills located all along the Saginaw River. There was also commercial fishing. But Norman had heard of the State Constabulary, and this caught his imagination. It seemed to fit in with his life, for he had been raised with horses.

His father and grandfather were horse breeders.

Norman's great-grandfather had come over from Ulster, Ireland, where he had fought under the flag of King William. Racehorse trotters were a part of his blood, and when he came to the new country in 1735 he brought some of his finest stock with him. He crossed over, landing in New York and making his way from there, via Canada, to settle in the new village of Tawas City, Michigan.

He continued to breed horses, and his son Lynus, Norman's father, followed in his footsteps. When the old man could not manage anymore, Lynus took over the work, assisted by his younger brother, Bill. His job was to take a stallion around the country to breed mares. He was also the racehorse driver, taking their horses as far as Syracuse, New York. It was a tough life, but the one they wholeheartedly chose.

The Ulster men and women were a committed lot. They had broken with their church at the time of the Reformation and had become determinedly Protestant. Stubborn and clannish, they set out on a course and stuck to it. They revered their forefathers and lived rigidly within the guidelines handed down to them. Compromise was unthinkable.

The baby Cynthia was reared in this tradition, and was taught early about her ancestors and what her family expected from her. She was not to lie, nor to steal, nor to do anything that would bring shame to their proud old name.

The old man Ryan lived to be 107, loving women and horses until the end. Cynthia's father, who would be the last Ryan of his line, faithfully followed in the footsteps of his grandfather. He, too, lived for women and horses until his death at 86.

When he died he would be buried in his great-grandfather's Orangeman's vest. The flag of King William of Orange and the sword that his great-grandfather had carried to battle were placed beside him in the coffin. The coffin, however, was draped with the Stars and Stripes because he had served proudly in the United States Army during World War I and the subsequent Russian occupation. But this is all ahead of this story.

Chapter 3

Eunice was very unhappy that, again, Norman was not with her for the birth of their second daughter. He had been away when their first daughter, Gladys, was born. It was bad enough when he was a constable, but now that he was in the service she saw even less of him.

When Cynthia was six months old, Eunice left her with her own mother and went to Detroit to visit her husband's Aunt Mary. She missed Norman terribly and the resentment was growing over his continued absence.

Cynthia's older sister, Gladys, would be cared for by her other grandmother, Sinthia.

Eunice eventually borrowed some money and started a restaurant in Detroit. Her anger at her husband had reached such proportions that she used her maiden name, calling it Sullivan's Restaurant.

Norman returned from the Mexican border campaign, where he had fought Pancho Villa under Black Jack Pershing, then promptly signed back up again in Lorain, Ohio. This was a terrible blow to Eunice and a turning point in the marriage.

When Cynthia was almost four, her mother brought her to Detroit to live with her. Cynthia knew her parents slightly because of their visits, but she had always lived with her grandparents and cried bitter tears when she had to leave them.

When her parents were having their frequent fights, she remembered her father sneaking her out in a car to take her to his own mother. Then she would again be snatched up and taken back to Eunice's mother.

Cynthia's stability was further shaken by the fact that her mother rented rooms over the restaurant, so there was no place to play. For a little girl who was used to doting grandparents and a yard to play in, it was tremendously confining, and in reflection she now describes it as "sheer hell."

For a youngster now barely four, she showed surprising determination in trying to alter her circumstances. She reasoned that if she were nasty enough, her mother would eventually return her to her grandmother.

She started to hate her mother, but Eunice was busy and never really noticed. Eunice's mother had introduced her to a couple of her boyfriends who had hopes of marriage. Little Cynthia would pinch them on their swollen war vaccinations, which angered them, and they would swear at her. Eunice would defend her daughter and reject the suitor, stating that she would never consider marrying someone who didn't treat her daughter with kindness.

What joy, then, to find that her father was coming for a two-day visit. Her mother warned her against talking about her boyfriends and carefully hid their pictures.

Norman was a very warm and demonstrative man. He hugged, kissed, and teased his little girl, and although she loved him very much, she never gave her mother's romances away, despite his questions.

Gradually she began to find something she could admire

in her mother. She loved her beauty, not knowing she would eventually become just as lovely. She learned to adore her mother's blue eyes and the golden blonde hair that reached her hips.

Eunice would use an oil lamp to heat the curling iron, then roll up her hair and produce beautiful waves her daughter would envy. Cynthia thought she looked just like the fairy godmother in her Mother Goose book.

When her father came he arrived on a horse, and he lifted her up beside him in the saddle to have their picture taken.

He asked her, "Will you, my Irish daughter, love horses as your dad does?"

She was so badly frightened, high in air on the back of the horse, that she peed all over his saddle. Her father kindly chose to ignore this.

Norman talked continually about the Kaiser, for the country by now was at war with Germany. This talk infuriated Eunice. She did not want him to go to war, but she also did not want Cynthia to overhear their quarrels. She would send her off to the movies.

Cynthia was sent by herself and would sit in the opera seats, but she was reminded of the situation at home, because they would show films about the war.

One night she did overhear them.

He said, "Precious, try not to make a scene, but I have been called back to service."

Eunice turned on him. "You're doing this on purpose. You're going so you won't have to be bothered by the girls and me. You're a man who wants a family but doesn't want the responsibility of one. It is the world you are out to see, but I warn you, I will not wait for you this time. If you go to war, then I will divorce you!"

He pleaded, "Precious, you and the girls mean the whole world to me."

Eunice snapped back, "If we mean so much to you, then you'll get out of the service. With your father dead, you leave a widowed mother, and a wife and two children. Certainly that is reason enough. You could go into a factory that makes war goods and still help your country."

He was horrified. "You'd have me lose my manhood, be a slacker? No, not even for my mother; not even for you and the girls. I am a man and I will serve my country as all the men in my family have done."

The argument ended there, and they all went out to the movies. As they emerged from the theater later, Norman was stopped by an Army officer who wished to talk to him. The sight of the uniform set Eunice off, and she grabbed Cynthia by the arm, running and dragging the child behind her.

Cynthia not only had overheard their argument but now was witness to her mother's rejection of her father.

She started to cry and shouted at her mother, "I hate you. I'll never see my father again!"

Eunice said cynically, "Don't worry, he'll be back."

Cynthia had seen and heard far too much to accept her mother's words. She loved her father so much. He was the only person in her life, other than Aunt Mary, who showed her tenderness and kindness. Her life had started to look up, and now she really wondered whether she would ever see him again. The old animosity toward her mother returned.

When her father did indeed come back, Cynthia, in her grief and anger, had reverted to the mean and nasty child continually at odds with her mother. For punishment, Eunice locked her in an empty room above the restaurant.

There was a rug on the floor, and I sat on it by the window. My only view was dull, showing only roof tops. I discovered that under the rug there had been placed newspapers, to act as padding. Seeing a small kerosene burner in the room, I decided I would open the burner and light the papers. I would set the restaurant on fire and burn it down!

I thought when they saw the fire burning through the ceiling of the restaurant, they would have to let me out. I started the fire and watched it grow. Smoke swiftly filled the room. It was hot, and no one came. My anger quickly turned

to fear when my eyes began to smart and I started to choke. I
wanted to call out, but by now I was gasping for air and unable
to make a sound. I was terrified.

Smoke was noticed coming out from under the door by
one of the roomers, who raced down to tell Cynthia's mother.
Her father had just come in, and Eunice screamed, "My God,
Norm, Cynthia's in that room!" She was so frightened, she
was unable to remember where she had placed the key!
Norman tore up the stairs and repeatedly threw himself
against the door until he had shattered it. He grabbed Cynthia
and carried her under his arm down the stairs. Taking in the
situation and blaming her, he accompanied every step down
with a resounding slap on her buttocks. It was the first
spanking she had ever gotten, and it was forceful enough to
effectively redden her behind. He finally let her go, and she
crept guiltily to the kitchen while the fire was being extin-
guished. Cynthia was with her Aunt Mary when her father
returned and went into the restaurant.

The place was crowded after the excitement, and, as the
fire had not harmed the restaurant, they had done a good
business, selling out all the pie and coffee.

Cynthia's father strode over to the cash register, where her
mother stood looking lovely and oddly composed, considering the circumstances. Before she could take in his intent, he
grabbed her by the waist. His face was red with anger, and he
shouted at her with a voice that shook. "It should have been
you that I spanked instead of Cynthia. To have locked that
child in that room alone. Well, here is when you get yours!"
He had spun her around, and he now sat in a chair and threw
her across his lap. Cynthia and Aunt Mary could hear all of this
in the kitchen, and, even though they were aware of his total
anger, they were surprised to hear the sound of hard spanking
and his voice loudly shouting, "Maybe this will teach you to
grow up." If Eunice cried, they didn't hear it for all the noise
he was making.

When he finished, he got up, dropping her to the floor. He

turned to the people in the dining room and said, "If there's a man here that wants to take me on, come outside." With that, he walked out the front door.

Eunice ran to the kitchen in a fit of temper, swearing she would have him arrested. Aunt Mary said, "Eunice, Norman was upset about you locking Cynthia in that room. This whole thing has frightened him. If someone hadn't noticed that smoke, she probably would have been burned to death."

Eunice hung her head and said, "Mary, the dinner hour is coming up, and I can't go back in the dining room and face all those people."

"Well," said Aunt Mary, "you'd better, because you know that you're needed. Who knows; maybe the men who saw this might change their ways. Maybe Norman has changed their style. Instead of wife-beating, they might consider a good spanking instead."

Eunice replied evenly, "I'm not his wife."

Aunt Mary raised her eyebrows and said, "Oh, I wasn't aware that you'd gotten a divorce."

Eunice's voice was stiff with her anger and humiliation. "Not yet, but I intend to." She then left for her duties in the dining room, leaving behind a little girl with a new piece of information to brood about.

Cynthia stood in the kitchen that she hated. She despised the army of rats which appeared and disappeared from the room. They would come out of holes under the stove and scramble up the pipes against the wall. She was depressed over the new altercation between her parents. She feared that her father was gone, this time never to come back.

Cynthia usually overturned a pail to sit on, but when she tried it she found that her bottom burned too much. Pails of peeled potatoes were placed on top of the big iceboxes. She used a lard can as a step to get on the table in order to reach the icebox. She managed to remove a pail of potatoes and lower it down. The water was very cold. She decided to sit in the bucket of potatoes and water. So, dress and all, she effectively cooled her bottom.

Cynthia sat as usual, watching Aunt Mary cook. There was little else to do, with no back yard and no playmates. She was a lonely girl, and now her ever-present feelings of insecurity were greatly intensified by this latest trouble. She sat watching the rats. They didn't seem to bother Aunt Mary, but Cynthia would watch them carefully, fearing that one would approach her. Her only consolation was Aunt Mary, who was always kind to her. Mary would talk to her as she cooked up the orders. She would tell her stories and try to amuse her. Sometimes, though, when she was terribly busy, she would have to beg the little girl to keep quiet so she could concentrate. Then Cynthia would keep quiet and long for a doll.

Later that night, after Eunice had closed the restaurant, she came to her daughter's bedroom. Cynthia silently hoped her mother's bottom hurt as much as her own did. Her mother looked down at her in despair. "What am I going to do with you?" Receiving no answer, she went out. Her mother had never slapped her, but then she had never kissed her, or hugged her, or shown any affection, either. Cynthia knew that if her mother were more like her father, she would try to act better. Her mother seemed unlikely to change, and she missed her grandmother very much. She felt so lonely. The only warmth she ever felt from her mother was when Eunice would occasionally let her come to bed with her. But this never lasted long, because her mother would complain that Cynthia kicked so much, she couldn't get any sleep.

Cynthia went over the events of the day again, particularly thinking of her mother's wrath. Feeling miserable, she got up and opened the door to her mother's bedroom. To her surprise, she saw her parents in bed, kissing. They stopped when Cynthia entered the room. Her father said, "Go back to your room. Father loves you and isn't mad at you any longer." She approached the bed and tried to get in. Her father decided to make fun of her. He pulled the blanket down from his wife, exposing her ample bosom. Taking a large breast in his hand, he pointed it at his daughter and said, "Does Cynthia want her mother's titty?" Cynthia ran from the room. She was being treated like a baby. She retreated back into her lonely bed, feeling rejected and not knowing quite what to make of her parents' behavior.

The next day Norman made a great effort to smooth over the troubled waters. He took Cynthia to the candy store and bought her candy and fruit. He helped his wife in the dining room and set dozens of rat traps in the kitchen. He and Eunice seemed to be reconciled when he left for camp. This, however, was not to last, for when he returned he told Eunice he was being shipped out. Eunice was livid. "You have dependents," she yelled. "You could get out of it."

He said, "It's too late. We embark from New York in four days and are on our way to France."

Cynthia had never seen her mother so angry. She went over to her husband and slapped him across the face, shouting, "I'll never wait for you again! I'll divorce you. Don't think if you come back it will be to me, because it won't work. You're nothing but a selfish bastard!" Cynthia ran out the door in tears.

Cynthia always had a little pocket money, because her mother let her keep it when she sold cigars and candy behind the counter of the restaurant. She got her little red purse and headed for the candy store next door. Her father was going away, and she wanted to buy him a present. She picked out a post card with silk embroidery on it. It showed a soldier with a little girl waving good-bye to him with a handkerchief. She also bought him an orange, an apple, and some suckers. She took them back to the apartment and found her father in his rocking chair. Cynthia sat up on his lap, and he rocked with her. Then she gave him his presents. She looked up to see whether he was pleased and found that he was crying. He leaned down and kissed his thanks to her, and said, "Baby, your dad's going overseas to fight for our flag. Now, you mind your mother and be a good girl until Father gets back home. Do that for me, promise?" He took her from his lap and got up. He kissed her good-bye and turned to take his wife in his arms. She backed away and spat out, "I hope that the first bullet gets you."

"Well, Precious," he said, "if it does, then you'll get a nice check from Uncle Sam." With that, he left.

It wasn't until Cynthia had gained some years and experience that she would realize her mother had desperately loved her father, and that her cruelty had stemmed from her overwhelming frustration in failing to keep him home.

Chapter 4

With Cynthia's father gone, life went back to the usual routine. Each evening, her mother would send her to the movies at six, while she worked in the dining room. The show would be over at nine, when the restaurant closed.

One night she sat in her usual side opera seat, and after the show she found they were having an amateur contest. Cynthia watched while they showed the prizes. They held up a Johnny Doughboy doll that looked just like her father in his uniform. It was as tall as she was, and she knew she just had to have it.

She saw a line of people waiting to go on stage and she joined them. The master of ceremonies was interviewing each contestant, one by one. Suddenly he spotted this tiny girl at the end of the line. Knowing the special appeal of small children, he stopped and went over to her, took her little hand, and brought her to center stage.

He asked her name, then asked the audience whether she belonged to anyone there. Not receiving a response, he said, "Little one, where is your mother?"

She replied, "She's in Sullivan's Restaurant, working."

He looked up and announced that since she was the smallest, he would let her go first, if the rest of the contestants thought it was all right.

Those in line had been laughing at this gutsy little personage and readily agreed. He smiled down on her and asked, "Do you sing?"

She said, "No."

He said, "Do you dance?"

She said, "No."

"Well," he said, "What do you do?" Not receiving an answer he asked, "Do you need any music?"

She said, "No."

By now the audience was completely captivated. The emcee decided the time was right for him to end the interview. Stepping aside, he said, "Well, little lady you just go ahead and do whatever you intend to do." Cynthia moved forward and with a loud and clear voice recited:

> Kaiser Bill went up the hill
> To take a peek at France.
> Kaiser Bill came down the hill
> With bullets in his pants.

Pandemonium broke out. The war was at its height, and feelings were intense. The crowd pounded and stamped its feet, and the sound of whistles and clapping resounded through the theater. It was Cynthia's first experience with applause, and she became terribly frightened. She thought she had done something wrong.

Cynthia ran off the stage and out the door. When she got home, she rushed to her room, jumped into bed, and covered her head with her blanket.

She was not aware that Aunt Mary had also gone to the show that night, arriving just as Cynthia was reciting.

When the contest was over, the emcee asked whether there was anyone there who knew the little girl.

Aunt Mary held up her hand and said, "She is my niece."

The emcee announced that Cynthia had won the doll, and an usher brought it down to Mary.

The next day Mary said to Eunice, "Do you know what Cynthia did last night?"

Eunice looked worried and said, "No, Mary, I never know what that minx will do from one minute to the next."

Mary handed her the box, and Eunice opened it and said, "Oh, Mary, she will love you for this."

Mary said, "I didn't buy it, Cynthia won it." She then proceeded to tell Eunice about the contest.

Eunice for some reason was not happy about the story. She seemed to feel that this was part of her daughter's unruly behavior.

Cynthia was now of school age but was often truant. She would be gone all day, then would show up at the time schoolchildren normally came home. Going to school frightened her; the traffic and busy streets were too much for a little girl raised in the country. The school finally wrote to Eunice, asking why her daughter was not attending school.

Eunice was extremely upset and confronted Cynthia about her truancy. She demanded to know what Cynthia did all day when she was not in school, and Cynthia admitted that she sat on the church steps until it was time to go home. Her mother scolded and threatened her with punishment, but Cynthia's wayward behavior continued unabated.

Her mother, in an effort to get rid of the rats, would call in the young and good-looking milkman to take the rodents from the traps and reset them. To safeguard herself from curious customers who might see the problem, she locked the kitchen door.

One day, Cynthia, unable to get in, went for help to the Sicilians who owned the candy store. She told them her mother was inside with the milkman and had locked her out.

They pounded on the walls but got no response, so they

concluded that Eunice was romantically involved with the man.

This juicy gossip soon spread through the neighborhood. When Eunice became aware that she was considered "loose," she decided she had lost all control of her daughter, and something had to be done.

She just could not let things continue the way they were. Cynthia needed discipline and someone who had the time to teach her.

She decided to send Cynthia to her own mother, who now lived in Bay City. Eunice had the restaurant to run; that was quite enough for any woman.

Chapter 5

So once again Cynthia was moved to a new home, at 309 Webster Street, in Bay City.[1]

It took very little time for Grandmother Sullivan to find that her work was cut out for her, but she was made of a durable fabric and was used to facing tough situations.

Melissa Sullivan came from another proud family. Her grandfather was the Reverend John Fisher, D.D., who had risen to the office of Bishop of Salisbury. His grandson, Michael Hylan, would become mayor of New York. John's daughter Susan, a first cousin to Queen Victoria, attended the queen's elaborate coronation. There she met Dwight Farnsworth, with whom she instantly fell in love.

Dwight belonged to a wealthy Catholic family which was

---

[1] The house still stands, the second-oldest in Bay City.

appalled over the union. Determined to marry anyway, the couple wed in a Protestant ceremony. Even this did not satisfy Susan's family, and the Fishers refused to accept their son-in-law. The pressures from their families proved too great, and the couple, full of sorrow, sailed to Canada, where they hoped to make a new start far away from their disapproving parents.

Some time after their arrival, a daughter was born, whom they named Melissa. Life in Canada was hard, and Dwight was finding it difficult to provide for his little family. Dwight and Susan talked frequently of their plight and thought that their fortunes might improve if they could go to the United States. They had little money, however, and could not afford the necessary legal fees. Finally, in desperation, when Melissa was four, they packed up as many of their meager belongings as they could carry and headed for Sarnia, a Canadian city on the bank of the St. Clair River. There, they walked to the water's edge and waded in. When the water became too deep, they started to swim, taking turns holding Melissa above the waves. They struggled with the river's current and gasped with the cold, but succeeded in reaching the town of Port Huron in Michigan. They were overjoyed to have reached the shore without being detected by the immigration authorities.

The threesome began their new lives in the town of Port Sanilac. Indeed, for a time it seemed that life held great promise for them. Dwight found work, and after some years they were able to buy a small farm. Their daughter was followed by other children, and they were happy with their life in this community.

Then came the great Sanilac fire.

In an instant, it seemed, the great, peaceful forest around them turned into a raging, voracious killer. When the couple's neighbor John Sullivan emerged from the forest into their yard, followed by a large number of families, he came upon a scene of fear and confusion. Dwight was trying to rescue what he could from the farm, and Susan was trying to figure out how to get the younger children down into the well. John snatched up two of the children, shouted to the Farnsworths to bring all the blankets they could find, and led everyone down into a nearby creek. There, he had them soak the blankets in the water and cover themselves.

They sat in the creek, shaking and sobbing, while the fire raged around them. Bending low over the water, they huddled under the wet blankets to escape the worst of the choking smoke. They were terrified by the roaring of the fire and the falling trees, but John's efforts were successful, and they all survived.

The fire lasted three days, burning thousands of acres of land and trees along with the area's homes and farm buildings. For the first time in Michigan's history, the Red Cross brought in disaster aid. It was a terribly cruel time for the little community. But the Farnsworths never forgot their generous neighbor who looked out for them and saved their very lives.

John Sullivan worked in the woods for a living. In his younger days he had been a logger, but an accident had claimed one of his legs to the knee, and he had turned to running a mule train, delivering supplies to the area. His wooden leg was almost entirely destroyed in the fire, and someone took a tintype picture showing him with his charred appendage. Copies were sold to the curious, and proceeds went to help local people get back on their feet.

Melissa, now an exceptionally beautiful young woman with striking auburn hair, took a fresh look at her neighbor and promptly set her cap for him. His size and strength, as well as his extraordinary heroism during the fire, made him an exceptional catch, regardless of his wooden leg. For his part, John found Melissa's beauty and unaffected charm irresistible. Their wedding was attended by throngs of well-wishers who had also survived the fire, with John's aid.

John built Melissa a large, Gothic-style house near the town of Lupton. (Unfortunately, this lovely structure burned down some years ago, taking with it the lives of two young boys.) The couple turned to farming, and found peace and harmony in their lives. Not that life was easy. Melissa worked right along with the hired help, and thought nothing of shooting an occasional bear and tanning its skin. She also made the acquaintance of local Indians, from whom she learned the healing properties of various plants. Melissa used this information to help her friends and neighbors.

It was to this strong woman that Cynthia was sent to be cured of her wild ways.

Grandmother Sullivan took her new job seriously. She recognized the problems and, in her forthright way, commenced the task of taking this rebellious child and rehabilitating her.

Many of Cynthia's problems Melissa blamed on the child's heritage. "If I knew the amount of Irish drops of blood that are in your veins, I would take a needle to you and pick them all out," she told her. "I know that you cannot help it that you are, unfortunately, mostly Irish; however, I'll do what I can to kill the wildness of it." Cynthia, of course, was terri-fied—and more than a little resentful of her grandmother's aspersions on her beloved father and her proud Irish ancestry. But resentful or not, Cynthia had little choice but to try to make the best of what at first promised to be a bad situation.

Melissa's plan was to structure Cynthia's life in such a way that she would have no opportunity to give vent to her wild ways. At least, that was what Melissa hoped.

Try as she would to make the best of her new life, Cynthia came to hate her grandmother's ways. Melissa dressed her in old-fashioned clothes which she made herself—long, baggy dresses trimmed in rickrack. Instead of pretty white anklets like the other girls wore, Cynthia was made to wear long black stockings and shoes. Once, her father sent her a pretty dress and new stockings, but her grandmother took the sleeves from her husband's old, red long johns and joined them to the tops of her knee hose to make long stockings. Cynthia's school-mates made fun of her clothes, and even the dogs chased her. Cynthia dreaded going to school. Teasing turned to ridicule and then to physical attacks from her classmates. At least the heavy coats that her grandmother made her sometimes saved Cynthia from bruises. She responded in the only way she knew how—with teeth and nails. So, rather than making Cynthia a subdued little girl, Melissa's tactics were turning her into a tough little tiger. The school-children now began to taunt her with an aberration of her name. Cynthia was shortened to Sin, and Ryan became rind. They would chant in unison, "Sin Sin pork rind." Or sometimes it would be, "Sin Sin pig rind," but that made little difference. She hated these kids and would fight them, but still the name stuck. Gradually she got used to being called Sin and even grew to like it, but for now it was a torment.

Cynthia's only comfort was her Johnny Doughboy doll, which she had been permitted to bring with her. She would hold his arms and make him walk with her. It was her only doll. Her mother refused ever to buy her one, and her grandmother was too tight with money to spend it for such foolishness. They never even had a tree at Christmas time. There were many trees that could have been cut down for nothing, but money would have had to be spent on decorations. The only extravagance in the house was a phonograph and some John McCormack records.

A few years later, a woman who had come to know Cynthia and whose children had grown too old gave her some dolls. For some reason, her grandmother hung them up in the parlor, out of reach. She would let Cynthia hold them on Sunday, but not play with them. After all, it was the Sabbath.

But not all of her life at her grandmother's was unhappy. Her grandparents loved the little girl and treated her as kindly as they knew how. Cynthia did have one friend. His name was Darrell Buck, and he lived next door. There were no other neighbors. One summer Darrell took some wood and wheels, and assembled an airplane. He and Cynthia would get in and pretend to fly. She remembers that she actually thought that this vehicle would take off, and they could go soaring across the sky. It was lots of fun playing with Darrell because he had such a great imagination.

This imagination was matched by the adults in the neighborhood, who wished to avoid any intimate topics brought up by their children. Any discussion of sex was absolutely taboo in those times. One weekend, visiting her other grandmother, Cynthia questioned her about where she had come from. Cynthia had overheard the girls at school discussing the answers they had gotten when they would ask their mothers. One mother told her daughter that she had been coming through their door one day with a watermelon. The fruit, heavy and awkward, had slipped from her hands. When it smashed to the floor and broke open, the mother had been astonished to find a darling baby girl inside. Another class-mate said her mother told her that she had had a large sunflower in her yard, and when it had opened up she had found her daughter. Sinthia, when questioned, told her grand-daughter that she had washed down the devil's rain trough into the barrel where they stored the soft rainwater they used to wash their hair. She told Cynthia that when she had arrived, she had had a handful of worms in one hand and frogs in the other. Cynthia thought this story was funny, but when she repeated it to Melissa, the old woman became greatly upset. Her Christian self was offended, and she declared that this was simply not so. "You must not think that you had anything to do with the devil," she declared. "Your mother found you inside a broken pumpkin." Cynthia and the other schoolgirls never questioned the inconsistency of these answers, perhaps thinking that each birth was unique.

The nice lady who had given Cynthia the dolls also gave her a real fur coat that her own daughter had outgrown. Cynthia was ecstatic. She paraded all around the house, and up and down the street. When she was visiting her mother for a few days, someone took her picture wearing the coat. What a contrast to those dull, drab, horrid clothes she was forced to wear! Oh, what she wouldn't do to be able to wear beautiful clothes again! And she made herself a little promise that, once she was out of this place, never would she allow herself to wear something that wasn't beautiful! When she was occa-sionally permitted a visit back with her mother, she begged and pleaded with her to go shopping. Her mother would buy her pretty things, and at last Cynthia could look in the mirror and not feel miserable.

But these visits were all too short. Her mother was busy with the restaurant and with her various boyfriends, and Cynthia only got in the way. Just as she was beginning to enjoy her new-found freedom, back she would be shipped to Grandmother Sullivan's.

During the time Cynthia lived with her Grandmother Sullivan, her sister, Gladys, was living with Grandmother Ryan. Gladys came to visit occasionally on weekends, but this did not always turn out well. One day Gladys decided that there might be treasure in the attic and went exploring. This raised the dust, and Melissa had just cleaned the house. Gladys was punished with a switch and sent home in disgrace. Another time, she pulled some of the sparkling green marble from the fireplace, making a mess. Again she was looking for treasure, and again she was punished and returned home. All she had found was an old calendar, which she quickly stuffed back behind the loose stone where she had found it. It is probably still in the house today.

The house on Webster Street was cool in the summer, and Cynthia thought it was beautiful. It certainly was much prettier than her bare room above the restaurant in Detroit! This was a real house! She used to walk from room to room, admiring the cranberry fixtures with the sparkling prisms hanging from them. The only thing she hated about the house was the fireplace in her bedroom right off the parlor. The fireplace had a grate with a devil's face on the front. When a fire was made, smoke and sparks would come out of his mouth. Cynthia found this awful devil's face frightening, and she would hide her head under the covers at night to keep from looking at it.

Gladys, living with Grandmother Ryan, had life a little easier than Cynthia. Not only did she have dolls to play with, but her life was not full of the onerous restrictions that Cynthia had to put up with. Gladys, who knew what it was like to live both with her mother and with Grandmother Sullivan, resisted any attempts to move her. Once, a social worker came to the house on Gladys's mother's complaint that her child was being withheld from her. Gladys promptly hid under the bed, and when she was dragged out, she kicked and scratched, screaming that if she was returned to her mother, she would kill herself! The social worker left, wisely concluding that they had better leave well enough alone.

On the other hand, the financial situation was better at the Sullivans'. Cynthia's meals were more wholesome, and she had "decent," if unattractive, clothes to wear to school. Melissa Sullivan was at least partly responsible for their better status. Norman, the girls' father, was still in the service, and the government sent a monthly check to Grandmother Ryan for the girls' upkeep. Melissa knew which day the check would arrive, and each month she appeared at the door to claim the check. Instead of fighting with her over it and demanding half, Grandmother Ryan would simply hand it over. When questioned about this, she would sigh resignedly and say, "Well, you know Melissa!"

Time went by, and Cynthia thrived under the orderly and relatively happy home life. By the time she learned that her parents had divorced, she was well settled in with her grandparents, and they were suprised that the news did not upset her too much. She really felt she was where she belonged. Her grandparents clearly loved her and had made her a large part of their lives. Thus it was very frightening when an epidemic of typhoid fever swept through the area, and Cynthia became a victim.

She was very ill, and the grandmother spent a great deal of time praying for her. Finally, her husband insisted that they buy her the coveted doll. Melissa purchased one made of kidskin with glass eyes that moved, but by now the child was far too sick to enjoy it, and even if she had been able to, the doll unfortunately had no clothes. A clear case of too little too late.

Cynthia and her grandfather had a daily ritual of raising and lowering their American flag. This practice was meaningful to both of them, for it was symbolic of his commitment to his country, and he had carefully passed this on to her. Her grandfather said, "You must live, for this old man needs your sunshine, Cynthia. Who would I have to raise and lower our flag each day?" He was close to tears.

The "dead wagon" came by each night, tolling a bell. The driver would stop when called and pick up another dead body at a home, or, sometimes, more than one dead body. It was a terrible time. The dreaded sound of this bell only reinforced the grandparents' fear for the young girl. She kept getting worse instead of better.

She now started hemorrhaging from the bowels, and their fear increased.

Her grandmother was in another room, crying and saying, "She can't make it."

Cynthia overheard, but did not fully understand. Weakly she called out, "I don't mind the typhoid fever. Maybe all my hair will fall out and grow back in all nice and curly."

What a surprise to have this interrupted by the arrival of Cynthia's father, who had heard that she was ill. He brought her a big basket of fruit, a big box of candy, and, foolishly, her sister.

Cynthia became even worse, finally losing consciousness. Her father called her mother to come, because their daughter was in a coma and not expected to live.

When Eunice arrived, she was on the arm of a new husband. He, too, was in uniform, which greatly upset Norman. After all, that had been their biggest source of disagreement.

Cynthia began to rally, and Norman soon left for the Fitzsimons hospital in Denver to help with the wounded with whom he had fought overseas.

Gladys used her sister's spoon one day to drink some broth, and soon afterwards she, too, became terribly sick with typhoid fever and nearly died.

Cynthia got better, but the recovery was extremely slow, and she missed two years of school.

Now there were new homes being built in the area, and among their new neighbors were the Owens. Oh, how Cynthia loved them. They had seven children. A daughter, Marguerite, was her own age, and the two became fast friends. When Mrs. Owen had a new baby, she let Cynthia hold it. This was even better than a doll, and she was thrilled. The mother also made room for her at their table and would ask her to eat with them. During this first world war, there was a terrible flu epidemic, and the Owens were victims. Mr. Owen survived, and so did Marguerite and an older sister. However, all the rest of that family perished, including Mrs. Owen and the new baby that Cynthia had held and loved. This tragedy upset her terribly. She felt as if she had lost members of her own family. It was a sad time.

Her grades in school were never very good. She did not want to be put back with younger kids, so she lied to the school authorities. After her long illness, she told them that she had been going to school in Detroit. Of course, having missed two years of school, the work was far too much for her.

One day she got into real trouble. She didn't know what a louse looked like, and when she saw one on her desk, she raised her hand to her teacher. The teacher said, "What do you want, Cynthia?"

Cynthia replied, "Mrs. Butterscotch, I've caught a book-worm. Aren't they supposed to make you smart?" The teacher came down the aisle, took one look, and slapped her across the face. Cynthia was sent to the principal's office, and he, in turn, sent her home. Of course, she didn't have lice. The louse had undoubtedly fallen from the hair of the girl who sat in front of her. There had been a real epidemic of them that year, but her grandmother would never have let anything like this happen to Cynthia. She had warned her, when the epidemic started, about not using anyone's comb, and she had Cynthia wash her hair quite often, after which she would inspect it. Her name-sake would not have anything that nasty on her!

There was a shed behind her grandparents' house with a wagon in it. Cynthia used to take the surviving Owen children and sit with them in the wagon. She would then proceed to catch and kill the lice she found in their hair. When Melissa found out about this, she feared that Cynthia might have them, too, and she poured kerosene on her head and wrapped it with an old stocking, which she made her wear all night. Then

Cynthia was forbidden to ever play with the Owen children again. She was crushed. Now the only time she saw Marguerite was when they walked to school together.

When Cynthia was about eight years old, she met a new girl friend named Dorothy Avis. They became fast friends, and Cynthia got to know the family well. The mother, Lottie, would invite the girls to have milk and cookies after school. Finding out Cynthia's circumstances, she invited her to call her Mama. Dorothy had a brother Warren who did poorly in school. His mother would shake her head over him. One day, out of his hearing, she said, "Poor Warren, with those big blue eyes and blond curls he looks so cute and so awfully dumb." Warren indeed was often put in the corner of his classroom with a dunce cap on his head and was made to face the ridicule of his classmates. The truth was that he had unusual intelligence, but in those days conformity was stressed, and someone who today would be in a class of gifted students was instead relegated to a corner or sent to the class for the slow. He was probably a dreamer, and this did not fit in with a teacher's strict discipline and regimentation. Certainly his dream and creation of Avis Rent-A-Car proved that Warren Avis did not lack intellect.

When Mr. Owen sold his house, and they moved away, Cynthia got to know the new people who lived there. The new owners had a son named Charlie, who became Cynthia's devil. He formed a gang of seven boys, and they took joy in tormenting her. They attended Fremont school with her, and when school let out each day, they would chase her home. They took particular pleasure if it had rained, and they could knock her down in the mud and force her face in it. She became the laughing stock of the school. This did nothing to improve her liking for this institution. Finally her grandmother went to the school and complained to the teacher, but the chases continued. Cynthia, as soon as school let out, would start running as hard as she could. But, try as she would, the boys would catch her and hurt her. She would come home crying, with a stitch in her side from running so fast.

One day, Charlie, as usual, ran after her, and she ran behind a house. She stooped down, hiding behind a cellar door. She saw Charlie looking in both directions for her. At her feet lay a two-foot board, and she quickly picked it up. Charlie was a good head taller than she was, but she was angry and desperate. He came around the corner, and without hesitation Cynthia brought her arms up and, with all her force, smashed the board down on Charlie's head. He dropped to the ground and did not move. She grabbed him by his short German haircut and started to drag him along the ground. Knocking him unconscious had not fazed her, and she was still angry, wanting further retaliation. She intended to drag him all the way home. She kept dragging, cutting through the yard of a cement company. There was a full crew of black men working, but she passed through unnoticed. She dragged him with her tiny fingers another block, past her own home. She stopped when she reached his gate and called out to his sister. The sister and mother came flying out, shouting, "What's the matter with Charlie!"

Cynthia said in a firm voice, "You were told to keep him from hurting me. Well, I guess you didn't do anything about it, so I hit him over the head with a board. When he comes to, you can tell him that if he bothers me again I will shoot him with my grandfather's revolver." With that, she turned and marched home in triumph.

She had thought this would end her ordeals, but the other gang members persisted. Just because she had cleaned Charlie's clock did not necessarily mean they should be afraid. One day, two of the members cornered her, pulling her between two houses that were built close together. They started in on her, kicking her and hitting her with their fists, but this time they were in for a surprise. With her victory over Charlie she had gained both confidence and grit. She now fought back with her feet and fingernails, kicking and flailing at them. When she was close, she also used her teeth. She was inflicting real damage on the boys. A woman came out of one of the houses to see what the commotion was all about, and the boys fled.

She had one more bout with a gang member before she was free of them. She beat the boy so badly that he fled from her and ran to a porch. She ran after him and beat the tar out of him. He never tried again.

This was one of the days when she was going to visit her grandmother Sinthia. For a nickel Cynthia could have ridden on the streetcar, but Melissa would not part with this coin. When she reached Sinthia's house, word had already gotten to the woman about the fight, and she said to the girl, "Cynthia, I have already heard about your fight. Well, my lady, let me tell you that one day you will pee on the wrong dog and get your block knocked off!"

Luckily this never happened, but her defense of herself and her feistiness in those difficult times as a youngster would remain with her for the rest of her life. She would forever stand her ground and defend herself against any adversity.

When Cynthia was twelve years old, her grandfather died. She stood at the grave site in the sleet and made him a promise. Taps was being played, and she said, "Grandfather, I will always remember what you taught me, and I'll never forget to love my flag and my country." Later in this story, you will recall this commitment and the fulfillment of this promise.

Chapter 6

With her husband gone, Cynthia's grandmother found herself in financial straits. Somehow she had to secure an income of her own. After a diligent search, she found a position as housekeeper for an attorney in Bay City, but, unfortunately, there would be no room for her granddaughter. Much as she regretted this turn of events, she closed her house and sent Cynthia to live with her grandmother Sinthia and her step-grandfather Bradshaw.

Mr. Bradshaw was a commercial fisherman and very kind. The move also reunited Cynthia with her sister, Gladys. They giggled together, remembering an incident when they were smaller and visiting here, and had needed to go to the toilet. They had been too scared to go clear back to the outhouse. They thought the empty house next door was haunted, as they would hear funny laughter, and sometimes they saw lights.

Their grandfather was looking out and saw them squatting in the back yard. He laughed and said to his wife, "I think the girls have just sprung a leak out there."

Constantly moving from one city to the other made schooling difficult. As usual, Cynthia lied to get into the grade with the kids her own age. Now she suddenly found herself in the eighth grade, where the homework was extremely tough. She had a friend named Wilhelmina, who had polio and was confined to bed. Cynthia would go to her house, place a ladder up against the house, and climb to her girlfriend's bedroom window. She would climb in and get the help she badly needed to complete her homework. Still, it was terribly tough. One day, Wilhelmina asked her whether she would go home and cook her something special for supper. Even at that young age, Cynthia was known for her good cooking. She certainly had good teachers. Her Aunt Mary had talked to her in the restaurant about cooking and had shown her how to make various dishes. She had also learned from her grandmothers. She went home to cook this special dinner, but before she had completed it she got a phone call that her friend was dead. A bitter blow, to lose a friend when you are so young. Without Cynthia's friend's help, life at school became really impossible, and she soon quit.

Not long after this, her mother once again requested that Cynthia come back to Detroit to live with her and her new husband. Shortly after her return, she became quite ill, and her mother put her in her own bed. She had a fever and was tossing about. All at once, she rolled right off the bed. Under the bed she saw a wooden box. Curious, she opened the lid, then quickly drew back in shock. The box was a coffin, and in the coffin was a stillborn baby clothed in Cynthia's new white lace dress that her father had recently bought for her. Cynthia quickly replaced the lid and got dressed. She knew where her mother hid her money, and she reached in and took enough to get back to her grandmother's. She couldn't live with a thing like that in the house.

When asked why her mother would keep a dead baby

under her bed, Cynthia said, "She badly wanted a baby by her new husband. When it didn't live, I think she couldn't bear to put it in the ground."

Now that she no longer went to school, Cynthia needed a job. Fortunately, she was taken for a girl much older than her tender age of fourteen, and she found employment working at a Coney Island, where they served hot dogs and chili.

Cynthia lost no time ridding herself of her old clothes and began buying flapper outfits for her developing figure. She was striking in these clothes, and suddenly she found herself being admired by the local young men. She would take most of her pay and invest in more dresses. She also was out from under the strictness of Melissa and started to use a little lipstick. This was the beginning of a lifelong obsession with apparel—certainly a result of her deprivation while living with Melissa.

With her job, her thoughts turned to transportation. She saved some of her money and eventually bought an old Model T touring car for $14.00. She asked how to get it started, then simply set off, learning how to drive all by herself. When she had more or less learned to manage the car, she drove right up her grandmother's steps to surprise her. The woman was astounded. When Cynthia turned fifteen, she would obtain her driver's license, but for now she traveled without one. This car not only provided her with a vehicle to get back and forth to work, but also gave her and her sister the means to get to the Saginaw River to fish. This was their favorite pastime, and they would dig for worms and catch yellow-bellied perch and walleyes. This not only was fun, but it was a big help during these hard times, because it put food on the table.

One day while Cynthia and Gladys were fishing in the bay from a rowboat, a sudden and violent storm came up. They could see another boat nearby with five occupants who were in worse trouble than they were. Horrified, they watched as the boat capsized and the people drowned. Suddenly Cynthia had an idea. She tugged off her bloomers and fastened them to the blade of an oar. She held this high in the air until it was seen by someone on shore, who sent a power boat out to rescue the girls.

This stay lasted only a little over a year, until, at their mother's insistence, Cynthia and Gladys returned to Detroit.

So once again she was uprooted. With only four years of education, she had a limited number of job opportunities, but she soon found employment working behind a lunch counter. She lived with her mother, and handed over her pay to her mother and stepfather. She had grown quite fond of this man and did not resent helping with her pay, as times were still precarious, and money short. The man was kind to her, sometimes sticking up for her when her mother was unfair. It was years before Cynthia figured out that her mother, like her grandfather, had not applied for a divorce but was just living with the man.

Cynthia enjoyed working behind the lunch counter, and she liked the customers. There she met a girl named Denelda, and the two became fast friends. Denelda had bobbed hair and adorable dimples. Although Denelda was older than Cynthia, it made no difference in their relationship, and they had great fun together. Cynthia introduced her friend to her real father, who was no longer in the army and had moved up north with his new wife. Norman, too, was unaware that his former wife, Eunice, had really never divorced him. He had been discharged from the army, and had turned to commercial fishing and rum-running from Canada. He was given the name "The Grey Ghost" by the locals, because of his ability to sail with no lights and unerringly find his destination.

Once, when Cynthia was visiting her father, they were chased by officers who fired at their car. Norman pushed her down, floored the gas pedal, and managed their escape. Soon after this, he took her into the woods and proudly displayed the two stills that he had set up to make moonshine. Norman also had a truck and frequently drove to Canada to purchase liquor. He would cover the liquor with ice and then top that with bass, which were legal to bring into Michigan.

The house that Cynthia and Gladys moved to had once

been a fine old mansion. Her mother had closed the restaurant after the stock market crash, as it did not pay to keep it open. Few had the money to eat out, and she could no longer make the payments, so she let it go. She and her new husband bought the house to provide them an income. Times were tough, and the girls worked hard to help their mother clean, for she now had much of the house rented out. Gladys stayed for about a year, then finally called it quits and returned to Grandmother Sinthia.

When Cynthia was fourteen, she met a handsome young policeman named Durwood Hudson and fell intensely in love. He was twenty-three. She told him she was eighteen, and since she looked it, he had no reason to question her. He would come in to see her at work and would pick her up to make sure that she got home safely.

Durwood was from the South and had lovely manners. He came from a large and very loving family. One brother, nicknamed "Jumbo" because of his size, was also a policeman and directed traffic. He was prominently displayed at the corner of Congress and Woodward, one of Detroit's busiest intersections. Another brother was an attorney, and his sisters, Anna Mae and Marie, were schoolteachers. Another younger brother came over to Cynthia's house one day and played with her little dog. That night, unbelievably, her dog died, and so did the young boy. He died of spinal meningitis. Cynthia felt so bad for the family.

This family was indeed special. They were warm and friendly to her. They enjoyed having her over for meals of fried chicken with biscuits and gravy. Even Cynthia's lack of education made no difference to them, and she greatly enjoyed their company. They always made her feel welcome and very special. It was a heady and exhilarating time.

About a week after she met Durwood, he told her he had been married before. It had not worked out, as his wife had a terrible temper and was violently jealous of anyone who looked at him. Durwood was very handsome, and Cynthia could see why women's heads turned when they saw him. He was over six feet tall, with dark brown, curly hair and very kind, soft, brown eyes. Cynthia did not tell her mother about his previous marriage because she knew her mother would not approve of her seeing him.

She felt very grown-up when she was with Durwood, and he drove an exciting car. It was a green Packard convertible with a rumble seat, large chrome headlights, and orange spokes on the wheels. On the back of the rumble seat was a spare tire with a wheel cover that said, "THE SPIRIT OF KING BEN." Cynthia thought this was terribly funny, because King Ben, a Mormon had been arrested in Harbor Springs for having so many wives. Durwood appreciated the fact that they shared a special sense of humor.

Cynthia's mother greatly liked her boyfriend. He was both respectful and generous, bringing her daughter small gifts of books and candy. Sometimes Cynthia suspected her mother actually was jealous, wanting Durwood for herself. Her mother would be so very charming, becoming almost flirtatious. She would keep Durwood talking long after Cynthia was ready and anxious to go out.

One night, Durwood brought her home from an outing, and they entered her house. Moments later, there was a knock at the door. Eunice answered it and was confronted by Durwood's ex-wife. She had followed them, and was screaming and threatening that if Cynthia kept seeing Durwood, she would throw acid in her face! Eunice was horrified and closed the door on the intruder. After Durwood had left, the ex-wife returned and told Cynthia she had better quit dating him. But Cynthia was in love and would not let this threat end her romance. She defied her mother, also, and continued to see him.

Durwood took Cynthia to the police firing range and taught her how to shoot properly. Often they went on picnics together, too, Durwood bringing ham sandwiches, pickles, deviled eggs, and Orange Crush. He would also bring a blanket, and they would lie down near the Rouge River and talk. She remembers how beautiful the trees were and how Durwood would name them for her. He had a deep love of God and pointed out to her how God had made each bird a different color.

Cynthia had no more trouble with the ex-wife, but the woman continued to make life difficult for Durwood, going repeatedly to his precinct and yelling at him. The other officers finally gave her the name "Dynamite" and kidded Durwood about this.

After six happy months of dating, Durwood proposed to Cynthia and she readily accepted, saying, "Let's run away together, out-of-state." She knew she was underage in Michigan and also knew her mother would never give her consent.

But the more mature Durwood, laughing sweetly at his impetuous little Cynthia, calmed her down and admonished her that "It just wouldn't be right."

One night, Cynthia descended the wide winding staircase in this former mansion for her date with Durwood. Her hand trailed along the beautiful, carved stair rail. She saw her mother standing and talking with Durwood. Suddenly, she knew from her mother's smug, self-satisfied face that she had just told him Cynthia's real age. This was confirmed when she reached the foyer, and he turned to her with a heartbroken voice and said, "Little one, we just can't get married. You're far too young."

Eunice said, "I don't put any blame on Durwood over this, because he simply didn't know, but I blame you, Cynthia, for lying. Do you realize that, if you'd run off out-of-state, Durwood would be guilty of breaking the Mann Act? You'll not see him again, even if I have to lock you in."

Cynthia said bitterly, "Yes, I remember the last time that you locked me in, and I remember the fire!"

Durwood gently stopped this exchange. He turned to her and said, "Don't worry, little one. I'll wait until you're older, and if you still love this man, then we'll still get married."

Now Cynthia's mother insisted she quit her job, so that there would not be any opportunity for them to meet. In its place, Eunice found Cynthia a job as a baby sitter with a wealthy family.

Cynthia had never felt that her waitress job was demeaning, but she certainly objected to being placed beside the chauffeur while the family or the children were sitting in back of the limousine. She thought it was humiliating. This, coupled with the breakup of her romance, caused her to seek a change in her life, so she soon quit her job. Her mother, however, made good on her threat and kept her locked up in the third-floor bedroom.

The house was a big, old mansion that had been converted into light-housekeeping apartments. Fortunately for Cynthia, the house kept her mother too busy to watch her constantly. Nevertheless, her hatred for her mother now returned like a storm in full force. She called Denelda and told her about her situation. Denelda still worked at the lunch counter where the girls had first met and became good friends. Denelda was seventeen and engaged to a captain with the State Police.

Cynthia asked Denelda whether she would drive her upstate to visit her father. She was finding it increasingly difficult to live with her mother and be locked up all day.

On another occasion, years before, Cynthia had tried to run away, but had been caught. She had been taken in front of a judge who threatened to put her into a girls' home for delinquents. She had never tried again.

This time, Cynthia had asked her mother for permission to visit her father, and Eunice had agreed to let her go for a brief stay. Norman was terribly pleased. Eunice had been granted custody of the girls, and he missed them.

Denelda readily agreed to drive her north to visit her father and his new wife. She had met Cynthia's father, liked him, and looked forward to a little vacation. They packed up the car. Cynthia was thrilled to be away. She had never liked Detroit, and now, with the prospect of having some time with her father, she was ecstatic! She was leaving behind the meanness of her mother, and this brought a smile to her face as they set off. It was good to get back together with Denelda, and they brought each other up to date on their lives. They laughed and kidded one another as they rode north.

Cars were slower in those days, and this was considered a long trip. They stopped for a bite to eat, then, as nighttime came, their talk grew more serious. Cynthia described her imprisonment in the bedroom and her mother's role in breaking her up with Durwood. Denelda talked of her boy friend and their plans, and said, "You know what? Sometimes I think I'm going to die young."

Cynthia said, "Now why would you think that?"

Denelda replied, "I really don't know."

Miles on their way, as they approached the town of Sebewaing, their jubilant mood came to an abrupt end when the lights on the car dimmed, and Denelda lost control on a double-reverse curve on a bridge. The girls' concern turned to panic when they realized that the car was heading for the railing of the bridge. The car hit the railing with a tremendous crash, rammed through it, and plunged over the side of the bridge and down into the river.

As the car came to an abrupt halt, Cynthia could hear the water and the sound of glass splashing into it. She felt intense pain and she could not see Denelda. She was in a panic.

Seeing a hole in the roof, she managed to escape through it and make her way to the river bank. She knew she needed help badly. She called out to Denelda over and over, but didn't get an answer. Looking desperately around her, she saw the lights of a farmhouse in the distance. She knew it would take a tremendous effort to get that far.

Cynthia realized that she was badly injured and losing a lot of blood. She started to crawl, but it was terribly painful. Further torment was a sheepdog who, smelling blood, kept biting her on the leg.

When she finally reached the house, the owners took her in and called a doctor.

In the meantime, Norman had begun to worry when his daughter failed to show up. He set out with a friend to see whether they could find her. He thought they might have had car trouble and been stranded along the road. They had traveled only about fifteen miles when they approached the bridge and saw the headlights shining up from the river. They raced down the bank, and, when Norman saw the car, he recognized it. He knew from the damage that anyone who had been inside would be badly hurt. They pulled out Denelda's body, but she was dead, and they could do nothing for her. They searched the car and around the area, but they could not find Cynthia.

Norman worried that she might have drowned in the river. Back on the road, Norman saw the lights of the farmhouse, and the two men quickly drove to it, hoping Cynthia might have survived and gone there seeking help.

His joy when he discovered her there, however, was short-lived when he saw her condition. She was in excruciating pain and bleeding from the mouth. The doctor arrived and treated her immediately. Her lung had been punctured, and a spoke from the steering wheel had ripped her leg to the bone. Her pelvis was broken, and the doctor had his hands full patching her up.

She lay on a bed in one of the bedrooms. Working swiftly, the doctor sutured her leg only to have the bed collapse, pulling out all the stitches.

The doctor had her moved and began again. When the stitching was finished, he applied a cast that covered her from her hips to her breasts. Her father had held her for the doctor, and now he looked up to him with beseeching eyes and asked, "Is my girl going to live?"

Cynthia looked up into the doctor's eyes. They were bleak. He shook his head and replied, "I hope so. She can't go to the hospital; it's too far away, and she'd never make it. You'll have to take her home with you and look after her carefully."

As Cynthia's father and his friend carried her out to his car, she looked at the sky and saw a falling star. She took this as a bad omen and said, "Father, please don't lie to me. I want to know if Denelda is dead."

He regretfully acknowledged that this was true and said, "The sky pilot takes them from here and there, and we don't know his reasons."

Cynthia was now not only in pain but also heartsick over her friend. How strange, she thought, that on this very day, Denelda had prophesied she would die young. How cruelly and quickly her prediction had come true.

Chapter 7

They took Cynthia home, where someone was always at her side. Her father spent the most time with her, and when he became overly tired, her sister, Gladys, who was also visiting, would take his place. He asked Gladys one day, "Who is this 'Durwood' she keeps calling for?"

Gladys said, "He's the man that she's in love with. Mother thought she was too young for a romance and broke them up."

Norman gave a quick bark of a laugh. "She certainly has a short memory. She was exactly the same age when she fell in love and married me! I'll get hold of her mother and arrange to get him up here. If Cynthia should die, she'll die knowing that she's a beloved woman. No woman is ever a real woman without the love of a man."

Then he asked Gladys, "Have you met his man, and is he worthy of Cynthia's love?"

Gladys responded with an enthusiastic "Yes!" Norman immediately left to go to the telephone office to put through a call to Eunice, who told him he could locate Durwood by calling the Canfield Police Station. Norman called and left a message. Later, the telephone operator came to the house, saying Durwood had returned the call and was on his way.

When Cynthia opened her eyes several days later, she saw her father by her side, and when she turned her head, there was her darling Durwood. She was lying on her back and had awakened in great pain. What a comfort to see those two whom she loved so much. Her father said, "Honey, you're going to be all right. Yes, Daddy's little girl is going to be all right, and when you get well and can walk again, I'll give your hand in marriage to this man. I'd be proud to call him my son-in-law."

Durwood took her hand and told her, "By the time you're able to walk down the aisle, I'll have saved enough to buy you a home." He then said teasingly, "My sister Mary will teach you Southern cooking so I won't starve to death." Cynthia was then given morphine and soon drifted off to sleep.

It would be a year and a half before she could get to her feet and manage a few steps. When she finally felt up to it, she started to drive her car again. Her father had gone to Bay City and towed it back with him.

One day she took her stepmother, Alicia, shopping. Needing gas, she pulled into a station but braked with too much force. The sudden stop violently threw Alicia's face into the windshield. The woman was in terrible pain, and Cynthia felt awful. She truly liked the woman and was appalled at what she had done to her. Her father had married once before, after he had broken up with Eunice. He had gone to New York and met a Ziegfield chorus girl whom he married and brought to Tawas City. There he operated a still, with the cooperation of the local sheriff. This worked out fine until he caught his wife and the sheriff together having sex. This he would not tolerate, and he divorced her. Cynthia had never liked her in the first place and was glad when her father got rid of her and married Alicia. The woman was very nice and did not deserve to have her face smashed. When they returned home, she saw the woman's eyes were blackened, and her father was furious. He demanded her car keys and took the vehicle away. He had the car dismantled and sold the parts to a dealer. When he got back, he gave his daughter her original $14.00 investment and told her that her driving days were over. She really could not blame him.

Her mother had come to see her a few times, but could not take her back with her and take care of her. Durwood came whenever he had leave, and she was very happy to remain with her father and plan her wedding. One leave, shortly after her first successful steps, Durwood announced he had to go to Kentucky to help move his mother and father north. All of his parents' children were in Detroit, and their parents wanted to be near them. He also told her he had left a girlfriend down there and he had to break off their relationship. He had asked her to marry him before he had met Cynthia. He felt the only decent thing he could do was to go to her in person.

Because Cynthia was still a minor and now able to walk, she was to be returned to her mother. The mansion was now lost in these depression times, and her mother lived in Flint. Cynthia was enjoying Durwood's letters and advised him about her new residence. After the move, the letters stopped abruptly. She worried that he had renewed his earlier romance, and as time went on and she still did not hear, she tearfully concluded that this was the only explanation. She became terribly despondent. She had lost her dear girlfriend, and now it looked as though she had lost the love of Durwood.

She was still on crutches but able to help a bit with the housework. She was sweeping the floor and had lifted a corner of the linoleum rug to sweep under it, when she came across the letters Durwood had written to her. Her mother had hidden them! Thank God she had discovered them. Why had she not suspected her mother's treachery? When his letters stopped, why had she not continued to write him, asking for an explanation? "Pride, that's why," she said to herself. "My damned Yankee pride, because I thought he'd gone back to that Kentucky girl."

She lost no time getting back to Detroit and sat in the police station waiting for him to come on duty. She would explain the whole thing to him, and they would be together again.

Her spirits were high, and when she saw him she felt the thrill of her old love returning. He asked her to come back when his shift was over so they could talk.

Later when they met, she explained about the letters.

Durwood's voice sounded strained. "Little one, I don't know how to tell you this without hurting you. Your mother came to me and said that after the accident you had suffered a nervous breakdown. She said your feelings had changed about me and that you wanted to break it off. She thought it for the best if I wouldn't try to contact you.

When I didn't hear from you, I figured she had been telling the truth. I was awfully hurt and started doing a lot of heavy drinking. I went back to Kentucky and ended up marrying my old girlfriend, Mary. I still love you, Cynthia, but Mary is expecting a baby, and I couldn't leave her now. When the baby is born I'll divorce her, and we'll get married, because I love you with all my heart."

Cynthia turned on him. "I don't understand how you could have done this. If you had truly loved me, you wouldn't have married. Well, you did marry her, and now you can just keep her!" Setting her crutches firmly under her arms, she stalked out.

Out of sheer spite, she now started to date Durwood's best friend, Johnny Hale. He was very good looking and ten years her senior.

We had only dated three or four times, but he was immediately infatuated with me and begged me to marry him. I was only sixteen years old. Certainly I didn't love him, but it offered an alternative to living with my mother, who was constantly slapping and punishing me for minor infractions. I remember once my mother claimed I had "sassed" her and

*then had repeatedly slapped me. I grabbed her wrist to make
her stop. My stepfather intervened in the tussle, saying, "She
is too old for this type of punishment." Yet my mother's
vindictiveness over petty things did not stop for long, and I was
looking for a safe harbor. Johnny certainly looked like a better
alternative to the life I was then living. There was also my
unhappiness over Durwood. Johnny said he knew I still loved
Durwood and told me he would be good to me and make no
demands. For some reason, Gladys didn't like him, but
Johnny had a good job, and my mother, always thinking of the
almighty dollar, saw he was ambitious and urged me to say
yes. Impulsively I yielded to Johnny and Mother's urging and
agreed to marry him. He was so excited, he raced right out and
bought me a lovely diamond engagement ring and a beautiful
circlet of diamonds for a wedding band. We drove to Bowling
Green, Ohio, where we could legally marry, as I was far too
young under Michigan law. After the marriage by the Justice
of the Peace we immediately set out for Pennsylvania to meet
his aunts. They were very welcoming and seemed happy to
meet me. Johnny and I slept apart. He knew I was not in love
with him and would not want any kind of intimacy.*

This marriage started out well but would eventually prove
to be a gigantic mistake. It was a foolish move, and she would
have many reasons to regret it. The urging of her mother and
the revenge she felt over Durwood would hardly be a healthy
foundation for a marriage. She was hurt over Durwood's
perfidy, and like a small child, she was going to SHOW HIM.

Through Johnny's aunts she learned that his mother,
Sarah, was in an insane asylum called Eloise in Wayne,
Michigan. They said she had been driven insane from the
tragedies that had occurred in her life. Her husband had died
in a coal mine disaster. Then her seven-year-old son and his
little boy friend had fallen into a coal mine shaft and starved
to death. When they were finally found, it was seen that they
had, in desperation, eaten the flesh from their own little
fingers! And this was not the end. Her fourteen-year-old

daughter had developed tuberculosis. On the way to Phoenix, Arizona, where they hoped to find a cure, the girl had started to hemorrhage and had died in her mother's arms.

Sarah eventually remarried, but was so depressed and despondent that the marriage soon was in deep trouble. Finally, in despair over the situation, her husband put his head in the oven, turned on the gas, and committed suicide. This was the final blow, and Sarah went to pieces and had to be confined. It was left to Johnny to bury his stepfather and face having his mother institutionalized.

Cynthia agonized over the horror of this story and wondered whether the mother, through someone's patience and loving care, might overcome her grief and return to a normal existence. She vowed to Johnny that she would try to help him rehabilitate her.

They returned to Detroit and rented a flat in the same building with her mother, at the corner of Third and Kirby. It was very convenient, as it was only two blocks from Mills Bakery where Johnny worked. The bakery had many trucks which would drive all over Detroit and park, so housewives could buy within a block or two of home. Johnny ran the ovens and knew more about them than any baker in the city. When the Wonder Bread Company on Grand River Avenue had trouble with its own ovens, he would be called to help out. He would come back home after one of these calls and say, "Wonder Bread, eat it and wonder what the hell you're eating." This was not true, but showed his loyalty to his own company, Mills. Ironically, years later he would switch to Wonder Bread, establishing the company nationally, and would rise to be president.

Renting close to work was handy for Johnny and nice for Cynthia too, as her mother had started a new family and had a little boy whom Cynthia could dress in cute sailor outfits, showing him off and playing with him. It was almost as good as having a child of her own. Other than that, she busied herself cooking and baking. Every day she made Johnny a butterscotch pie. Oddly, he never seemed to tire of them. She also busied herself cleaning house and doing her crocheting and embroidery. Also, she learned the painstaking and time-consuming task of making hand-stitched quilts. Of course, she also shopped. Johnny was generous, allowing her to buy anything she wanted, so she started to fill their closets with her new clothes. True to his word, he left her alone, and they slept apart. If there was any irritant in their beginnings it was only that he hated to wake up in the morning and would respond to her calling him by throwing his shoes at her.

Durwood remained friends with Johnny and would often come over to visit them. Durwood's sister Mary sometimes came with him, and she continued to give lessons to Cynthia in southern cooking.

Durwood's wife had their baby and needed blood. When Cynthia learned of this, she offered herself up, as she had the same blood type. She went to the hospital and lay on a table beside her while they did a direct transfusion. This she did only because of the woman's need, and not because her feelings toward Durwood had softened.

True to her word, Cynthia had Johnny drive her to Eloise mental hospital every week to visit his mother. Sarah was very depressed and angry, and the visits were painful and quite difficult. One day Cynthia took her out of Eloise for a trip to the dentist. They traveled by streetcar, and suddenly Sarah turned on the conductor and began hitting him. She thought he was Grover Cleveland, whom she blamed for the hunger during the depression. Cynthia pulled her off the man and off the streetcar. They were then forced to take a cab.

Cynthia and Johnny moved from their flat when they found an attractive house for rent. She had fun furnishing it and making it comfortable. One day she was in the basement, where there was a sink. They had also installed a stove and put up shelving for all the jars of food she had canned. It was cooler down there in the summer, and she was busy canning tomatoes, unaware that the landlord had come over for the rent. When he knocked and no one came to the door, he let himself in, searching for her. He finally came down into the basement. Without saying a word, he proceeded to grab her, obviously wanting to have sex. She broke away from him and grabbed the furnace poker. This threat did nothing to turn him away, and she began to beat him with the poker. He backed off and ran for the stairs, but she was too angry to stop. She followed him as he left the house and raced for the car. He jumped in, but before he could get the vehicle started, she took the poker and smashed his windshield. Of course, under these circumstances they could not remain in the house and they shortly moved away.

Johnny, too, had a temper but was not always the one at fault in various skirmishes. One day they were driving out to see her mother when Johnny stopped to mail some company papers. He had parked a few feet from a cab stand, and a cab driver started a fist fight with him. The unfairness of this angered Cynthia, and she reached down on the floor and grabbed the crank. She jumped out of the car and ran up to the fighting men. She raised the crank high in the air and, with both hands, brought the crank down on the cabby's head. She had successfully knocked him out, and they sped away.

Cynthia kept up her visits to Sarah at Eloise, but felt the mental hospital was hardly a place where a woman could make any headway with her depression and subsequent violence. Inmates would grab her, and she would become angry and scream and lash out in turn. Cynthia thought the old, drab, urine-smelling building—and close proximity to the other patients, who were even worse—was harmful. Cynthia visited her for about a year, then decided they would just have to bring her home if there was to be any hope at all.

Cynthia and Johnny tried their best to bring her the love and attention that they thought would bring about even a small transformation from what she was, but it was all uphill. Sarah would go into rages, and would lash out and put on her clothes and try to run away and "get lost." She had to be watched every moment, and with Johnny at work this proved to be an insurmountable task. After a few months, Sarah came after Johnny with a knife. The couple decided their efforts were in vain, and Sarah was returned to Eloise. Cynthia had tried valiantly to stick with it, but it obviously had not worked.

She also now had another monumental problem. Shortly after they had brought his mother home, Johnny began to demand his marital rights. It was now that Cynthia began to realize the extent of her mistake in getting married to Johnny and her foolish reasons for doing so.

Johnny suddenly became highly interested in having sex with me, but in a way that I had never heard about—anal intercourse. I was appalled and filled with disgust. I rejected this and all his other ideas and demands. I couldn't understand why these things would interest him.

Gradually I came to understand that normal sex with me had, oddly, no attraction for him. I begged him to leave me alone, because I would never consent to be a willing partner in these acts. He told me I didn't need a man in bed but would rather have a horse. He was trying to play the role of a stallion, and I wouldn't tolerate this treatment.

He indulged in normal sex with other women, and I couldn't understand why I was the exception. I was such an innocent. I didn't even have the words in my vocabulary to describe what he wanted or what would be a proper label to describe his appetites.

I once came out of the bedroom to find him on the davenport with the girlfriend of his best friend, who was staying with us. They were making love the way I had always heard it was done.

When I later referred to this incident, Johnny became livid with rage. Placing his hands around my throat, he proceeded to choke me until I nearly lost consciousness. I couldn't understand him, and my fear of him increased as he became more and more abusive.

I finally threatened to leave him, and he countered with a threat of his own—that he would kill me. I asked him why he had married me, and he grinned as he spoke. "I wanted you because I knew you were still a cherry [a term used at the time for a virgin] and I intended to be the first." But he never made any overtures, and my virginity remained intact throughout the marriage.

The one thing that did get shattered was my pride. I left him, but he knew my route to and from work. One day he rushed up into the streetcar where I was sitting. Brandishing a sawed-off shot gun, he forced me off.

He insisted I return to him, and I was in such fear, I felt I didn't have a choice. The marriage struggled on for years, but it was not a real marriage at all. Having me back was not enough, and he would have many sexual liaisons.

When I found he had gonorrhea, I realized our relationship could not continue.

I was terribly depressed. I stood on the bridge to Belle Isle and considered jumping off into the Detroit River. The police came up and asked me what was the matter. I told them about my problems, and they said things were bound to get better and that ending my life was not the answer.

They kindly drove me to my mother's house. She made me get down on my knees and swear I had not been "up to something."

I went to a doctor because Johnny said I had given him the disease. He tested me and found the results were negative. He told me to bring in a pair of my husband's unwashed shorts so he could test the stains.

I had left where we lived, but I broke back in and got the undershorts. I took them to the doctor, and the test proved positive.

I had suffered too many years with this nightmare. I became desperate and finally summoned up the courage to end it all with a divorce. I suppose a psychiatrist would have a field day with his behavior. Johnny really gave me a clue to his strange behavior when he admitted he had never had a virgin. He was so proud of the ownership, that to possess one was the ultimate, and to deflower me (our expression at that time) would have been to give this prize away. He simply couldn't bear to actually lose this precious possession that he *could show off. I was the big blue ribbon, the trophy on the mantel, the Olympic gold medal.*

Cynthia went back to her mother. She was still underage, but it was not long before she knew that she would never be able to live with her mother again. Eunice threatened to call the authorities. Undaunted, Cynthia decided to take the risk. Whether Eunice actually made good on her threat, Cynthia never knew, because that was the last she heard of it.

Cynthia moved into the home of her girlfriend Ann. Ann was just the kind of person she needed at this time. She was the soothing type who enjoyed mothering. Durwood continued to come and visit her. Now he thought there might be hope, when she left Johnny, but she was adamant about any further relationship. "I said I never wanted to see you again, and I haven't changed my mind. You can't have your cake and eat it too. I will never settle for seconds. If you have a brain in your head, you will understand I am all through. What you had is gone, and what we have had is over!"

Durwood would return again and again, to no avail. She continued to reject him, and the arguments were sometimes quite heated.

Durwood was persistent, but Cynthia never budged. He came one day, and her anger was particularly vehement. She railed at him when he pleaded with her. The room seemed to vibrate with her vindictive clamor. Defeated, he left.

Durwood had been promoted and now rode a motorcycle. When he left Cynthia that day, he was quite late getting to his call box. His supervisor was waiting by the box and was extremely angry. He chewed him out, and for Durwood it had been far too much for one day. He swung and hit the lieutenant.

Durwood was called before the "board of discipline" and given time off. He started drinking heavily. He continued to drop by and try to convince Cynthia of his love for her, but she continued to reject him. She told him in no uncertain terms that he might as well give her up, because she would never change her mind. He begged her; she refused him again. The scene was quite ugly. He left.

Cynthia and Ann made plans for a little dinner party. Ann had invited her boyfriend, Jack Armstrong, a police reporter for the *Detroit Times*, to join them. He was very late in arriving, and when he finally came he apologized to them. "I had a story to cover about a Detroit policeman. As near as we can get to the story, there seems to have been a marital mix-up of some kind. Seems he was in love with some other girl and was in a mess over it., He went into an old carriage house. We found an empty fifth he first must have downed. Anyhow, he climbed up to the hayloft, put a rope around his neck, and jumped."

Cynthia and Ann looked at each other. Cynthia turned to him and asked anxiously, "What was his name?"

He looked into his notebook, frowning as he kept flipping back and forth over his pages, and finally he replied, "Durwood Hudson."

Chapter 8

Cynthia's life would begin again, but she felt numb, and the shock of these events would continue to haunt her for years. She would think of Denelda and Durwood and blame herself for their loss of life. She would cry and call herself the "kiss of death." She was a long time living with these two tragedies and dealing with the part she had played in them.

Years later her mother would speculate about what Cynthia's life would have been like had she not interfered and played God. She herself had married young, and to a man in uniform who was very attractive to women. She told Cynthia of the women who were constantly chasing after Norman, fascinated by his good looks, further enhanced by his uniform. She said she had never really caught him cheating, but he was such a flirt, she had been constantly jealous and miserable.She tried to justify her interference with Cynthia's romance on the grounds that she was just trying to save her from the heart-break she had experienced worrying over these women.

But Cynthia remembered the boyfriends at the restaurant and her mother's great admiration of Durwood, and she remained skeptical.

As time passed and she found herself struggling with self-reproach over the tragic events, Cynthia began to examine just who and what she was. She was reaching maturity, and with it came a new feeling of responsibility for her actions. She was no longer the little girl who could set a building on fire and feel no regret. She distanced herself and looked back on her past and her heritage with an open mind.

Her grandfather had loved to tell her about her ancestors and their origins. He would describe her as a "Blue Belle Yankee" and tell her to "Never forget what you are, because life is hard, and you have to be very strong in order to take what it has to offer and then keep going."

Cynthia remembered these words and thought about them carefully. She evaluated her relationship with Durwood and the fact that he had actually killed himself over her. She thought of her grandfather's words and realized that, unlike Durwood, she would never have done this to herself. "I am a Blue Belle Yankee!" she said to herself, "and far too strong to let anything or anyone destroy me."

With this new understanding of herself would also come the realization that Durwood had been the weaker of the two. Her mother was wrong; it would not have been the uniform that would have spoiled their union, but her own strength of character.

Cynthia was now working as a counter girl and found a room close to her work. She liked waiting on people and was very popular with the customers. They enjoyed her friendly manner and the good service she provided.

She saw a great deal of her friend Ann, whom she had met through Johnny Hale. Ann tried many times to fix her up with dates, but Cynthia was reluctant to get involved again.

She watched some of the other counter girls having dates

and sometimes having affairs. It seemed to her that she had gotten into enough trouble without getting involved with sex. She had wanted to "go all the way" with Durwood, but that was with the single aim of getting pregnant so her mother would have to give in to her marriage. He, fortunately, was too much of a gentleman to take advantage of her.

Other than that, she thought these girls were stupid to let themselves be used one day and passed by the next, like pay toilets.

She worked at her job and she also tried working out her life. She had so many emotions to deal with. She had to cope with her grief and she had to cope with her bitterness. She did have a few dates, but they were strictly evenings out. There didn't seem to be room for romance.

Chapter 9

One day Ann called and invited Cynthia to have lunch with her at The Ringside. Ann loved this spot because it was a hangout for reporters, and she was sure to bump into her steady, Jack Armstrong.

Jack had tried to get Cynthia to date his buddy, but she had always refused. She was still trying to get over Durwood's death. Cynthia arrived early, and passed through the bar and lounge and then between the wrought-iron grill dividers to reach the dining room. She was the only one in the room, and she proceeded to go to the far end where she sat at a table, her back toward the dining room. In front of her was a public phone booth.

The waitress came, and she ordered a martini. She waited for it to arrive and when it did she took a sip.

She heard a noise and looked up, expecting to see her

friends. Instead, she found herself looking directly into the eyes of an extremely handsome man who had come to the phone booth and was placing a call. Their eyes seemed to lock in place. Neither one lowered them, and when he was finished with his call, he came out of the booth and stood at her table. Pointing a finger at her, he spoke: "Do you know I'm going to marry you?"

Cynthia did not answer. She had years of experience at lunch counters dealing with men and their "lines."

However, this time she was speechless. She was amazed at herself for staring at him. This was so out of character for her. She had been so struck with the sheer weight of his magnetism, she had lost control of herself.

Cynthia loved clothes and instantly recognized his sharp, conservative appearance. She took in his six-foot height, his wonderful head of curly hair, and the gleam of his white teeth.

He walked past her with the grace and pride of a panther.

With some effort, she regained her composure and then became indignant. How conceited of him, to think she would be bowled over by his words. She did have to admit, she had been quite taken with his looks. She thought that whoever had invented the expression "tall, dark, and handsome" surely had had him in mind.

Cynthia took a larger drink of her martini and got up. She walked up to the bar and saw her friend Tommy. Ann appeared, and Tommy turned to the new arrival and said teasingly, "Cynthia has just found an admirer. A minute ago, 'God's gift to women' stepped out of our phone booth and talked to her. He's a nightclub manager and also an emcee. He's been asked to manage this place and was here to look it over. Watch your step, Cynthia," he grinned. "This man has so many women chasing him, you'll get trampled in the rush."

Ann asked him what the man's name was.

"His name is Herman Prujansky, but everybody calls him 'The Turk' or just plain 'Turk.' That's because he's so popular with the ladies. They claim he has his own harem. There's no question but that he wants Cynthia to add to his list. Before

Turk left, he stopped and asked the bartender who she was and what he knew about her."

Cynthia feigned indifference. Harem, indeed!

She would be damned if she would ever have someone she had to share. She turned away but had trouble getting rid of the image of that incredibly handsome face.

Cynthia was working now as a waitress in a club called The Cellar. One night a gas main blew up, and the place was out of business. Cynthia was also out of a job.

Through friends, she learned there was a job opening at The Paddock for a food and cocktail waitress. She lost no time getting over there, and with her experience and nice appearance, she was immediately hired by the bartender.

The job was explained to her. She would serve dinner from six until ten. The kitchen would then close, and she would serve drinks until the club closed. The club offered two shows a night and had a smart clientele. She was to report the next day at five, early enough to learn where everything was and to set up the tables.

Cynthia reported for work and found it was a very pleasant job. She was just clearing up from some late diners when she came face to face with the man who had been in the telephone booth at The Ringside, and she remembered that he had been offered the job there as the manager. The shock also registered on his face, then he grinned at her with those wonderful teeth and said, "Well, so you finally found me."

Cynthia was very indignant. This man certainly was egotistical. Found him, indeed! She said, "I certainly wasn't looking for you. A gas main blew up where I was working, and I simply needed a job and found this opening."

He was still smiling, and, with a twinkle in his big brown eyes, said, "God bless that gas main!"

Ignoring him, she quickly returned to her duties. She stuck to her work and managed most evenings to avoid him. She recalled the bartender's words when she saw with her own eyes how he was chased by women. Well, one thing was for sure: she wasn't about to join in the chase.

Often she felt his eyes on her, but she would avoid looking at him, afraid that she would again be caught staring at him. It was not too difficult, because the place was popular, and it kept her busy.

Besides being the manager, Turk would double up on his duties and also emcee and sing. When she knew she could not be seen by him, she would try hard to get ahead in her work so she could listen.

There was so much more to this man than his attractiveness. Others at work would talk about him, and she learned he was Jewish. He was extremely well-liked among the Jewish customers. Cynthia had never been around Jewish people and was pleased that they treated her with such warmth. She worked hard to be attentive to their needs, and they responded with compliments and generous tips.

When the kitchen closed, she then had to work at the long bar. This was always filled with stag men. Cynthia had never had a job where so many men had tried to date her. But then, she had never worked a dinner club before, and wondered if they were all like this.

One evening she came to work and, passing down the aisle between the bar and restaurant, saw Turk sitting with a woman and a little boy who looked about six years old.

He stopped Cynthia, saying, "I would like you to meet my son, Marvin, and my former wife, Helen."

She chatted briefly with them, complimenting them on their good-looking son. After a bit, she excused herself and started work.

When the club closed that night and her work was finished, she removed her uniform and got dressed to leave. On her way out, Turk intercepted her and invited Cynthia to join him and his friends for dinner at the Brown Bomber Chicken Shack. The Brown Bomber was, of course, the famous prize fighter Joe Louis. Cynthia accepted and found that Turk was actually with another girl. They were joined by an older man named Sam Rubin, the attorney who owned The Paddock.

This was the era of blind pigs and black-and-tan night

spots. The country was saddled with prohibition, but the police were sympathetic toward the owners of these clubs and averted their eyes, knowing they were selling liquor. As long as there was no trouble, the law kept its distance. These clubs encouraged patronage by both blacks and whites, and the blacks themselves policed their own neighborhoods. A girl could walk safely down these streets alone at night with no fear.

If someone had predicted then that this same Detroit would for years be known as the murder capital of the United States, Cynthia would never have believed them.

Joe Louis had hired his old childhood friend Sonny to stand at the entrance and carefully screen the customers. Some were courteously turned away at the door if Sonny sensed they were drunk.

Cynthia was glad she had accepted. The Chicken Shack was a very popular spot to go after the bars had closed, and soon the place became crowded with bar owners and musicians who were looking for some fun of their own. Some of the boys would bring their instruments in with them for a jam session.

The two races mixed here with dignity and good humor. They were served family-style with good southern-fried chicken, and agreed that there was no finer eating in the entire city.

What a lot of fun! With everyone coming in after hours, she was able to meet and mingle with entertainers whom she had only heard about. They sometimes sang with the impromptu band, which thrilled her.

Finally, it was late and time to leave. When she indicated that she was going to call a cab, Sam insisted that they escort her home. Before they got to her door, they entered the neighborhood where Sam lived in an apartment hotel, and he suggested a nightcap at his place. He said he had a new suite and wanted them to see it. Cynthia wondered whether she could quite believe him, but she sat quietly, listening to the others agree. She finally said yes when she realized that to say no would cause the others to cut short their evening. She didn't want to be known as a killjoy.

Sam led them to a building that she knew was exclusive, renting only to professional people. He collected his mail and key from the desk clerk, and they went to his apartment. Sam was very cordial, expertly mixing their drinks. He walked with her to the living room, which she admired.

Then he led her over to a painting and asked her whether she had ever heard of Vincent Van Gogh. She admitted her ignorance, and he then proceeded to tell her about this artist and why he was Sam's favorite. He explained that Van Gogh was the first painter ever to make the colors move before your eyes. She really could not see them move but was not about to admit it.

He pointed out how the artist used swirling brush strokes and intense yellows, greens, and blues for effect.

She found this all new and quite interesting until she became aware that they were alone in the living room. Suddenly she knew that Turk and the girl had vanished into the bedroom.

She wondered how long it would take Sam to make his move. If he told her to shack up or else, she was prepared to take the "or else." He made the pass, and Cynthia rejected him with a firm "No!" She informed Sam that she was leaving and turned to the door. Sam said he could not let her go down alone—that if she went out through the lobby by herself, the desk clerk would think she was a call girl, which was not allowed in a place like this. Sam assured her he would not touch her and said he felt that Turk and the girl would be leaving soon.

Cynthia sat in a chair by the door and laid her head back. She could hear the heavy panting and movement through the bedroom door. It seemed to go on and on. Sam was dozing in a chair across the room, and soon she, too, fell asleep.

Cynthia woke up when she felt a kiss on her lips. It was Turk on his way out the door. He had left the girl asleep in the bed. Sam asked her if she would mind waking the girl up and taking her home. She reluctantly agreed, not really wanting to have anything to do with her. She had known her for some time, as she was Cynthia's dentist's assistant. She knew that the girl was nothing but a tramp. Cynthia would see that she got home, but she felt above her and would have been embarrassed to be seen with her.

Cynthia saw quite a lot of Sam after that. He respected her and soon was pouring out his marital troubles to her. His ownership of the club and her sympathetic ear brought him out night after night.

He had dated the same girl all through high school, until it became an expected thing that they would end up together. They had married and both enrolled in law school. Sam and Melba had struggled together in their first years to get a start in their field, and this had been hampered by the birth of two children.

When success had finally been theirs, his world had fallen apart. He had thought they had the perfect marriage and the perfect life. They adored their children and had a mansion in an exclusive section of Detroit called Sherwood Forest. They owned a lovely yacht and, of course, The Paddock.

The worry over money was well behind them when Melba had started an affair with a prosecuting attorney. Sam placed most of the blame on the fact that his wife had never dated anyone but him.

Cynthia listened but privately thought this was a weak theory. She was more inclined to think that, with Sam's law practice and business dealings, Melba had felt neglected.

It all had finally come to a head when his wife, after a violent quarrel, had shot and killed the prosecuting attorney.

Melba had been charged and brought to trial. The testimony had brought out the fact that this man had cheated her out of an enormous amount of money. The jury had voted for acquittal, and she had been freed, but Sam had never invited her to return to him.

Sam and Cynthia went out a few times to dinner. They would talk, and she would urge him to go to Melba and ask her to come back. She said she felt that Sam's wife was wrong in sinning against the marriage, but that Sam still loved her and should find it in his heart to forgive her. Perhaps reminded of the mistake she had made with Durwood, she told him he was letting his pride get in the way of a solution.

Turk watched them go out together and would make remarks to her. After all, she had rejected him, and it was still a sore point. He hinted that he thought she and Sam should get married, and then, he supposed, she would be his boss.

Cythia told him what the situation was, explaining that she was simply a crying towel for Sam while he tried to sort out his life.

Sam urged her to meet Melba, but she thought he simply wanted to display her so that his wife might feel jealous. She finally agreed to a meeting at The Paddock. He was still finding it difficult to ask his wife back. He loved her, and the children needed him, yet the words stuck in his mouth.

He thought that Cynthia was smart and that perhaps she could gauge Melba's feelings and bring about a reconciliation.

Cynthia met with Melba as Sam had arranged. They instantly liked each other and talked at length. Cynthia then went to Sam and talked to him. "Your wife is a lovely woman. She told me she had made a God-awful mistake. She wants to come back and she needs you, Sam. They have found out she has an advanced cancer of the cervix. Take her back in joy for the time she has left."

Sam rushed out of the room to be reunited with his wife, and Cynthia tiptoed out through the kitchen.

Cynthia had been having great difficulty with a persistent customer who wanted to date her. She had found that the kitchen exit was her answer when she wanted to evade him and his offers of a ride.

The kitchen was closed for the night, and she made her way in the dark. Cynthia bumped into a large body, and her arms were suddenly pinned to her sides. A hand brushed the wall and found the light switch. It was Turk. His face turned from a look of anger into one of delight. "Well, so I finally got you in my arms. What in the world are you doing, creeping around in the dark?"

She explained that she was bothered by wolves at the bar and that this was how she got away from them. He told her that he thought she was smart to do this because "the bar is full of the Purples, and no place for a lady."

He was, of course, referring to the Purple Gang, who had gained a reputation for their gangsterism. They had held up a truck in their youth near the Eastern Market. The cargo had contained boxes of purple sweaters, and when they had appeared together wearing their booty, they had been given the nickname and would be called that for the rest of their criminal lives.

Turk asked her if she would like a ride home, and she gratefully accepted. Once she was seated in the car, he asked if she would like to take a ride out to Belle Isle to see his trained hyena. She agreed, and they drove around the island for a while and talked. It was far too dark as yet to see any animals.

They parked by the fountain and watched the far-off lights through the spray and the ships that were passing by on the Detroit River. As they continued to talk through the night, she found him intelligent, interesting, and a lot of fun. He was attractive in so many ways, that she was sorry she had avoided him for so long. When daylight came, she was surprised that the time had gone so fast.

Cynthia and Turk headed for the zoo, and when they reached the hyena cage, Turk called out to the animal, pretending that he was an old friend. He was very funny, and she was enjoying herself. Finally he called out to the hyena, asking it to roll over. To her amazement, the animal actually rolled right over and emitted its crazy laugh.

Turk turned to her. "Didn't I tell you that I had a trained hyena?"

Cynthia answered, "You must have been here many times with many girls to have taught him that!"

Laughing together, they returned to the car. He told her he had the evening off, and as it was also her night off, perhaps she would like to go out with him. He had tickets for the amateur prize fights. He explained that they were called the Golden Gloves competitions.

She had never seen a prize fight, and he had behaved so well through the night in the car that she felt she could trust him. He was also so much fun that the evening was sure to be a success.

When he picked her up that evening, he handed her a little pin shaped like two gold gloves. She thought it was darling and thanked him. She supposed that a lot of women would be wearing one like it as an expression of their love of this sport.

Turk carefully pinned it on her and told her that he had won it himself in another Golden Gloves competition. "I was doing well until the night my mouthpiece fell out. I quit right there. I loved my teeth too much to have them knocked out."

They went to the fights and then on to get a late snack. Turk saw a friend of his and called over to him. "Hymie, could you lend me your car? Mine is getting something minor fixed. We came in a cab, and I need a car." Hymie came over and gave Turk his car keys.

Turk said to him, "Don't expect it back right away, because this pretty lady and I are going to Monroe and get married."

Cynthia giggled. He really was so funny.

His friend laughed, saying, "Turk you've been going to get married every night that I've known you."

Turk responded, "Hymie, this time it's different."

He turned to Cynthia and explained that he had to go to Monroe to see the mayor. "He is a friend of mine, and I need to ask him for a favor. Would you go with me? We should be back by noon, so we'll have time to get some sleep before going to work."

She agreed, and they left, speeding along the highway. Soon a patrol car stopped them, and the officer asked him why he was speeding. Turk told him he was in a hurry because they were on their way to get married.

The policeman said, "I don't blame you. She sure is pretty,

but if you want to enjoy the honeymoon, you'd better slow it down."

After they drove off, she asked Turk whether he always got away with things by thinking fast. She called him a con man, and they laughed together. He never did answer her question.

Chapter 10

They arrived early in Monroe. They entered the city hall, and Turk left her in the waiting room while he was ushered into the mayor's office. Soon he came out with the mayor and introduced her. As they turned to leave, the mayor wished them luck.

This struck her as a rather odd remark, but she quickly forgot it when Turk said they were now going to another building. They crossed the street, entered, and stood before a desk with a sign that said County Clerk.

The man looked up, and Turk said, "We have come for a marriage license."

Cynthia's eyes flew open. She spoke up, "No, we didn't!"

Turk explained to the clerk that she was terribly nervous. Taking Cynthia aside, he said, "Look at all the girls wanting your man; you're so lucky to catch me."

She was indignant. "Now listen to me, Turk, you're fooling yourself if you think that I will marry you."

The clerk looked bewildered. He took an application and placed it on the counter, then took a pen and proceeded to ask Turk for their names. When he had all the information, he handed the form to Turk.

Cynthia continued to protest, but Turk ignored her. The clerk's eyes got bigger and bigger.

Turk thanked the clerk and led her out of the building.

They quarreled all the way back to the mayor's office. He accused her of not wanting to marry him because he was Jewish!

She denied this and said, "I would marry any man that I loved, but I do not love you!"

He declared, "You have fun with me, you like me. That's a good start."

The mayor had arranged everything for them, even granting permission for them to marry without the required blood test.

Suddenly they were standing before the mayor. Cynthia was still protesting, and Turk was laughing. She continued to argue as the mayor started the ceremony. Turk was so forceful. His eyes sparkled with amusement at her surprise when he produced a wedding ring! He slipped it on her finger, and suddenly she heard herself say, "I do."

On the way back to Detroit, she placed the marriage certificate on her lap to read it over. She found it hard to believe she had let him talk her into this. She thought about the police officer and how smooth Turk had been. Somehow she felt she had been conned. One thing came to mind that was very satisfying. Last month she had turned eighteen, which made this marriage legal, and her mother could do nothing about it!

She looked down again at the certificate. Suddenly she let out with a big "ho!" She started to laugh and laugh.

Turk wanted to get in on the joke.

She explained to him that according to the license, he had married a Kathleen Ryan and not her at all.

He was firm with her. "If you will just shut up for a minute
. . . you had the poor clerk so confused that he didn't know
where he was at. But let me tell you, Baby, I am your husband.
You stood before witnesses . . . before a man who could marry
us, and I don't care if you had said that you were John Doe, you
are my wife!"

They drove on in silence until he asked in a low voice,
"What will your folks say when you tell them you have
married a Jew?"

She told him truthfully that she had no idea.

She thought about it. The only Jews she had ever known
had owned the big grocery store where her grandmother
shopped. She remembered that when she had typhoid fever,
they would send over gifts of large oranges for her. She had
once heard someone say the Jews had killed Christ, but she
had never believed it.

They stopped at a small roadside stand for lunch. Turk was
running out of money, so they had to celebrate their union over
hot beef sandwiches.

They finished, and he drove them to the hotel where he
lived. The desk clerk looked up when they came in, and his
eyebrows rose.

Turk introduced her as his wife, but the clerk had a look on
his face of smiling disbelief.

Turk turned to his bride and had her produce the wedding
certificate. The desk clerk's face showed complete shock. "Do
my eyes deceive me, or am I actually looking at a genuine
marriage certificate for the great Turk? Oh, how the women
will cry when they hear this news! The great Turk hooked, oh
my."

Turk laughed and said, "Yes, and she never even tried to
hook me."

Cynthia wondered to herself if perhaps this had been part
of her appeal.

They entered his room. Knowing that she had no luggage,
he swept the spread from the bed and put it in her arms. "There.
You can shower first and put this around you."

She showered and traded places with him and then climbed naked into bed.

I listened to him in the shower and lay there thinking how quickly life had changed for me. It was just one month ago that I saw a complete stranger who pointed his finger at me and said he was going to marry me. Was this fate? If it was, then fate sure was funny.

I felt a little embarrassed over what was to come. I wondered what it would be like? He probably thought I was worldly wise, and I actually knew nothing!

He came from the shower and climbed in naked beside me. He was a very gentle lover and I felt everything was working out well.

Something apparently was different for him, however, because he stopped and asked me, "How long has it been since you've been with a man?"

I told him I had never been with a man, and he was astounded. He became very excited over the fact that he was the first.

We resumed our lovemaking. I was wonderfully happy; it was as thrilling as people said it was. Our breathing quickened and we were swept up in a glorious climax.

He told me I was his first virgin and that he would cherish me forever.

I told him that he might be the first, but if he didn't treat me right, he would not be the last.

He started making sweeping promises, starting with a fur coat for every day of the week, but I cut him short.

"I don't want your gifts, just yourself, and I won't share you with either drink or with other women."

He promised me that I would never have to worry. He said he had known he just had to have me, and would need nothing else, for I would fill all his needs. We cuddled together and we slept.

Turk called the club and told them to call in for replacements for them. He claimed he was going to throw his clothes out the window and swore he would not go out of the room for a week.

Turk just about kept his promise. He had newspapers and all their meals sent up. He claimed that, with his job, he was just worn out with the public and wanted to really get to know his wife.

Cynthia also had questions. She asked about his parents, and he said they were the old Orthodox Jews, and he worried about springing her on them all at once. "They wanted me to marry a nice Jewish girl. They wanted me to remain with my own people, but that is one thing I can never do. I decided long ago, I would never marry a Jewish girl just to please my parents. These girls think of themselves as princesses and want to be waited on, hand and foot. I've never met one who would lift her hand to help her man. So many of my friends married Jewish girls, but they all have gentile girlfriends that they keep in apartments. The wife gets the mink and diamonds, and the girlfriend gets his love and her rent paid. Well, I think that's a false and shoddy way to live, and it's not for me."

Cynthia had told the truth when she had said that she did not love him.

He had also told the truth when he had said having fun with him and liking him was a good start.

She found that he was very smart and great fun to be with. And he was very caring and tender in bed. Slowly she began to fall in love with him. Eventually this love would blossom into the most important thing in her life.

It was hard at first. She had left a childhood so filled with hurts that she found it difficult to trust anyone.

She did find one blemish in this otherwise idyllic relationship. Turk insisted she quit work and stay in the apartment. He may not have wanted a Jewish princess, but he also did not want a working wife. She missed being at the club, but he would not even let her come in to visit. He explained that he was so busy there, he could not take the time to ward off her admirers, who would want to talk to her and paw her.

She objected, saying she had managed very well in the past without him, but he was adamant.

Cynthia loved clothes. She had been making good money but had never given one thought to putting anything into the bank. Every cent was spent to put pretty things on her back. Turk loved taking her out and showing her off, but he became upset if he thought her dress too sexy. He started to forbid her to wear certain outfits. She certainly had the figure to catch the eye. She was nearly five-foot-five with a thirty-eight-inch bust and thirty six-inch hips. She weighed ninety-six pounds. Turk was terribly proud of her figure but would get upset over any dress that he thought showed it off too well. Her prominent bust line displayed over a low-necked dress would send him into a tirade.

Once in a while she would defy him and put on a dress she especially liked, one that he had forbidden her to wear. When she would get it back from the dry cleaner, there would be a scorch mark on the seat from a hot iron. She would complain to the cleaner about this, and he would blame it on his press man. The cleaner would then pay her for ruining her dress.

She had lost several dresses before she found out that it was her husband who was to blame. The sax player in his band owned the cleaning shop and was just following his boss's orders. The band thought this was very funny.

Cynthia quickly became bored with nothing to do. It soon became obvious to Turk, too, that she needed more in her life. He had introduced her to a couple who were old friends of his. He suggested that Mollie, the wife, might help her find them an apartment. He had already moved her clothes to the hotel. It had taken four trips in his car.

Chapter 11

Mollie agreed to go apartment-hunting with her, but they had no luck. Every time she went to see an apartment, Mollie would speak up and announce that Cynthia's husband was Jewish. She would then be told they did not rent to Jews. Cynthia wondered why Jews were rejected, and Mollie, who was also Jewish, told her that Jews were thought of as dirty housekeepers.

Cynthia said that she had heard the term "dirty Jew" but never thought it was true.

Mollie said, "God forbid that we are dirty; we Jews are a clean race. Kosher means clean!"

Turk wanted to live close to his work, and that section had many lovely apartments and apartment hotels, but each and every one that Cynthia went to turned her away. She knew better than to try to rent one without telling the manager. Turk had a prominent nose and would be instantly identified as a Jew. They would then be told to move out.

Suddenly Cynthia had an idea. She told Mollie about an old Jewish man named Sol whom she had met while working as a waitress. Another waitress there was always calling everyone an old putz, and Cynthia thought that sounded cute. Sol was a regular lunchtime customer of hers, and one day she called him an old putz.

They had gotten quite friendly, and he knew her well enough to know she had made a big mistake.

He admonished her. "My dear young lady, you don't know what you are saying. That is a very bad Jewish slang word. It means the tool that a man uses to pass water. You should never use a word from another language that you don't know."

She told Mollie she had just remembered Sol and was going to call him and see if he would help. She knew that Sol owned the Hoffman Building, the Whittier Hotel, and many apartments. Cynthia said he could hardly write his name, but he was extremely smart.

They found a phone booth and looked up his office number. When she got him on the phone, she identified herself as the waitress who had called him an old putz. She told him she had married a Jewish man and of her difficulty in finding anyone who would rent them an apartment.

Sol was glad to hear from her, calling her "my little darling," and was very sympathetic about her problem. He told her he would give her a choice of some lovely apartments and not to worry about the rent, because he would make sure they were affordable.

Cynthia was ecstatic and told Sol how grateful she was for his kindness. She could hardly wait to tell Turk.

So she found an apartment, after all. It was already furnished, but she would have the fun of finding things to put in it to make it cozy. Turk let her get anything she wanted for their new living quarters, and for a while this managed to keep her busy. It was fun, shopping and arranging the apartment, and she eagerly looked forward to Turk's return each night. She had never thought that love and sex could be this perfect.

Their love life was spectacular. Turk said that the sight of her turned his knees to rubber. He found that the slightest touch during the night brought on an immediate reaction. He was tired all the time because he was losing sleep. He finally got the manager to take their bed away and bring up twin beds. This only lasted a week, for he found he missed having her with him. He would wake up and then have to cross over to be with her.

He was amusing, even in the middle of the night. He would get up and stand between the beds, pounding his chest and shouting, "Me Tarzan, me want Jane!" Then he would slide beside her and over her, and it was wonderful.

Cynthia could also be fun. They had not been married long before he became ill and went to the doctor. He was having difficulty sleeping, and the doctor prescribed sleeping pills. When she woke up in the morning, he was still dead asleep. She had purchased a set of kelly-green pajamas for him, but he would only wear the top. The weather was warm, and he had slept without any covers. She looked at him as he lay on his back and got an idea. She carefully got up and found a length of red ribbon. Gently, so as not to disturb him, she tied a bow around what she describes as his "willie." Later he woke and went to the bathroom. She heard him roar with laughter, and he came back out. He paraded around, grinning as he postured and posed. He finally declared he was going to go out in the hallway and knock on the doors of the other tenants and show himself off. He said he was going to ask the other people, "What should I do with a wife who ties up your joint like it's a president." He even went so far as to go to the door and grab the handle as if he were in earnest. The idea set Cynthia off into uncontrollable laughter as she pulled him away. Even though he was sick, it set the tone for the day.

Now, with everything in place in the apartment and only a little housework to do, she found she was bored. She had been working steadily since she was twelve, never once calling in sick. She liked working in a restaurant. She enjoyed people and missed being around them.

Turk was unbelievably jealous. He told her she was never to be around any man besides himself. At first she was flattered by his attitude, but it would became a fire-breathing monster.

When she was in a nightclub sitting on a bar stool, and an old friend came up to talk and perhaps put an arm around her shoulder, she would learn about Turk's temper. He would yell at the fellow to take his hands off his wife! This happened twice. When he found that his friends enjoyed teasing him by touching her on the arm or back, he knocked them cold. So she had to learn quickly to respect his will, or people would suffer for it.

Cynthia tried to talk to him about it and convince him that he had nothing to worry about, because she was a faithful wife. She told him that he embarrassed her with his actions. She pleaded with him to curb his temper and open up his eyes to what he was doing to her. Certainly the fact that she had been a virgin when he met her should tell him something about what a fool he was to think she would suddenly start granting favors. She told him she was so completely satisfied in her own bed, with her own husband, that she was not even tempted. But the jealousy continued unabated.

Cynthia was downtown shopping when she ran into her friend Myra Wolfgang. They had met when Myra had recruited her into the newly organized Hotel and Restaurant Employees Union. She had not wanted to join, but without being a member, she would nor have been able to get a decent job.

They greeted each other with warmth. Myra asked her where in the world she was keeping herself, because no one seemed to see her anymore. Was it true she had married the Turk? She said it seemed as if every woman in Detroit had the hots for the big, handsome devil.

Cynthia told her she had indeed married him and had known he was popular with the women, but had not been aware of the titles tagged to his name. Since then, she had found that, because of his popularity as an emcee, he was called the Night Mayor. She had also heard him referred to as Mr. Detroit.

They decided to stop somewhere for coffee so they could catch up on the news. Myra told her she really had not believed it when a friend had told her Cynthia had married Turk. "My folks and his are very good friends. They came over from the old country at about the same time. They meet together at their club every Saturday night, so I was sure they would have said something."

Cynthia explained that Turk did not want to upset his parents and had not told them yet. His father had worked hard when he had come to America and had eventually owned a distillery. In 1929, when the crash came, he had lost everything, suffered a heart attack, and then had a nervous breakdown.

Turk could not bring himself to admit to his father that he had married a gentile. He was afraid that if he told him he had married outside of their faith, it might bring on another heart attack.

Myra could understand that, but she could not get over the fact that no one ever seemed to see Cynthia anymore. Laughingly she asked, "Does Turk keep you under lock and key?"

Cynthia's face was serious when she said, "The answer is yes. Myra, I really love him, and he is very good to me, but I am very unhappy. I have always worked and have always been a free soul. Now, suddenly, I find I have a restrictive boss who will not let me out of his sight. He made me quit my job, and I hate sitting around the apartment every night, waiting for him to come home from work. He is so jealous, he only allows me to see a couple of girlfriends. I'm not used to being idle and I'm bored to death."

Myra had the perfect solution. She told Cynthia about a new German singing club called the Concordia that had just opened in Detroit. She thought Turk might agree to let Cynthia work there because the membership was made up of only older people. They formed a singing society, and people from all over the United States came to participate.

She explained that Cynthia's job would be to act as hostess during the lunch and dinner hour, when the club was open to the public. However, when the dining room closed in the evening, the public was asked to leave.

She offered to intercede for Cynthia by going to Turk and talking to him. Cynthia readily agreed. She knew that Myra was a strong woman. If anyone could talk Turk into something, it would be Myra.

Years later, Myra, then Myra Breckenridge, would become the president of her international union.

Chapter 12

Turk was at the club rehearsing some new acts when Myra approached him and explained that she needed a favor from him. She told him how she had organized a new German club and that she needed Cynthia to work there.

Turk had heard all that he wanted to and said, "Absolutely not."

Undaunted, Myra continued to present her case. She explained that the club was made up of members who were from the old country—older people who would appreciate Cynthia's good manners.

Turk said, "Sorry, Myra, but no way. She's not to work. She's my wife, and I will support her."

Myra was persistent and pleaded with him to back down. She finally asked him if he would consider just letting Cynthia help her out until she could find someone else.

Turk thought about this and finally relented, but said he would first have to look the German club over.

This was at least a partial victory, and Myra and Cynthia were elated.

The German club was located in an old building erected at the turn of the century. The inside, in contrast, was quite new and quite splendid. Upon entering, one was impressed with the wide, oak circular stairway and the hand-carved handrails. The landing had a Tiffany glass window of many colors, emblazoned with a crest. The carpeting was a rich royal blue, and a lovely crystal chandelier hung above the landing, the prisms sparkling with reflections from the lights. At the top of the stairway were large white doors which, when opened, revealed large banquet rooms that could seat from three to four hundred people. There was a bar and a dance floor in front of an elevated bandstand. The walls were wainscoted in oak with flocked wallpaper above. The ceilings were beamed, and the tables were set with real linen tablecloths and, startlingly, real sterling silver flatware! Clearly, no expense had been spared. Here, too, were many crystal chandeliers, breathtaking in size.

Turk could not help but be impressed, and when he saw that the clientele were, as Myra had said, all older people, he at last gave his consent.

Myra told Cynthia to use her union card with her maiden name on it, explaining that the Germans didn't like Jews. She further cautioned her not to admit she was married to a Jew.

With this job, Cynthia's life took a definite turn for the better. She got up each day with a real purpose. The added income was a welcome bonus, too, because she and Turk were terribly big spenders. He drove a white Cadillac convertible and swore he would always drive a convertible. He later amended this because he thought he might become bald someday. (He did not.)

Cynthia drove a burgundy Lincoln Continental with burgundy leather upholstery. The added money helped them greatly with their large car payments.

She loved her new job, and she loved still more the

activity and independence it brought. Turk gradually accepted the fact that she worked, and Myra never did look for a replacement.

They had the same day off, and Turk started to take her out to dinner at his club when they had a special movie star as the entertainer. During this time, women were expected to wear formals at night. Cynthia had purchased a beautiful new dress with a hoop skirt and a low neckline which she was eager to show off to her husband. It was made of a changeable lavender taffeta, which went well with her blonde hair. She had the hairdresser arrange it in the new style—all piled high with four long curls hanging down her back. She had thought up a new idea and bought a length of lavender ribbon, and, after pinning her grandmother's cameo to it, had tied it around her neck. She looked anxiously in the mirror and was pleased with the effect.

The weather was bitter cold, and she was glad to wear her new mink coat. Turk, on their wedding night, had promised he would cherish her and give her a fur coat for every day of the week. He was starting to make good on this promise.

Cynthia took a cab to the club, where she had arranged to meet Turk. She had dressed all up for him and she could hardly wait to hear his reaction. She was delighted when he greeted her and commented on how beautiful she looked. They had dinner and were later joined by some of Turk's friends. Each one took turns taking her out on the dance floor and joking with her about how burned Turk was getting at the attention they paid to her. She did not really notice; she was too busy enjoying herself.

The evening ended, and as they started home he proceeded to attack her. He accused her of flirting with the men and behaving like a hussy! She indignantly denied that this was so and became just as angry as Turk. It was unjust of him to find fault with her when she thought the evening had gone so well. They drew up to their apartment, and he was still berating her, saying she had really finished herself that night and he would never take her to the club again. He told her to get out of the car, that he would be back later.

Cynthia had the key to the apartment and went in. Her Irish was really up, and she decided she would retaliate by locking him out. She knew that if she let him in, he would have gotten over his anger and then she would forgive him. Up until now they had always settled their differences in bed. He would be especially loving and tell her he knew she was angry, but that he could not sleep without holding her in his arms. The next morning she would wake up all warm and cozy in his embrace, and the fight would be forgotten. Well, she was not going to be so forgiving this time!

Cynthia was fully determined she would not let him in. She went to bed, and when the bell rang and rang she simply turned over and did not answer. Then the telephone rang, but she did not answer that either. She was going to punish HIM for once.

It was noon of the next day when she again heard the doorbell ring. This time Cynthia answered it. She supposed he had spent the night at his parents' house or had checked into a hotel. She was wrong. He had instead returned to the club and gone to sleep on the chaise longue in the ladies' room, using his overcoat as a blanket, but it had not been not enough to keep him warm through the night. He had came back to the apartment with the beginnings of a cold. Over the next few days the cold got worse, and he really looked sick. She was worried about him and finally convinced him he had better see a doctor. Her worry was confirmed when it was found that he now had pneumonia.

She received the news at work and rushed to the hospital, but he was still in the emergency room, where they had him under oxygen. His family arrived at the same time and they were all told that tests had been taken and that the results were very bad. He had a hole in his lung which had caused it to collapse.

When Cynthia was allowed in to see him, she forced herself to look calm. Turk looked so scared lying there, and it tore her up inside. He apparently thought her calm face indicated that she did not take his illness very seriously. He informed her that he had been bleeding from the mouth. "You see, Baby, what your temper has done? You have killed your old man."

Turk's parents came in. The doctor also had called Cynthia in, addressing her as Mrs. Prujansky. This was a revelation to his parents, because they had been told that he was only living with a shiksa (gentile). His mother's mouth compressed into a fine line, and her face expressed her distress at this news. Turk looked up at her and grasped her hand. "Mama, don't be upset. Yes, we are married and she is my very life. She is good to me, Mama. Please be kind to her and, as you love me, love her."

Cynthia saw the woman's face change. She turned to Cynthia and said, "If you love my son, when he leaves the hospital you will let him come home with me so I can nurse him."

Cynthia thought about the hours she would be away at her job, and also about their apartment with the drafty corner windows, and she reluctantly agreed. Her mother-in-law was pleased and thanked her. She told her to feel welcome to come and visit Turk while he recovered from his illness

Turk was hospitalized for a month before he was released, and Cynthia visited him every day. When he was discharged and went to his parents' home, she tried to visit him regularly, but Cynthia felt very uncomfortable there. His family and relatives spoke Yiddish, and she could not understand them. She felt angry at being left out of their conversations. It was obvious, too, that they were talking about her, and she thought they were very rude. Her mother-in-law took her aside and explained the situation to her. "My sister and my brother, please do not feel bad, but as yet I cannot find the courage to tell them my Herman has married a gentile. We're from an old and proud Jewish family. We're descendants from the ancient line of Katz. Now I think I am coming down with a cold myself, and I don't want you to catch it, so maybe you'd better not come to visit my Herman for a few days."

Cynthia was angry and deeply offended. Did her mother-in-law think her blood would contaminate theirs? Katz, indeed! Did that make her a dog? She was also suspicious about the cold coming on, but she could hardly call the woman a liar. Furthermore, she couldn't see any point to be gained by her lying. She was polite to the woman, but after she left the house, she muttered to herself, "I'm a Blue Belle Yankee, and my heritage is just as important to me as the Katz line is to you!"

Her good friend Mollie was staying with her for company during this difficult time. Mollie answered the bell from the lobby when it rang the next morning at 4:00 A.M., and listened to the speaker. Cynthia was frightened. "They're coming to tell me that he's dead!"

Mollie said, "No, he's not dead, he's on his way up." Turk then came into the room and announced that his parents had been going to put him on a train to Phoenix without letting her know. The doctor felt the climate out there would help him recover.

He had sneaked out of the house and had purchased a ticket for her on the same train. "I can't go out there alone. Without you, Baby, I'll die."

She agreed to pack up and meet him at the train station, and he left.

Chapter 13

Cynthia was frantic. She turned to her friend. "Oh, Mollie, what am I going to do? We just moved to this apartment. I bought all new furniture, and I don't know what to do with it. Who knows how long we'll be gone? I'll have to give up this apartment, and I've just hung up my new drapes. They are custom-made, and I can't take them back."

Cynthia was very nervous, picking things up only to lay them down again. She called Ann, who promised to come right over. When Ann arrived, she joined with Mollie in taking charge.

They helped her pack and told her they would store the furniture for her and see whether the new tenant would buy the drapes.

They knew that the doctor thought Turk would do better in a warmer climate, and they told her to concentrate on getting him better and to leave the rest to them. Cynthia was very grateful. She knew she was lucky to have such good friends.

She took a cab to Michigan Central Station and boarded the train. She sat in their compartment and waited for Turk. When he arrived, he was so terribly weak and white that she was frightened. She immediately helped him undress and got him into the lower berth.

During the entire trip, Cynthia only let him get up to go to the bathroom or sometimes sit up in the compartment. She would go to the dining car and return with their meals. They would sit together and watch out the window and comment on the changes they saw as they traveled further and further west.

Gradually a bit of color returned to his face, but he was still very weak. He had lost a great deal of weight, and his clothes hung miserably on him. Turk was always so careful about his appearance, and to now be reduced to looking like this broke her heart.

As they rode, they discussed their individual situations. Money was going to be tight. Some time earlier, Turk had finally decided to go on his own and have his own nightclub. He had borrowed money from a dentist friend who had agreed to back his new venture. He had bought an empty factory building at the corner of Fenkell and Wyoming. Turk had redesigned the building himself and had named it the Trocadero. He had had a raised dance floor put in and a bar that was separate from the dining room. He had turned it into a fabulous nightclub, seating five hundred people at a time, and the entrance was always full of people waiting to get in. Just inside the door was a life-size placard of Turk with his gorgeous smile and his hand outstretched as if he were going to shake your hand. This unique greeting immediately put people into a good mood. He had hired a good chef, and soon the word got around of the fine dinners that were served. He had the best entertainment and spared no expense in getting the big-name entertainers that people wanted to see and hear. Among the top names he featured were Lena Horne, Martha Raye, Mildred

Bailey, and Tony Martin.

It had taken all he had borrowed, plus whatever Cynthia could give him after their living expenses were paid. He had taken his brother in as his assistant, and when he had fallen ill, Turk had put his brother in charge. He worried because there were so many facets to running a nightclub.

Help was always a problem. Just when things were going well, you would get a few waitresses who would quit, or you would find that the bartender was helping himself to the till.

Entertainers had to be lined up and ads run to draw the crowds.

His brother did not have Turk's background, and Turk felt frustrated about walking away and leaving him in charge. He also had given him the job of selling their cars. They would need every penny they could scrape up.

Cynthia also had a problem. She could hardly admit to having a husband that no one at the Concordia knew existed. She would want her job back, so she had called and made up a story about a sick mother who was not expected to live. They had been nice and wished her luck.

Cynthia and Turk arrived at the depot in Phoenix at four in the morning. A single cab stood outside. When their luggage was all loaded, the driver asked where he could take them. When he found they had no reservations, he was shocked. He said, "Folks, this is the height of the season, and the hotels are full. I guess you don't have a choice so I'll at least check, but I don't know if I'll have any luck."

He stopped at three hotels, but they were all full. He finally said, "Well there's one more place called The Lures that I can try, but if you can't get in there, I just don't know what to tell you."

He pulled up in front of a large, white stucco structure. Cynthia could see it plainly by the street lights shining on it. There was a balcony all around it, with large cement urns filled with colorful flowers, and there were lovely, white willow rockers on the front porch.

The cab driver went in and returned to say they were in

luck: there was a vacant room. They thanked him for his persistence on their behalf, and when they had paid him, they got out and entered the hotel.

It had been built in another era, and Cynthia thought the interior looked like a set for an English movie. They followed the bellhop down a red-carpeted corridor. On the walls were old paintings of cowboys. Cynthia thought it would not take a lot of imagination to envision the appearance of one, gun in hand. They were taken to their room, and Turk immediately noticed that the entrance held the only door. He asked the bellhop about a bathroom and was told that it was ten doors down the hall and shared by all the guests. Turk was aghast.

When the bellhop left, they inspected their new quarters. There was a highboy—the largest that Cynthia had ever seen—a commode with pitcher and bowl, a brass bed, and a willow rocker. Turk opened the highboy and discovered a slop jar with a lid and a lace cover. Turk had never seen one, but Cynthia had lived as a country girl for so many years that this was a familiar object.

She explained it to him. "You're supposed to use the jar at night when you need to relieve yourself. You then place the lace cover over the opening before putting the china cover on top. This keeps the cover from making a noise and disturbing the other guests."

Now Cynthia thought she would have some fun with him. She recalled a description she had read in an old-fashioned book long ago. She repeated what she had read as if it were fact. She said, "In the morning there will be a chambermaid who will knock on our door. She will be all dressed up in a black uniform with black hose and shoes. She will have a tiny white cap on her head and a little white apron. She will come into our room to take away the chamber pot to empty it, and then tidy up the room."

She was just teasing him, but, much to her amazement, in the morning a maid appeared at their door, and she was dressed exactly as Cynthia had described her. Turk thought that Cynthia was so smart to have known about this and told her so. She did not enlighten him.

When they had showered and dressed, she told Turk to rest while she went exploring to find some place to buy their breakfast. She would also call the doctor who had been recommended to him and make an appointment. She set off down the main street, which passed their hotel. Coming to a cross street, she saw a dime store on the corner with Navaho Indians weaving their colorful cloth. She thought they were beautiful people; they reminded her of the gypsies she had seen in northern Michigan when she was little.

Next to the dime store was a restaurant, and Cynthia entered and placed her order. After buying a newspaper, she made a phone call to the doctor's office and made an appointment for that afternoon. When the food was ready, she returned to the hotel.

Turk looked bad. His eyes peered over great purple pouches. His once-proud body was shrunken, and he moved with an effort. She loved him so much. He was such a handsome man, and she wondered if Christ had looked like him. After all, Christ was a Jew. She wondered if her thoughts were blasphemous and she silently prayed for forgiveness.

Cynthia and Turk had something very wonderful together. It was as if each one of them was simply an extension of the other. If she entered their club and came up behind him, he would be instantly aware of her presence and reach his hand behind his back to clasp hers, even though the place was carpeted, so she knew he had not heard her. It was extraordinary.

She remembered another strange incident. Once while working at the German club, she was suddenly filled with panic. There was no explanation for her fear, but she hurried to a telephone and called the club. When she asked for Turk, she was informed that he had had a violent nosebleed and had been rushed to the hospital.

Turk agreed they had something special together. He likened it to the relationship between his mother and father. Cynthia knew nothing of this. Her association with his parents had been brief, and she was still bitter that his mother had lied to her, wanting her out of the way and Turk out of the state. Thank God he had come to her and told her of the plan. He had been in terrible shape, and she wondered whether he would have made it through the train trip without her help.

Chapter 14

Cynthia and Turk set off in a cab to see the doctor, with whom they were immediately impressed. He was a former Mayo Clinic doctor who now specialized in lung problems. His name was William Furst, and, although he was young, he inspired confidence. After having Turk undress, he did a scope of his chest and showed Cynthia how the lung had collapsed and how the pressure had caused the heart to move over. He said, "There has to be a hole in the lung to cause it to collapse like this."

He sounded grim.

He then took an x-ray and said, "I'll want you to return tomorrow. Now tell me something about yourself and your normal activities."

Turk replied, "I'm a singer and nightclub emcee in Detroit."

The doctor immediately cautioned him. "I don't want you to sing or even raise your voice above normal. And you're going to have to avoid sex—you just might die in the act. It's all right for you to walk around a bit, just take it easy. But you can eat anything that you want."

When they returned the next day, the doctor again had him undress and he repeated the procedures of the day before. When he finished he told Turk to get dressed and asked Cynthia to follow him. He took her into his office and had her sit down. He looked very sober as he said to her, "I've never seen a lung so bad. I wish I could tell you your husband will live, but, in all honesty, I can't. It was a good idea to come to Phoenix where the climate is better, but it might be too late. Are you still staying in the hotel?"

Cynthia said yes.

The doctor continued, "Well, I have a suggestion. I think it would be better if you moved across the street from this office. I know the owner of an apartment house there, and he has a vacancy. I would like your husband close by in case of emergency."

Cynthia agreed that this sounded like a good idea. The doctor gave her the address of the apartment and told her to bring Turk in to see him twice a week, and to get him to take it easy because his lung was bleeding.

Turk had gotten dressed, and they returned to the hotel. When she had made him comfortable, she told him about the apartment and said she was going then to see about renting it.

Cynthia left and found the owner. The apartment had formerly been a big, old home that had been divided into two units. She was very pleased with it. The living room was large, and the kitchen quite cosy. There was only one bedroom, but off the living room was a screened-in sun porch which also contained a bed.

She thought this would be just the ticket. She would put Turk on the porch and have him take advantage of the sun. There was also steam heat, which pleased her, as the nights did get fairly cold. Cynthia paid the rent and hurried back to the hotel. She told him all about what she had found and how nice it was. She was excited and could hardly wait to install him in their new quarters. She told him about the sun porch and how she thought that it would be beneficial to him.

The next day she packed, and they moved. As soon as she got Turk settled, she went into town to shop for supplies. She bought food and several old-fashioned nightshirts. They were the type that reached to the ankle and had slits up the side. She even bought a piece of flannel to make him a nightcap. Turk clowned and laughed at this getup and asked her, "Do you really think I'm going to wear these things?"

She said, "Turk, my grandfather always wore these, It helped to ward off the chill of our cold, Michigan winter nights, and I insist you at least try them."

He laughingly agreed, then confessed several nights later that he had never slept so well.

A few days later, Cynthia ventured out the kitchen door into the garden and found a flower patch surrounded with bricks. She took several of the bricks into the house, washed them clean, and placed them in the oven to heat. These she wrapped in a towel and put under the covers by his feet, for added warmth at night.

Perhaps Turk gave in on these changes because she was now on her own turf. After all, she had even known about the chambermaid at the hotel, hadn't she?

At any rate, she knew he enjoyed the fuss she made over him. He cheerfully donned the ridiculous nightshirts, for, really, who was there to laugh at him? Just thank God the boys back in Detroit could not see!

Cynthia got up each morning and walked several blocks to the bakery for fresh coffee cake, rolls, and fresh-squeezed orange juice. She would return to fix him a large breakfast and serve him in bed. She made him stay there until one o'clock in the afternoon, when she let him get up to shower and dress

Sometimes he would spend time writing to friends or to his brother to see how the club was doing. Later they would take a bus to El Centro Park. This was a lovely spot, with miles of green lawn and a man-made lake with canals that wound around for several miles. They would sometimes rent a little electric boat and go for a long ride. They went to the park every day and would lie on the grass in the sun, reading the newspapers that they were able to get from home. When they were through reading, they would discuss the news and talk about themselves and their future plans. They also, now with more time on their hands, filled each other in on their beginnings. Cynthia told him of her erratic and sometimes painful childhood. Turk told her of his background, starting with the story of his parents, George and Rebecca. They were from czarist Russia and had had to flee from their land when the warring Tartars started a mass pogrom, attacking and murdering Jews. Turk's father had seen his parents, brothers, and sisters trampled to death under the hoofs of the Tartars' horses. He and his wife had hidden in the sewers in their town of Odessa until they could emerge and make their way to France. From there they eventually had immigrated to the United States.

Turk told her of his long association with a man named Jimmy Hoffa and their mutual regard for each other. He also told her about growing up in the same neighborhood where the Purple Gang lived. His parents had never known about his association with them and would have been greatly upset. He told her he had been friends with them, and continued to be, but had never had any thoughts of joining in on their escapades and criminal acts. When they hijacked the truck with the purple sweaters, as a friend he became a recipient of one himself. Talking to him, she now learned he had actually acquired the nickname of Turk when he was quite young, because of his dark complexion.

Soon Turk became tanned and more healthy looking, but the doctor continued to watch him closely. After some months had gone by, he again tested Turk and became very alarmed when he found that the lung was filling with air. He said it was far too soon and he feared it might collapse again.

Cynthia was not worried. She no longer heard the slurp

sound of the water that lay outside the lung. The wheezing had stopped, and she felt encouraged. Many visits later, the doctor also decided his lung was indeed beginning to heal.

Dr. Bill, as they were now invited to call him, started to take them with him when he had a call to make on the outskirts of Phoenix. He served on the Board of Health and would donate his services to the Mexicans there, who were so very poor. Poor they were, but also very polite and very proud. They might not be able to pay the doctor a fee, but they would give him gifts, sometimes a beautiful dog, in repayment. He did not have the heart to refuse their offerings, but he was sometimes hard put to know what to do with each new present.

One night Turk had gone with Dr. Bill, and Cynthia had stayed behind. She was sitting in a big armchair with her legs tucked under her, embroidering, when they returned.

Turk came up behind her and, suddenly, something dropped in her lap. She thought it was a rat! She screamed and wrenched herself from the chair.

Caught off balance with her legs still under her, she fell to the floor. Turk and Dr. Bill were convulsed with laughter. She calmed down and took another look at what had frightened her.

It was a small animal, no bigger than her hand. The animal's body was covered with gray skin, and it had bulging brown eyes with a bit of yellow hair between them. She was amazed and asked, "Is this a dog?"

Dr. Bill said, "Yes, it's a breed called Mexican hairless, and it will never weigh more than three pounds."

Cynthia was tickled with this cute baby, and she picked up the frightened puppy and cuddled it to her.

Dr. Bill looked around. His eyes took in the one bed through the bedroom door. He immediately became quite serious and said, "I thought I'd given you strict orders not to sleep together. I warned you about having sex."

Cynthia denied they were sleeping together. Turk spoke up and said, "She's right, I don't sleep in a bed at all. Cynthia simply hangs me up on a hook at night."

Cynthia took the doctor into the cold, screened-in sun room and said, "This is where I have Turk sleep. Back in Michigan, when they find children with lung problems, they send them to open-air schools, right through the bitter winter. They have the kids bundle up in heavy, warm clothes and sit outdoors for their classes. They'd be breathing the clear, fresh air, and this would cure them. I thought if it worked for those children, the fresh air might be the answer for Turk."

The doctor was amazed. "Your husband's recovery has been so rapid, I can only conclude that you are really onto something. I'm so impressed, I'm going to suggest they try this treatment at the hospital."

A few days later, he told them he had called a meeting with other doctors, showing them the initial x-rays and then the recent ones. The doctors thought the recovery incredible, and they all agreed to try this treatment on their own patients.

They had been in Phoenix now for a year. It was nearly Easter, and, with Turk feeling so well and the Michigan weather turning warmer, they considered returning to Detroit.

They consulted with Dr. Bill, who said he thought Turk's health would hold up. So their trip came to a close, and they packed up their belongings. Little did they know then, Phoenix would play another part in their lives and turn their marriage upside-down.

Chapter 15

So once again they were back in Detroit. Turk went right back to the club to see his brother and find out why absolutely no money had been sent to him in Phoenix. He and Cynthia had known when they left that money would be tight, but when nothing had come from their investment in Detroit, the situation had become even worse than they had anticipated. His brother gave excuse after excuse, but his answers simply did not add up. Their quarrels were constant and often escalated into great shouting matches. If their father was there with them, Turk worried that these fights would cause his father to have another heart attack. Eventually, he learned that his brother had taken the money and bought himself a new Cadillac and an enormous new home. That put an end to their association. Turk closed the club and took the liquor license with him.

He now started another nightspot, naming it simply The Show Bar because of the stage he had built in back of the bar. It was the first of its kind and soon became very popular. The money to start this new enterprise came from a loan by Martha Raye, though Turk was careful not to disclose this information to Cynthia.

Cynthia, of course, immediately went to the Concordia to see whether they would give her back her job.

The Germans were close to their families, and they expressed concern and sympathy over Cynthia's mother's supposed illness. Cynthia had hated to lie to them in the first place; now she had to make up more lies to support the first lie. She told them her mother had been terribly ill but, luckily, had survived after all. They told her how happy they were for her and said they had not replaced her but had let the head waitress fill in for her. The head waitress liked being hostess, so they offered Cynthia a job as waitress.

Cynthia was extremely pleased because waitresses earned good tips, and she and Turk needed the money. Turk's brother had long since sold their cars, but that money was gone, and they both needed transportation.

Although Turk had never wanted her to go to work, they now had doctor bills to pay as well as the storage rent on their furniture.

Cynthia and Turk took a suite at the Detroiter Hotel rather than renting an apartment; they wanted to be sure that Turk could handle the change in climate.

The Concordia had never hired anyone before who was not German. Her old union card, listing her last name as Ryan, however, made her more acceptable. An Irish battalion had fought on the German side during the First World War.

The manager of the singing club was Ernest Beverton, a very colorful character who wore lederhosen, knee length pants made out of soft leather and held up with embroidered suspenders. With these he wore knee-high hose and a Tyrolean felt hat with a brush made of deer hair sticking up on the side.

Cynthia had, by now, been around Turk and his Jewish

friends long enough to have picked up the low German they spoke to one another. This was important, because she could understand the customers when they spoke it. She liked the manager very much and liked working at the club. There had been, however, one unhappy experience in the club before she had left for Phoenix.

She had been working in the dining room and Ernest had introduced her to Baron Von Wirtzburg, who had belonged to the Purple Hessians during World War I. She later learned the baron had made his escape with the Kaiser into Holland, following Germany's defeat.

Ernest had been anxious to please this man and had told her to take his order for something from the kitchen.

She had said she would be glad to, and, turning to the baron, she had asked him whether he would like to see a menu.

He had emphatically said, "No!" She had been startled by his dictatorial and officious manner, but, careful not to show her distaste, she had kept her face perfectly bland. She had thought he looked just like the Kaiser with his clipped hair and beard. He had a gold cane, obviously carried for effect, and when he had talked to her he had emphasized his words by striking the gold head on his other palm.

He had demanded a steak tartare and, in a blunt guttural voice, had described in detail how it should be made.

They were to take ground steak and make it into an oval shape. They were then to press down the center, to make a cavity, and put in four raw eggs. Over this he wanted chopped onions. On the side he would have boiled potatoes with sour cream.

Cynthia had gone to the kitchen and told George, the cook, what the baron wanted. When it was ready, she had taken the platter out to him and also brought a basket of black pumpernickel bread.

She had set down his platter and put the bread on the table.

The baron had summoned up all of his arrogance and bellowed angrily at her, "Girl, I did not order bread." With this outburst, he had taken his cane and knocked the bread to the floor. "Now," he had said, "you vill pick the bread up."

If he had looked at her, he would have been warned, for her blue eyes had turned to ice.

She had reached in front of the baron and taken the platter of steak tartare, raised it high, and neatly overturned it on his head.

The baron had let out with a roar. He had sworn at her, screaming that he was going to kill her. A shocked Ernest had hurriedly come out from behind the bar with a towel and tried to wipe away the broken raw eggs, meat, and onions that were streaming down the man's face.

When he had stemmed most of the flow, Ernest had taken Cynthia aside and told her that, even though the man was wrong to have tried to humble her, she should not have done this. He had said he feared that the board, when they heard about it, would fire her.

Cynthia had made her escape to the kitchen. She had told George what had happened, and he, too, had worried that she would be asked to leave. But she had not felt a bit sorry. The man had been insolent and had gone much too far. True, she could have just ignored the bread and left the room, but leaving would have never given her the satisfaction she then felt.

She saw the whole thing again in her mind, with all the food sliding and dripping, and poor Ernest, with his rolling accent and Alpine outfit, jumping anxiously from one foot to the other while trying to mop it up.

Suddenly she threw back her head and brought forth peal after peal after peal of laughter, until she was exhausted. It really was so terribly funny, and she could hardly wait to tell Turk.

The board did hear about the incident but wisely weighed its options. They knew the baron had been abusive to other waitresses and that he was noted for spending little money in the club. Cynthia, on the other hand, was known to be their most efficient and sought-after waitress. The manager had liked her from the start. George the cook had nothing but praise for her. He realized she often made him look good by throwing on an apron when things got hectic and seeing that the food emerged from the kitchen fast, while it was still hot.

When she kept her job, the other waitresses silently applauded her. She had done what none of them had dared. The old baron was nothing but a vain, dominating, bullying bastard. It had taken a Cynthia to stand up to him, and they admired her for it.

The next Saturday night, Cynthia was at work, and who should walk into the dining room but the baron. This time he had a lady with him.

Cynthia was flustered but tried to keep her face calm and friendly. He approached her and, reaching out, took her hand and kissed the back of it, in the old-world style.

The baron turned to the lady and said, "I was out of sorts the other night and was quite rude to this lady."

He turned back to Cynthia and asked her to forgive him, and she smilingly agreed, glad that this unfortunate episode was finally resolved.

Chapter 16

Many of the German families had sent their sons back to the homeland to stay with relatives and learn of their heritage. Some of these parents now began to have second thoughts. They read in the papers about the political unrest overseas, and they started to send for their children.

One evening the baron came in and announced that Germany and England were at war. He was very loud when he declared that it was about time Germany struck back at the unfairness of the Versailles treaty, which had taken away over 25,000 square miles of German territory. He bragged that Germany would blow England "right out of the ocean."

Cynthia was indignant but kept her face impassive.

The atmosphere began to radically change as the young men began to return from Germany. When the U.S. entered the war, the baron was quick to boast that Hitler would take care of not only England but the U.S. as well.

The new young members eagerly agreed with him. Some of the older people were now feeling regrets that they had allowed the boys to go to Germany in the first place and get caught up in Hitler's rallies. Most loved their adopted country and were upset over this new attitude, and they stopped coming to the club. They claimed these boys were like a pack of rats ready to follow the Pied Piper.

Cynthia worried that Turk might be called into service and told him so. He assured her that with the history of his lung, it "wouldn't happen in a hundred years." But, much to his surprise, a couple of months later he did get called up and was sent to Chicago.

Cynthia was sitting alone one evening, embroidering, when suddenly she heard a noise. Startled, she looked up, and there was Turk framed in the doorway. She jumped up and ran to him. He had her in his arms, and she was so glad to see him that she started to cry. She had missed him terribly. Turk admonished her, "Now, that's no way for a lady to act."

She said, "Turk, how did you do it?"

Turk looked down at her. "Baby, I just missed you so much I went A.W.O.L."

She stepped back. "Oh, no! Turk, this is war-time. They'll shoot you for desertion!"

He laughed and said, "Now, Baby, you know your old man better than that. They took me with my medical lung record, but later found I had inherited my father's flat feet. My brother has the same thing, and he'll be turned down, too. There's no place in the service for flat feet, so they have now registered me as 4-F, which means unfit for military service."

Cynthia couldn't stop crying, she had missed him so much. Turk took her back in his arms again and patted her.

"Oh, Turk," she said. "You're always teasing me. I'm so glad to have you back again."

He took his handkerchief out and wiped her eyes. Then he gave her a lingering kiss. "Come on, Jane," he grinned. "Tarzan's back." He led her into their bedroom.

Cynthia chose not to tell Turk what was going on at the club. If he knew how anti-American and anti-Semitic it had become, he would tell her to call it quits. She overheard so many dreadful things while she waited on the tables. When the Japanese entered the war against her country, the talk increased. The young people became more prominent and began to salute each other, clicking their heels together and raising their arms with the new cry of "Heil Hitler."

As the club changed, so did she. Now she began to actively try to overhear all she could. If she was interested in the conversation at a table, she would fill water glasses still three-quarters full, pick up lost napkins, and pass the bread individually to each diner. She was learning more and more and was appalled by the intensity of the feelings that permeated the club.

She would occasionally run across pamphlets that were being distributed by the newly formed German-American Bund that held meetings in the basement. She would watch carefully to make sure she was not seen, and slip the pamphlets surreptitiously into her handbag. She really had no plans to do anything with them, but simply took them, wanting to learn all she could about what was going on.

Cynthia began to feel more and more that she was leading a double life. At work she had to listen to words of hatred against her government and the Jews. Then, when the club closed each night, she would go home to her own loving Jew and hear of the concern he and their friends had about the war. It was bewildering, and she held it all inside her, where it churned and fermented into a proof so high it began to poison her.

One evening, the other waitresses were all busy in the dining room, and she was asked to take a tray of beer down to the Bund meeting. When she entered the room she saw a man standing by a wall where there had been placed a map of Detroit. He was pointing out to the group the locations of all the post office substations. What was this all about? She was about to place the tray on a table when a man rose up and knocked the tray from her hands. It went down with bottles and glasses crashing and beer pouring out on the floor. He was savage. "How dare you bring us Jew beer! You go back to the bar and tell them that never again will we be served with Drewry's, they must now only serve us Stroh's!"

She returned to the bar, got the replacements, and went back to the meeting room with what he had demanded. She did her best to clean up the mess without making too much noise or calling attention to herself. This was finally just too much, and she was anxious to have the evening end.

She and Turk got off work at about the same time, and they had been invited to a late surprise birthday party given by a friend for her husband.

When they got there, Cynthia had several drinks. She was still upset over this latest incident at the Club, and when the hostess went to the kitchen to prepare a late night supper, she followed her in and had still another drink.

She and the hostess were the only gentiles. Cynthia did not tell the group what had happened that night, but she did talk about her fear that Hitler was going to take over the country. She could not seem to stop, and finally Turk told her to shut up. "Baby," he said, "you're becoming a bore. You know you can't have more than one drink, because that little brain of yours starts to get rattled."

She was incensed, and left the room and got her coat. She went outside and got in their car. To hell with them! They had no idea what was going on. Well, she was not going to stand around and see it happen. She would go to Canada and join the Women's Armed Services.

She drove to the Ambassador Bridge, which links the U.S. and Canada, but was stopped on the other side by the Canadian Customs official, who asked her to get out of her car and come into his office.

She was a woman traveling alone, and it was four o'clock in the morning. He asked her where she was headed. She said, "I am entering Canada to join the Canadian army." She opened up to him, telling him she knew she had had too much to drink, but she was so worried about the club where she worked, and the Bund that had formed, and she felt she had to do something!

Cynthia explained what had been going on, and her frustration over the fact that no one believed that Hitler really could take over the country.

He listened carefully to her and then said, "I'm going to give you some advice. Why don't you go back and see if you can't do something about exposing this club for what it is. This, I think, would be a greater contribution to your country. If you will give me your name and address, I will have someone with the authority to investigate the matter contact you."

This made sense, and she gave him the information and thanked him. Satisfied, she went to her car, turned it around, and went back to her apartment.

As she crawled silently into bed, Turk woke up, reached for her, and asked, "Where in hell have you been?" Before she could answer, he again admonished her about having more than one drink, saying, "Baby, you just can't handle it. I'm tired, and we'll talk in the morning."

She was tired, too, and happy to nestle in with him. It had been a night of great anxiety, and she was glad to be encircled within his arms and to go to sleep.

Chapter 17

When they woke up it was afternoon. The doorbell had rung, and Turk quickly got up to grab something to cover himself. He told Cynthia, "It's probably someone for me, so stay in bed." As he was leaving the bedroom, he paused to ask, "How does your head feel?"

She called out to him, "If you find it, will you bring it back to me so I can scratch it?"

She turned over, arranged the covers around herself, and prepared to go back to sleep. When she heard Turk come back into the room, she poked her head out of the covers and was surprised to see a look of fright on his face. He whispered hoarsely, "What the hell did you do last night? I just let in an agent for the FBI and the police reporter Ray Girardin."

Cynthia's heart jumped. She leaped out of bed and called out over her shoulder, "I'll explain when I come out." She hurriedly went to the bathroom, quickly brushed her teeth, put on a robe, and ran a brush through her hair.

The men were all in the living room. Turk looked pale. Obviously he thought the FBI was nothing to fool around with. The agent explained that Ray Girardin was with him because he often helped the FBI in their investigations. This was the same Ray Girardin who would, years later, become Detroit's police commander.

The agent questioned her about the story she had told to the customs agent. She had a terrible headache, so she had to make a special effort. She knew she had to convince them about the Bund right then. She thought she would probably never get another opportunity, if they didn't believe her. It was a big help that she knew Ray Girardin. She had met him and his wife at The Ringside when she used to go there with Ann. It was there, also, that another police reporter had told her about Durwood's suicide.

Cynthia asked them to sit down and she recounted as earnestly as she could all she had seen and heard during her employment at the Concordia. She explained how the club had changed from an innocent singing society to an anti-American organization, after the Bund had formed.

She showed them the purloined pamphlets. One, in color, showed a picture of George Washington crossing the Delaware. It explained that he was German and that many of the early settlements were built up by Germans. These Bund members felt the United States really should be a German territory.

Then she told them about the map of Detroit and how they had pinpointed the post office substations. She expressed her fear that they were planning to blow them up. She told of the intense anti-Semitic feelings that the membership openly expressed. Finally she related the incident involving the "Jew beer" and how she had decided at that point that something had to be done.

They listened attentively to her recital, and when she was through, the agent asked her, "Do you think you could get us into the club so we can plant a wire in the meeting room?"

"Well," she said, "this is my day off, but I'll be going to the club tomorrow, and I can let you in."

She agreed to meet them at the John R entrance behind the Wolverine Hotel at eight the next morning. Cynthia asked them, "How long do you think it will take to place the wire?"

The men shrugged, and finally the agent said, "It depends on how difficult it will be to conceal it."

She cautioned them. "The cook comes in at ten o'clock, and if you aren't gone, I'll ring a buzzer to warn you. You get ready to leave, and I'll help you get out."

They thanked Cynthia for her cooperation and left. Turk was beside himself. "What the hell have you gotten yourself into?"

"Turk," she assured him, "I'll be very, very careful, so don't worry."

She did not admit to him she was scared stiff herself. The tension was not helped, either, by her goddamned hangover!

The next morning the two men appeared on the dot of eight, and she led them to the meeting room and left them to their work. She stationed herself as a lookout and waited. She had no idea what was entailed in wiring a place, but she hoped they would hurry.

An hour went by, and Cynthia began to get very anxious. Her hands were sweating and she kept wiping them off on her dress. Another hour passed, and, right on schedule, in came the cook. She stayed out of sight and rang the buzzer. The cook was banging pots and pans, and Cynthia swiftly tiptoed down to lead the men out.

Finding they had just finished their work, she quietly led them up to the landing. They were only six steps from the exit when George, the cook, appeared at the head of the stairs.

Cynthia stopped in her tracks and her heart began to pound. Her mind raced. She spoke to George.

"I opened early and found these two men waiting to get in."

Ray Girardin picked right up on her cue, saying, "We'd

heard there was good German food served here."

George beamed and said, "That's right, and I am the cook, but we don't serve before noon."

Ray asked, "Is there a bar where we could wait and have a few drinks?"

Cynthia said, "Oh, yes, we have a bar and I'll be glad to show you the way." She walked away with them in relief. It had been too close.

At the bar, the men gave her instructions while she served them. She was told she had been assigned a telephone line at the post office. She was to call and ask for line fourteen if she ever needed them or if she had anything to report. She could call and reach them either day or night.

Cynthia poured a glass of beer and took it to George. "This is from those two nice fellows who came in to have lunch."

George was pleased and asked no questions. She knew then that they had not raised his suspicions.

Over the next few months, she saw even more changes taking place. It was no longer a happy club. Large groups now came in to join the Bund. They put up a big picture of Hitler on the wall; the American flag was removed, and the Nazi flag with its swastika was put in its place.

Cynthia was the only lead the FBI had. They told her they had known there was a movement but had had no way to get information on it before.

Although they offered to put her on the payroll, Cynthia refused. "No, I don't want any money. This is my way of helping out my country."

She told them about her grandfather and the promise she had made to him as she stood by his grave. They were impressed by her story and the fact that she would not take the money. She got the impression that this was unusual.

They were also worried that eventually someone would find out she was married to one of the hated Jews, and suggested that it might be safer for her if she moved away from Turk temporarily. Cynthia regretfully saw the wisdom of this, and that night when she told Turk what they had said, he laughed and said, "Now I have my own Mata Hari."

Then he turned serious. "I should be the one who is fighting these people; I am the Jew. I should be the one taking the risks instead of you, but Baby, you go ahead with the job that you're doing. You're my soldier on the home front, and I'm proud of you."

The FBI continued to warn her about living with Turk. They feared that if her marriage were discovered, the Bund might easily suspect what she was doing. Then—branded as a spy—her days would be numbered. So Cynthia moved away from Turk and continued to gather information, reporting regularly to the FBI. Gradually she began to realize that there was much she was missing. She witnessed only the meetings in the dining room. What she needed was to form a relationship with an insider. She began to flirt with a member of the little group of musicians who were employed there, thinking this might get her into the inner circle. She picked on Franz, the violin player, and flirted outrageously with him. His brother played the violin, too. They had a man playing the grand piano and another who played the bass viol. They were talented and played well together. In keeping with the club, they played only German music.

Cynthia began casting glances at Franz, arching her eyebrows, and giving him winks. She would walk past him provocatively, and he was not long in responding. Soon he started singing German love songs over the microphone, looking straight at her. From there he progressed to holding her hand. His brother clearly approved. Then he asked her to join him for meetings, held after the club closed. They were held in different parts of Detroit, and she could not go until she was officially a member of the Bund, so she applied for membership.

Swallowing her distaste, she practiced clicking her heels and giving the Nazi salute with a shout of "Heil Hitler!"

Cynthia was accepted and was made to swear she would lose her life, if necessary, for the Fuhrer. She promised, with all the feigned sincerity that she could muster.

There was one member named Hans who she thought saw right through her. He had cold blue eyes, and she felt he was not fooled at all. This terrified her, and she did her best to avoid him, praying she would not be discovered.

Cynthia was living now in constant fear. Even the FBI agents warned her to watch her step. She was getting in very deep, but to back off now, she thought, would surely look suspicious.

Her flirtation and romance with Franz was paying off. He proudly told her of his part in the Bund. He, along with his brother and the bass viol player, worked in a war plant during the day. They had access to blueprints that the Bund wanted. They would take their musical instruments to the plant, find the blueprints, and hide them in their music cases. After work they would go directly to the club and turn them over to the Bund to be photographed, returning them to the plant the next day before they could be missed.

She related this to the FBI as soon as she could. The agent said this was a really big break and commended her for doing an incredible job.

She wondered if her grandfather knew what she was doing. He would be so proud.

Chapter 18

Over the next weeks and months, Cynthia attended many meetings with Franz. Often the Bund would have speakers who would boast of the new Germany under the leadership of the Fuhrer. Hitler's plan, they said, was to take over the United States, following his conquest of Europe. One speaker said that after Hitler took over, he would eliminate all the Jews and Negroes. This brought the audience to its feet, clapping and cheering.

Cynthia joined in with the crowd, but even as she smiled and clapped, her thoughts were centered on what she really thought of the speaker. She imagined what his face would look like if she suddenly got up and announced that she was married to a Jew and that he was wonderful!

One night the club was holding a special banquet at which the French Ambassador was to be a guest. He was pointed out to her when he came in, so she recognized him later when she glanced into the dining room. The man was being lifted out of his chair by four Germans. Each had grabbed an arm or a leg, and they took him out through the club entrance and threw him down the flight of stairs.

When the four returned to the dining room, Cynthia ran down the steps and helped the little man sit up. She checked him over and satisfied herself that there were no broken bones. He was dazed, however, and she went to the curb and hailed a cab. The cabby helped her get the ambassador to his feet and into the vehicle.

Cynthia returned to the club and realized she had been seen. She spoke to the men who were watching her and quickly explained, "I helped that man because I was afraid that someone would see him lying out there and call the police. I was worried it might wind up in the newspaper and bring on an investigation."

They bought her explanation and told her she was smart to have thought of this. Why the ambassador had been invited, she never did learn. She did, however, find out later what had happened. At the banquet, an announcement was made that Hitler was offering free passage money to anyone who was young enough to fight in the German army.

The French Ambassador had spoken up and said that anyone who went would be foolish, because they would only wind up as cannon fodder. He had predicted that Germany was going to lose the war, and with that statement his welcome had ended, and he was seized and thrown out.

She was now calling the FBI quite often with reports on the increasing activities of the Bund. One day, the agent said he had a special request to ask of her. Could she possibly find out where they kept the printing press that ran off their subversive literature?

This posed a difficult problem. It was not something you could casually ask about. Immediately, it would raise suspicion as to why she wanted to know. She worked on the problem in her mind for weeks, but could not find a plausible explanation for asking anyone. Since it never came up at the meetings, she was afraid she would just have to tell the FBI she was unable to get the information. She knew they would be disappointed, but it just could not be helped.

Soon after, Franz asked Cynthia whether she would like to go with him for a weekend at a lake near Pontiac. She accepted, and much to her surprise found not only that the cottage was owned by Violet, the head waitress, but also that the elusive printing press was housed there!

Violet was very active in the Bund, and Cynthia found that the members came out to help on weekends, working all night on Saturday and all day on Sunday.

That weekend, they were printing maps of Detroit with positions and instructions for its takeover. They folded the maps and put them in bundles to be passed out to the various workers in the city who had promised their cooperation. Again, the postal substations were identified, and all police stations. When she returned from the weekend, she called her post office number and excitedly told the agent how she had found out about the printing press.

The agent was delighted and told her this was a really lucky break. He explained that they needed to know where it was so they could confiscate it when they finally cracked down on the Bund.

In addition to her FBI informant work, Cynthia had joined the Red Cross early in the war and had eventually become a lieutenant, with a crew of twelve women. She drove an ambulance, and their training was designed around giving aid to children and the elderly in the event that Detroit was bombed. She attended two meetings a week and learned how to make bandages and give first aid. She was concerned about what Franz would think of this, but he said it was fine to aid the old and the kids. He also told her her training might come in handy if Germany dropped parachutists over Detroit. She would have the perfect cover for rescuing the soldiers and driving them to safety.

One day, Cynthia and her crew were practicing lifting

bodies onto stretchers, when she experienced a terrible pain in her side. She managed to get to a phone and call her faithful friend Mollie, who said she would leave immediately and take her to a doctor.

Mollie did not lose any time, and neither did the doctor, who said, "Well, young lady, you have a very hot appendix here, and it's got to come out at once."

Cynthia begged for time. "I can't go into the hospital right now. I have things to see to that are terribly important."

The doctor was worried. "Well, I can tell you, we'd better get you in before it bursts."

She refused, saying, "I'll try to clear things up quickly and I'll let you know just as soon as I can."

Cynthia was entangled in the many facets of her life and needed to loosen all the knots and straighten out the strings.

She went home and called the club, telling them she was in great pain with appendicitis. It was unusual for her to call in sick, and they were kind and sympathetic.

I'd been working at the Concordia and reporting on the Bund to the FBI for over two years. It was time for me to end this double life and get back to some kind of normalcy. I knew the government was planning to close in on the Bund soon, and I needed to distance myself from them. If they were rounded up and jailed, and I wasn't taken, it would not take much for them to figure out who had been the spy in their midst. It was a perfect time and a perfect excuse to be away when the ceiling fell in.

If I were in the hospital or healing from the operation, they would think it was just a lucky break that kept me out of the net. Their organization was so large, I doubted every last one of them would be picked up, and if the word went out to one of them that I'd played a part in this, I'd be a marked woman.

I also needed to break off with Franz and get back with Turk. I missed him so much. The times that we did see each other were spaced too far apart, and our meetings were necessarily furtive and secretive.

Finally, I needed to give the FBI my latest findings before I was hospitalized. I contacted them with the recent information I had just learned. The members of the Bund had bragged that a mini-submarine had positioned itself at the mouth of the Saginaw River. The object was to surface in the dark, let their sailors onto shore, and blow up the Dow Chemical Company. Dow supplied powder for ammunition, and the loss would certainly hurt the war effort. The sailors were also to demolish Consumers Power, which supplied electricity for as far away as Detroit. This loss would severely cripple the factories. Then, too, they planned to destroy the DeFoe Company, the builder of sub chasers and landing craft.

I had in the past supplied them with information about Max Shloeffen, who was one of the Bund's top leaders. Now I also learned he was harboring an escaped German prisoner, a former Luftwaffe pilot.

England sent many prisoners to Canada, but this one had gotten away, into the protective arms of Max. I later read in the paper that Max was tried for treason and hung. The paper said he was the first to be hung for this offense since the days of George Washington. Did I feel guilty about being responsible for his death? Not a bit.

I knew I had made a substantial effort toward bringing these people to justice. The FBI had made it clear how brave they thought I was, to take such tremendous risks for my country, and said how grateful they were to me.

I felt very proud.

Chapter 19

Cynthia's next step was to see Turk and tell him that she was going to have to be hospitalized soon and about the latest developments at the Concordia. She couldn't wait to tell him that her spying days were coming to an end and that she could move back in with him. He would be thrilled! She would have to carefully work out how she would accomplish leaving the club, but she did not have a lot of time. The darn pain in her side made that all too apparent.

Turk's new business was downtown on Woodward Avenue, close to the Detroiter Hotel. This, then, was where she headed to find him. She had been there only a few times. It would have been hard to explain why she was there in the first place, and of course she was always afraid the Bund would connect her with Turk.

Cynthia entered and saw once again how lovely it was,

and how innovative. The large room had its booths, tables, and chairs all done in white French provincial. The large bar was built in a half-circle, with real butterflies inlaid under the clear glass top. Behind the bar, under the ceiling, was a large dome covered with red velvet and decorated with white fleurs de lis. Under this dome the band played. The walls were covered with red flocked wallpaper, and overhead was a crystal chandelier with large glittering prisms.

Cynthia loved it here and had found it hard to keep away. She went over to the bar and sat on one of the stools. Mike, the bartender, greeted her; he was an old friend. He said, "Turk's gone out for something to eat, but he should be back shortly." Mike turned away to wait on a customer, but had only gone a few steps when he returned. He said, "Don't look now, but are those men peeking through the Venetian blinds friends of yours?"

Cynthia stole a glance and instantly recognized the eyes. "Oh, damn," she said, "a couple of Nazis." She jumped off the stool, saying, "Tell Turk I love him."

She hurriedly left and saw Franz and George ahead. She caught up with them and squeezed between them, asking if they would like to buy her a beer.

They all stopped at a bar, and when they had finished their beer and George had left, Franz took her by cab to the Hofbrau House by the Belle Isle Bridge. She had never been there before but had heard the food was all Bavarian, and very good.

Cynthia thought it was ironic that the restaurant was owned by the same Max Schloeffen whose name she had recently turned over to the FBI. She wondered whether he kept the escaped prisoner somewhere on these very premises.

She made herself quit thinking about this and began to concentrate on what she was going to tell Franz. They ordered something to eat, and when they were alone, she turned to him and said, "Franz, I have something to tell you. I never believed that I'd fall so madly in love with you. You've become my whole life, but now I must forget you, because I'm no good for you. Maybe I'll just have to kill myself."

"You see, I am married to a Jew, and he beat me up and kicked me out, and that was when I went to work at the club. Tonight I went to The Show Bar to see my husband and to ask him not to make any trouble for me, since I was seeking a divorce."

"He wasn't there, and then I saw you and left. I know you've told me you love me and want to marry me, but you can't want me now, having been married to a Jew. You must think about what Hitler would say!"

Franz turned to her and put his arm around her shoulder. "Oh, my Liebchen [darling], he would understand just as I do. Those Jews can make you do anything, even marry them. It will not make a difference to me, I love you so much."

She smiled tenderly at him. "Oh, Franz, you're so wonderful and so very understanding."

Inside, she churned with frustration. She was not out of it after all. "Shit!" So much for her dramatic revelation.

Now she had another matter to handle. "Franz, I called in sick today, and I'll be going in shortly to have my appendix out."

He was concerned. "Oh, my *Liebchen*, I'm so sorry. Tell your Franz which hospital you'll be in."

She said, "Oh, I didn't think to ask the doctor, and he didn't say." This was a lie, but what was one more, after the hundreds she had already told? She did not want him at the hospital. She wanted him out of her life! She sweetly said, "As soon as I find out, I'll let you know."

She woke the next day and ran to the bathroom to throw up. The pain was bad, and she kept straining and retching, even when there was nothing more to come up. She brushed her teeth and rinsed out her mouth, all the time holding her hand to her side.

Cynthia slowly got dressed and fought against the pain. It only got worse, and by early afternoon she gave up and called her friend. "Oh, Mollie, come get me quick, the pain is killing me."

Mollie, her ever-dependable Mollie, must have broken the speed limit, for she arrived long before Cynthia expected her. Mollie scolded her.

"Cynthia, you were a fool for waiting so long."

Cynthia did not mind her words. She knew her friend was worried, or she would never have spoken to her like that.

When they reached the doctor's office they were greeted by a roomful of books in boxes and general disarray. Clearly, the doctor was vacating his office. He came out, and Cynthia spoke up.

"Well, I've finally had enough and you can yank my appendix."

He raised his hands in consternation. "I've been drafted, and have to be at the induction center tomorrow. I need the rest of today to finish clearing out this office."

He took her in the examining room and checked her. The doctor looked extremely worried and said, "Well, what I warned you about has happened. Your appendix has ruptured. I'll contact the doctor who's replacing me and turn you over to him."

He turned to Mollie. "You'd better contact her husband so he can sign her in." Mollie put in a hurried call to Turk. He was in and out much of the time, and she sighed with relief when she got hold of him.

Turk told Mollie he would leave immediately and meet them.

They were about to go, when the doctor stopped them. "I'm calling for an ambulance. You may both ride together, but she is not in any condition to go in a car."

He called for the ambulance, then placed a call to the doctor who would be taking over. When he had completed the arrangements, he turned and told them the doctor's name. He assured them that this doctor was extremely capable. "He's from Austria and received his training in Vienna. He is a specialist, and I consider him even better qualified than I am."

It never occurred to either one of the women that this doctor was from the same country as Hitler. They were also ignorant of the fact that Deaconess Hospital, where she was

going, was located in a German section of Detroit and run
mostly by German personnel.

The ambulance arrived, and she was taken away. It was
typical of Mollie to ride along and not show concern over how
she was going to get back to her car.

When they reached the hospital, Turk and the doctor
were both waiting. She was taken in for a quick examination,
then told they would operate on her as soon as they could get
her ready.

Turk rejoined her and comforted her as best he could. He
took her hand in his and said, "Don't be afraid, Baby. Your
Pops will be right here, waiting for you to come out. I love you,
Baby, and I miss you. My arms have been so empty without
you. When you leave this hospital, you're never going to go
back to that German club. I want you with me, Baby."

Cynthia answered, "I've already decided not to go back
to the club, but I'm scared to death one of the members might
find me. The FBI is about to clamp down on them, and I'm
worried they might connect me with them."

Turk said, "Look, Baby, I'll protect you. When you leave
this hospital I'm going to take you to live on Twelfth Street,
where you'll be safe while you recover from this operation.
This street is in a solidly Jewish neighborhood, and any
German who entered would be torn apart like a herring. Even
Hitler and his army wouldn't be safe there."

She looked up at him and said, "Turk, please believe that
I've always loved you."

He recognized she was speaking from fear. "Baby,
you're not going to die. You're going to be just fine."

The attendants then came in, and she was wheeled away.
They gave her a shot, and she asked whether she could have
a spinal. Cynthia had read about this new method in the paper,
and she was afraid that under ether she might say something
about the club. The doctor agreed, and it was administered.
She watched them as they painted the area where the incision
was to be made.

When she lost feeling, they started the operation. She

watched as they used tongs to bring up the sopping, bloody appendix. She thought it looked like they were picking pieces out of a watermelon.

Suddenly she thought she felt pain and said, "Pass the ether." The mask was placed over her face, she took great deep breaths, and soon there was blessed oblivion.

When she woke, she was in her room and could hear two nurses talking. This in itself was not disturbing, but as they continued, she realized they were speaking in German! She was terrified. She decided she must have talked while under the ether. These nurses would know she had betrayed the Bund and they would want revenge.

She opened her eyes, and one of the nurses said in a pleasant voice, "So, you finally decided to wake up." But the nurse did not fool her with that sweet voice. Cynthia knew they were planning to kill her, and she was not going to die without putting up a fight.

She screamed at them. "Get out of my goddamned room, you dirty, Brown Shirt Nazi bastards!"

One nurse ran out and appeared minutes later with Turk, who comforted her. "You're all right, Baby. Don't be upset."

He did not understand, and she became hysterical. The doctor was summoned. He wanted to give her a shot to calm her, but she refused. She turned to Turk and in a frightened voice said, "For God's sake, Turk, don't let him give me a shot."

The doctor acquiesced. Then Cynthia demanded of her husband, "Now get those goddamned Nazi nurses out of here!"

He did as she asked, then told her, "I'll provide private nurses for you around the clock."

He hired the nurses for her but she was still fearful. She refused to eat any food, worried she would be poisoned. She pleaded to go home. She was so filled with anxiety that she was rolling from side to side, despite the tube which was draining out the infection. The nurse called the doctor to tell him what Cynthia was doing. He came into the room and said,

"I have no idea why you're so afraid, but I think you'd be better off out of the hospital. I'm going to let you go home."

Cynthia left by ambulance with her private nurse. The driver lifted her and carried her inside and onto the bed. He had been gone only a short time when the phone by her bed rang. The nurse asked her whether she could reach it, and Cynthia said yes and picked up the receiver. She said, "Hello?" A man's voice spoke to her. "I'm with the FBI."

She cut him short. "How do I know?"

He said, "Call the post office number that you were given, and I'll answer."

She hung up and rang the post office, and he answered, assuring her that he actually was an agent. He said, "You needn't have worried in the hospital, because we had you under constant watch all the time, even by your private nurse. We were worried, because the doctor had two interns working with him who came from Canada. We suspect they're Nazis."

She was amazed at this information. She was too startled to ask him how they had even known she had been admitted. Later she would wonder whether they had had her followed, to protect her. There did not seem to be any other explanation.

Johnny Hale.
Their failed marriage left her virginity intact.

Turk Prujansky.
A man she could not share.

Rex Anderson.
The man she thought she married.

Rex Anderson in drag.
What she later discovered him to be.

Bernie Sakosiac.
He lost out by his unreasonable jealousy.

Bill Neery.
He possessed more than a cheating heart.

Chapter 20

Cynthia made a concerted effort to get better quickly and get back on her feet. Turk received a call from Dr. Bill in Phoenix. He told Turk that his brother owned a big restaurant in Phoenix called The Mission, and he asked Turk to come out and manage the place.

Turk was enthusiastic and quite willing to give up The Show Bar. Cynthia also liked the idea. She missed the wonderful climate out there and the openness of the countryside. Detroit was too congested for her taste, and far too noisy.

Soon they were boarding the Rock Island train and heading west. She relaxed and rested her head on the back of the seat. There was another reason for her to get out of Detroit. The FBI had finally closed in on the German Bund a week earlier. The newspapers had been full of the news, listing the hundreds of arrests that had been made. She had recognized many of them. The information she had supplied the FBI had filled a nineteen-page document with lists of names and activities. She had done her job and was glad she had, but now it was with great relief that she was leaving the area.

Turk turned to her.

"You know, Baby, I never realized how involved you were with the FBI and how deeply you'd gotten into that Nazi Bund. You took an awful chance, and I'm really lucky to get you back."

She looked at him with surprise.

"Oh, Turk, can you believe I was just thinking about them, too? I'm so glad that we're leaving Detroit. I've been worried that someone might connect me with those arrests."

"Well," he said, "that's all behind you now, so you can relax." He was right, it wouldn't do to dwell on it.

She was glad to get Turk out of Detroit, too. Some weeks earlier she had heard rumors that he was seeing a Hollywood movie star named Martha Raye. Upset, she had called him and told him what she had heard.

He had said, "Baby, you know how people talk. There's nothing to it. There'll always be those who are jealous of anyone in show business and try to make trouble. How would you like to meet Martha yourself? She's giving a party tonight at the Book Cadillac. It's her birthday and she wants to celebrate. Baby, she's a lot of fun, and I'm sure you'd like her. All this talk is just silly, and you can go with me and see for yourself."

Cynthia said, "O.K., where shall we meet?" They arranged a time and place before hanging up.

I called Mollie and invited her to come along with me.

She was my best friend and I thought I just might need an ally. I went to my closet and scrutinized the contents, finally selecting a dress I considered glamorous. I dressed with care and took a lot of time with my hair. I was really nervous. If this woman really was competition, I wasn't about to come off looking second-best.

We met at the hotel and rode the elevator to Martha's suite. The door was open and we walked in. Turk took us over to Martha and introduced us to everyone. Martha was very gracious and saw that we got something to drink and places to sit. I'd been prepared to not like the woman, but despite myself I was soon caught up with her charm. I watched Martha and Turk carefully, looking for any sign that they had cultivated more than a friendship.

It was tough being married to a man who was so goddamned handsome! I was aware that Martha was also giving me more than a once-over. Well, lady, I thought, if you are interested in panning for gold, you had better find some new territory, because I've already staked out my claim

Turk had said it was Martha's birthday, so I had bought her a gift. I gave it to her, wishing her a happy birthday. Martha opened the package and showed everyone the white leather diary I had bought her. She said, "Why, thank you very much."

I said, "You're welcome," and then added, "Just be careful never to write anything in it that you wouldn't want anyone else to read." The group laughed. The evening continued, and there always seemed to be someone handing me a new drink. After the first one I started to pour them out into a vase of flowers.

I seemed to be the only one there who wasn't connected to show business. They were telling a lot of inside jokes, and I simply couldn't catch on to most of it. Several times I saw that Martha was watching me and my reactions, or rather my lack of reactions. I wondered if she thought that I was an idiot for not catching on and joining in the laughter.

Later I got up and went to the bathroom. The bedroom door was ajar, and I saw the man who had been introduced to me as Eddie Condos standing there with a newspaper reporter kneeling in front of him. I slipped past the door and returned to the living room and kept my mouth shut about what I had seen. Many years later I learned that Martha had married him, which greatly confused me.

It was getting late and Turk excused himself, saying he was going to take his usual Saturday night steam bath.

Mollie said she was tired, and Turk offered to drive her home. Martha turned to me and said, "Well why don't you stay over tonight and visit with me?"

I said, "Sure," and soon all the other guests left. Martha then said, "How would you like to try on some of my clothes and jewelry?"

I said, "That sounds like fun, I love pretty clothes." She led me to her bedroom and opened the closet. I picked out outfits and tried them on. It was fun. It reminded me of when I had played "dress up" as a child. I found that my big bust was not surpassed by Martha's and that the gowns fit perfectly. I not only tried on dresses but also her jewels and furs. I commented on a particularly pretty gold bracelet and she said, "Isn't it nice? It was a gift from Al Jolson."

I paraded around in the gorgeous finery, and we laughed together like a couple of kids. She asked me, "Don't you envy me having all these beautiful things?"

I said, "Not a bit. Where in the world would I wear them?"

She responded, "Well, maybe you don't envy me for my clothes and furs but I can tell you that I envy you your husband."

I said, "Martha, you can look at him, but don't touch. We're living apart right now because I'm doing some secret work for the government. We'll be getting back together soon, because my work is almost done, and I can tell you that he is my whole life."

Martha made no comment. It got late and she loaned me a nightgown. She was awfully tired because she had done a show that evening before giving the party. She sat brushing her hair and said, "I'm so tired that I'm having trouble even doing this."

I said, "Why don't you give me the brush and I'll do it for you."

Martha recoiled from me and her face looked shocked.

"No no, that's all right, I can manage."

I backed off. I wondered if she thought that I was one of THOSE. I excused myself and went to bed.

I found out the next day that Martha had seen me pouring out my drinks in the flower vase. Turk told me she had asked, "Is she really that naive or is she putting on an act?"

Turk had laughed and replied, "It's no act, Martha, she really is."

I thought back about this as the train churned on. No, I wasn't as näive as they thought. I could see how much fun Martha was, and how very vivacious and attractive. She would be a temptation to any man, and I was glad to get Turk away before she was again booked somewhere in Detroit.

This trip was very different from the one they had taken when Turk was sick. Now he joined her in the dining car and played poker in the club car. He was smart enough to know that many professional gamblers rode the trains, looking for easy prey. Even a pair of white-haired ladies, looking perfectly innocent, could be working as a team. Turk wisely stuck to penny ante.

They had been lucky to get a compartment, where they did not have to sleep sitting up. Wartime travel was difficult. They traveled with shades drawn at night so they would not be visible in case of enemy attack. Often they were sidetracked while they waited until a troop train, with a higher priority, was given clearance. Every train station had its share of soldiers. Often Cynthia would wave a greeting to them, and they always smiled and waved back. She wondered how many of them would ever see home again. She knew she had been lucky. She had had her own tour of duty and had managed to live through it.

She did not spend as much time in the club car as Turk did. He was not a drinker and had never taken up smoking, but he loved to gamble. He always managed to round up players, and he spent most of the time playing, until finally they reached Phoenix.

Chapter 21

Cynthia was happy to see the town again. Despite Turk's illness, the couple had had a closeness in working together to restore his health. They had also made friends here and were happy in anticipation of being reunited with them.

Cynthia and Turk quickly settled in and went to work. Dr. Bill had set his brother up in business, but his brother had been called into the service and no longer could run the restaurant. Turk and Cynthia divided the duties. He would be the manager and handle the payroll and bookkeeping; she would take charge of the help and do the ordering. They worked different shifts, taking turns between the day shift and the night shift.

Eventually they would sell their interest in The Show Bar to their old partner and buy The Mission.

They had left their cars in Detroit to be sold. Coming here was a good move. Back in Detroit, Turk had again developed lung problems. When Dr. Bill had contacted him, Turk had thought the business presented to him a chance to get away from the cold climate. Being a drive-in with carhops, The Mission allowed you to order from your car. The parking lot was huge, covering a city block. Business was extremely good and the parking lot was always full.

The Thunderbird air base was large and not far from the drive-in. Also out in the desert was an armored tank training camp. The town was straining at its seams with all the servicemen and their wives.

Cynthia found she had to constantly interview girls for jobs as carhops. Most of her girls were married to servicemen, and when they would be transferred, the wives would follow. But she did have several girls who were local and dependable. Months passed, and she and Turk felt that all was going smoothly.

One day Cynthia was approached by a military policeman from the base. He said, "Lady, we have a problem."

Cynthia looked perplexed. "What sort of problem?"

He said, "You'd better start watching your girls, because I hear they're selling sex in your parking lot."

She was indignant. "That can't be. They're a bunch of nice girls."

He insisted, "Lady, every drive-in in Phoenix and the rest of the United States is having the same problem. Now, you'd better watch it or you'll be closed up. We're not going to have a bunch of tramps infecting our base with venereal disease."

He left after she gave him her promise to see about it.

That night, when her shift was over, she made as if to leave but actually positioned herself in a dark place to watch the parking lot. She saw one of her favorite waitresses approach a car. The waitress talked briefly to the occupant, then reached out her hand and accepted some money.

Well, this was strange. You usually got paid for the food after you had brought it to the car. Next, the girl took hold of the handle of the car's rear door, opened it, and proceeded to enter the car. The driver followed her into the back seat.

Cynthia was appalled. She had never checked before. It had never occurred to her that something of this sort might be going on. She felt bad, for she really liked the beautiful carhop, but it made no difference. Cynthia had caught her cold turkey, and she would have to go.

When the girl got out of the car, Cynthia emerged from the building's shadow and called all the carhops together. She said, "I had an M.P. here today, complaining he had heard girls were selling sex in this parking lot. I just witnessed this for myself, and the girl is fired. I won't be accused of being a madam: If any of you are also doing this, let me tell you I won't put up with it." With that, she dismissed them, telling them to go back to work.

From time to time she would check on them again, but she never saw a repeat of this incident.

Their lives continued to be busy as their first year stretched into two. Turk had sent for his parents and Cynthia was glad. They had finally accepted her, and she had grown really very fond of them.

Her mother-in-law had once said, "Cynthia, you're like a wart on my hand, I've gotten so used to you."

She took Cynthia with her to meet the local rabbi. The meetings were held in a store-front, because Phoenix had no synagogue.

She teased her daughter-in-law. "I brought you here because the rabbi is going to get you all wet and then he's going to rub you all over with kosher salt and then you'll be Jewish."

When the rabbi had gotten in front of the group, Cynthia's mother-in-law suddenly reached over and, with a large safety pin, closed the neck of Cynthia's blouse, so he could not look down at her ample breasts.

She whispered to Cynthia, "Now, darlink, the rabbi can keep his mind on what he's saying."

Cynthia didn't see her in-laws all that often; she was too busy. When Turk wasn't on duty at night, he would sometimes visit them.

A lot of his time would also be spent visiting the various bars while Cynthia worked. Phoenix had no nightclubs then, and he would spend the evening gambling.

Turk joined the Chamber of Commerce and met a big contractor named Andy Womack. They struck up a friendship and were soon talking about working together.

Turk told Cynthia, "Womack wants me to run a restaurant for him. Andy already owns about fifty motels and The Parkway restaurant. We're planning to change the restaurant and turn it into a real nightclub, with dinner music and a floor show."

Cynthia said, "Turk, we've got more than we can handle now. I don't even like Andy Womack."

Turk argued, "Baby, he's going to give me a piece of the business. It's bound to make us a lot of money. There won't be anything like it in Phoenix."

Cynthia continued to argue, but Turk was too excited about getting back into the nightclub business to listen.

He joined Andy in renovating the restaurant and, eventually, running it. Cynthia saw less and less of him.

Cynthia was at The Mission one day, talking to one of the carhops. "You know what I'd like to do someday? I'd really love to learn to ride a horse."

Someone behind her spoke up. "If you'd really like to learn, I could teach you."

Cynthia turned around in surprise and asked, "Who are you?"

The man gave his name and said, "I'm a rodeo rider and I could teach you. I wouldn't charge you, but you'd have to rent your own horse."

Cynthia was ecstatic. She made a date to meet him at a local riding stable, where the man kept his own horse.

The rodeo rider was thorough, making her learn the basics before he went on to the finer points. He was a tough teacher.

One day he said to her, in disgust, "Are you going to ride a horse the right way or are you going to ride like a goddamned dude? You don't trot a western horse. You walk him or you gallop him. It's one or the other."

Cynthia loved it and was a good student. After a few months, the rodeo rider said he had taught her about all that he knew, unless she wanted to get into rodeos.

That held no interest for her at all, but she continued to rent horses and ride out on the desert. She loved it and it was helpful to have another interest, since she saw so little of Turk.

Turk and Andy were very involved in the Chamber of Commerce and the Kiwanis, which was planning a big parade. Andy asked Cynthia whether she would like to ride behind his daughter, who would lead the parade. She refused, saying she could never leave the drive-in that long. She disliked the man and also disliked some of his business practices. She wanted no part of him, and no part of his goddamned parade, either.

Turk had worked the morning shift at The Mission, then Cynthia came in to replace him. She was at the cash register and had lifted the cash drawer to put in a check, when she noticed a letter addressed to Turk.

She opened the letter and read it. Much to her distress, she found it was written by Martha Raye. It told Turk how much she missed him and how glad she was that he and his friend were coming to California. Of course they were to stay with her.

Seething, Cynthia turned to one of the five counter girls. "Judy, would you please take over the cash register?"

She got in her car and drove to The Parkway. When she found Turk, she told him she had found the letter and had read it.

Turk said, "Well, ever since I told Andy about all the movie stars I'd met in Detroit, he's been just crazy to meet some of them. Yes, we're going to Los Angeles for two weeks."

Cynthia said, "If you go, don't expect me to be here when you come back. I always said I wouldn't share you, and I meant it, Turk."

"Look, Baby, this is just something I have to do. I'm in trouble. I've been gambling, and I'm in debt to the mob for six thousand dollars. I need to please Andy and see if he'll loan me the money. If I don't get it, the mob will take me for a ride. I have no choice."

An idea began to form in her mind. She remembered that when they had taken over The Mission, they had had offers of money from both an ice cream company and a bread company if The Mission would change over to their brands. She now wondered: if she went to those companies and threatened to quit doing business with them, might they offer her a bribe? It was worth a try.

The next morning she got dressed, pulling on a figure-revealing yellow sweater. She went to both companies and, sure enough, she soon had four thousand dollars in her purse.

She was trying to think up how she would get the rest, when she saw the man come in who changed records in the jukeboxes and extracted the money. He also would be getting the change from the four pinball machines and the cigarette machines. She knew these companies were run by racketeers, but she also knew they made a lot of money.

The Mission always got a commission for allowing these machines in their building, but the commissions were not what she was after now.

She approached the man and leveled with him. She told him that her husband was in trouble with the mob and that she needed three thousand dollars. She had decided to get seven thousand altogether.

The man listened to her story and said he would be right back. She figured he had left to make a phone call.

When he returned he said, "O.K., lady, we figure you're good for it. Here's the money, and we won't press you for it. We'll just take it out of the commissions you normally get. You won't be getting any more commissions until we get paid off." She agreed and thanked him.

Cynthia took off immediately for The Parkway and again went in search of Turk. When she found him she said, "Turk, if I pay off your gambling debt for you, will you promise me you won't go to California with Andy?"

He said, "Baby, where would you get that kind of money?"

Instead of answering him, she persisted with her own question.

"Do I have your promise?"

He laughed and said, "You win. If you can come up with the money to bail me out, I not only won't go to California, but I'll promise never to go to places where they gamble for such high stakes again."

With his promise, she handed him the six thousand, reserving one thousand needed for The Mission's bank account. She had to explain how she had gotten the money, and Turk laughed, telling her how clever he thought she was.

She could relax now. She had saved Turk from the mob's retaliation, and she had his promise not to go to Los Angeles.

She wondered how Martha had found out where Turk was and how to contact him. She was not about to question him, though. After all, she had his promise that he was not going out there, so he would not be seeing Martha after all. Cynthia was going to let well enough alone. She was not about to rock the boat.

Two weeks had passed when she got a telephone call from her mother-in-law. "Cynthia, why are you letting my Herman go out to California with that Andy Womack."

Cynthia assured her. "Don't worry, Mama. Turk has already promised me that he isn't going."

Her mother-in-law said, "Then why has he been all afternoon packing his bag?"

Cynthia said tightly, "I'll see why."

She sped out to The Parkway and confronted her husband. "Why are you going to California after you gave me your promise?"

Turk said, "Baby, Andy was so disappointed when I told him I wasn't going. He had been so excited about meeting all those stars that finally I just couldn't back out."

Cynthia was livid. "You're not married to Andy, you're married to me! I told you before that if you go, you'll not have a wife to come back to. Now tell me, what is your final word!"

He said, "Baby, you'd never leave me. I told Andy I would go, and, yes, I'm going."

She left Turk without saying another word and drove back

to The Mission. She sat behind the cash register and thought about what had happened. How could he love her, and still break his promise and go off to Martha. She felt so sunk. All those years when he'd told her he loved her. The words must have been lies! Now what the hell was she going to do?

She thought about her threat and the way Turk had brushed it aside. The cook came up to her with a request. She got up and went with him into the storeroom to get something.

She had formed the habit of hanging the "fly-boys'" jackets there. No liquor could be purchased in town after eight at night. Often, a boy would place a bottle in his jacket in case he had a chance to stay all night and wanted to take a bottle to the motel. The boys were always looking for girls who would share a motel room with them. Among themselves they would quote the Ogden Nash couplet: "Candy is dandy, but liquor is quicker."

She took care of the cook's request, then turned to the hanging jackets. She found a pint bottle and took it. She wrote a note. "Sorry, but I need this more than you do." She folded the paper and stuck it in the jacket pocket with a ten-dollar bill.

Cynthia left the storeroom, helped herself to a glass, and entered the ladies' room. She filled the glass halfway up with the whiskey and added water. She said "bottoms up" to her reflection in the mirror, then downed the drink and made another. She repeated this ritual until she had emptied the whole pint. She was not aware that alcohol is a depressant.

She had taken her anger and hurt and built a fire under those feelings, and the flame was soaring. She grabbed her purse and called to her dog, Pancho. She stalked from the restaurant, got out her keys, and started up the car.

Chapter 22

Cynthia had no destination in mind as she fled away in her old car. She lacked both plans and direction. She reached the intersection with a five-way light. Each of the five roads led to a different state, and she simply took the first road with a green light. She had only the change from a twenty, a few clothes she kept in the trunk of her car, and her Mexican hairless dog.

She traveled simply to gain distance. Without a road map she had no idea where she was going, and she certainly did not care.

She felt terribly betrayed. Turk's attraction to Martha apparently had not faded. Cynthia remembered telling him on their wedding night that she did not want a fur coat for every day of the week, but only a husband she would not have to share. Bitterly, she remembered he had given his promise, but the only one he had kept was about the furs he had given her. She set her teeth. Furs were a poor exchange for the fidelity she had desired.

She drove on and on. She was in the desert, and passed no little towns or evidence of anyone living out there. Way off in the distance she finally saw lights. It turned out to be a gas station, and she turned in.

The attendant came out, and she asked him to fill up the tank and check the oil.

It was still wartime, and gas was carefully rationed. She wondered how far she would get with only two gas stamps.

The attendant said, "Lady, where are you headed?"

She answered, "Whatever direction I'm going, is where I'm headed."

He saw as she opened her stamp book that after leaving his station she would be left with only one stamp.

He told her, "You're headed for California, but you'll never make it. There's not many travelers in wartime and you're running out of gas stamps. You're gonna be found dead out on the desert."

She spoke up.

"I don't think anyone would care."

He was very concerned. "Look, lady, if you want you can stop for the night with me and my wife."

She thanked him but said she was going on.

He refused to take her gas stamps or her money. He explained that he could get away with it because he fueled big trucks and her single tank would not be noticed. He said, "That will help you on your way, and, believe me, you're going to need all the help you can get." She thanked him and, with determination, drove away.

Cynthia continued through the night with her dog cuddled beside her. After some hours, she saw a light flashing for her to stop. It was a California State Policeman, who told her to get in his car. They proceeded up a ramp and onto a bridge, and parked by a bridge house. He took her inside, invited her to sit, and handed her a tin cup filled with hot black coffee. She took it gratefully, for she was nearly frozen with cold. Her old car had no heater.

She realized that he must think the situation odd. She was traveling alone with a dog. This was unusual in wartime, with gas rationing. Also it was late at night, not your usual time to take a trip. Then there was her attire. She was dressed in a western buckskin riding skirt, a western plaid shirt, a light-tan Stetson, brown riding boots, and a brown-and-white cowhide fur vest. Certainly not your usual traveling clothes.

He waited until she had drunk some of the coffee and quit shivering. He asked her for her driver's license, and she produced her wallet from her purse, opened it up, and handed it to him. He carefully inspected the license and still holding the wallet said, "O.K., lady, let's hear your story."

She blurted out her whole miserable tale and swore that she was telling the truth. She named someone he could call for confirmation and told him vehemently that she was not going back.

The officer opened her wallet and checked its meager contents. He looked back at her and said, "You know I could put you in jail for vagrancy, don't you? But I'm not going to do that. I tell you what: You can stay here for the rest of the night and stay warm until morning, when I go off shift."

She asked him where she was, and he explained that this was the bridge over the Colorado River which separates Arizona from California. He said that in the morning when she crossed the bridge, she would be in Blythe, California.

She looked him over carefully. He was an older man and had really been quite kind. She felt safe with him and agreed to stay until morning.

The bridge house had large windows and a huge spotlight that lit up the swift-moving water below. A machine gun pointed downward.

The officer kept his eyes on the river, and she asked him what he was looking for.

He said, "There's a Japanese camp just up the river, and my job is to watch for anyone who might escape. I'm supposed to watch for anything in the river that's floating down. If I see boards, straw or tree limbs that someone might be using to hide themselves and get past here, I'm to open fire."

If he thought she was shocked by all this, he was mistaken. She had seen and heard enough of the Bund activities to know there was real danger in the country. She knew nothing about the Japanese, but she sure as hell knew about the Germans.

It would probably have been safe to tell him about her work with the FBI, but they had sworn her to secrecy, so she decided it was best not to divulge anything.

The night ended, and with it came the change of shifts. The new officer came with his light flashing to alert the one on duty that this was not a civilian to be checked out. When the two men were together, the older officer explained Cynthia's position and said he was going to have her follow him over to Nick the Greek's greasy spoon. He thought she might find work there, and he drove her back to her own car.

It was a Chevy coupe of ancient vintage she and Turk had found in Phoenix. She always seemed to be sent on errands and needed a car.

She got in, started it up, and followed the officer in his car.

Detroit had gone from car production to war production, and cars—even a 1930 model—were hard to find. Fortunately, it used little gas, or she would not have gotten even this far.

The officer led her first to a gas station to get a fill-up. He told the attendant to put it on his bill.

This put Cynthia instantly on the alert. She was not sure she wanted to be obligated to him. She was, however, short on gas and short on money.

She kept her mouth shut, but privately thought she had better watch her step.

While they waited for the fill-up, he showed her the town. There was not much to see. There was a four-story hotel, a two-pump gas station with a sand drive, a general store, and a small, square restaurant.

He took Cynthia in and introduced her to Nick, the owner,

telling him that she was headed for California but had run short of funds. The officer said he hoped Nick could give her a temporary job. Nick asked her whether she had had any experience and seemed pleased that she had.

He said that due to wartime, he no longer got travelers, but that a new air-training base had fliers who would come in for a bite. He said he could not pay her more than ten dollars a week, but he could provide her meals and a room.

Her discomfort over the free fill-up at the gas station was increasing, but she thought she had better play along until she could form some plan. The policeman was just too interested in her welfare, and she was wary.

She put on a bright face and thanked them both, telling them she was very grateful.

Nick went into a back room and came out with sheets, pillow slips, towels, and a broom. He told Cynthia her room was right behind the restaurant, then asked if they were hungry. Before she could say she was starved, the policeman spoke up and declined, saying, "Thank you very much, but I have to take off or my old lady will think the Japs have got me."

He did take the time to walk with Cynthia to her new room. She was shocked, but tried not to show it. It was a just a shed, like the kind you'd put tools in back in Michigan.

It had four posts set in the sand and was built four feet off the ground, with steps leading up to it. It was made of unpainted boards without even a curtain to cover the single window. There was no sink and no toilet. She realized that whoever lived here would have to go to the restaurant to use the toilet.

By now, the officer had the look in his eye that she had been expecting. He told her he would stop by to see her before he went on duty that night, and then he put his arms around her and kissed her.

Cynthia smiled and thanked him, calling him a wonderful man for doing all he had done for her.

After he was gone, she made a great show of sweeping out the shed. A room, indeed! She then went back to the restaurant, to see how she could make her escape. She asked for a drink of water, and sneaked looks out the windows to find her best escape route. The main road ran down from the bridge and passed in front of the restaurant. This would take her to California, but this she rejected as being too obvious a choice. The officer might decide to follow her.

Behind the restaurant, and behind the dozen shacks that Nick passed off as rental rooms, was a sand road she thought she could get to without being detected. She went back to the shed and told her dog they had better get some sleep, since they had been up all night. She prayed she would wake up in time to avoid the officer. She threw a sheet across the bed and fell right into a deep sleep. When she woke, the sun told her it was late afternoon.

Cynthia looked out the door, and no one was in sight. The back door of the restaurant was closed. She grabbed her dog and ran to the car. She wrenched open the door and started it up. She tore away, turned left onto the sand road, and went like hell!

When Cynthia felt she had put enough distance between herself and Blythe, she slowed down. She thought she must have a guardian angel watching her. She had gotten two tanks of gas free, and still had a little money and the gas stamps she had started with. So once again she was on her way.

Chapter 23

When Cynthia felt safe and saw a truck stop, she pulled in and got a hamburger for herself and Pancho. She did not stay long, and resumed her driving into the night.

Hours passed, and she thought they surely would come to a town, but she found nothing but desert and mountains. It was black out, and she needed to go to the toilet. She stopped, leaving the motor running and the key in the ignition. Squatting squaw-fashion, she relieved herself.

Before she could get back into the car, the wind slammed the door shut, which, on those old cars, made the doors automatically lock. Now she was in a fix. She had not seen a single pair of headlights during all those hours, and as she stood by the car, she thought her guardian angel had finally deserted her. The motor was eating up her precious gas, and she was beside herself.

She was afraid to walk anywhere for help. She had seen the coyotes sometimes kept at roadside zoos, and she was really afraid. She remembered her grandmother back in Michigan warning her to be home by dark, because of the timber wolves that sometimes attacked their horses.

She had also heard that in this part of the country, the diamondback rattlesnakes would come out at night and curl up on the road. The pavement retained the heat that beat down during the day from the sun. She was too terrified to try to walk around to find a rock to break a window.

She had also heard that the wartime maneuvers had moved the mountain lions from their usual habitats, and that there were new reports of attacks. She was very cold but too frightened to make any move.

Unbelievably, she saw in the distance a bit of light that eventually turned into a pair of headlights. She was desperate, and as they approached, she spread-eagled herself in the center of the road. An army convoy truck came within only a few feet of her before it stopped.

She ran to the driver's side, but her teeth were chattering so hard that it was difficult to talk and tell him what had happened to her.

The driver got out and immediately assessed the situation. With a tire iron he smashed in the window so she could get inside her car. Then he turned to her and said, "You're a very lucky girl I didn't follow my orders. I'm to stop for no one! If anyone gets in my way, I'm supposed to run them down. I could be court-martialed for not following orders, but I just couldn't do it."

She assured him she would not tell a soul. He talked to her for a few more minutes. She learned that it was midnight and that there was a town ahead named Needles. They both drove away after she thanked him repeatedly.

Just as he had said, the town appeared, and she saw a bar and restaurant that was still open. She stopped and ordered a hamburger and a beer. Turk had always said that if you were lost or in a strange town, you should always seek out either a bartender or a cab driver.

She asked the bartender where he thought she could find work. He said there was a town ahead called Las Vegas. He said, "It isn't very big, but a new air base named Nellis is nearby, and the servicemen flock to town looking for food and entertainment. There's also a big tank-training camp and a big magnesium plant. I don't think you'll have any trouble getting a job there as a waitress."

The information gave her encouragement. She set off in her cold car with the broken window.

She had traveled some distance when she came to Boulder Dam. She was surprised to find she had to wait in line. She viewed the others waiting, and could not believe the touring cars loaded with children, and crates of chickens tied onto running boards. Every available space was filled with something. This was the time of the great drought that produced the dust bowl so sadly portrayed in John Steinbeck's *Grapes Of Wrath.*

When it came her turn to cross, she found she had to be searched. Apparently they were worried about sabotage, and the search was thorough. Her car was then searched, and she was told to get back in and follow a jeep across the dam.

She saw that a machine gun was aimed at her and was following her all the way. It was very frightening. She was relieved to get that over with and be back on the highway.

Cynthia arrived in Las Vegas and slowly drove down Fremont, the main street. She was not impressed. The whole town was only five blocks long! She passed the Sans Souci Hotel and thought that it looked like a flophouse, then saw the Apache, which she liked a lot better. She parked across the street and entered the Apache lobby. The place was awfully old-fashioned, but it looked very clean, so she took a room. She got her key and went back out to get her Pancho and a few pieces of clothing from the car.

Cynthia returned and climbed the stairs to her room, then took a shower and fell into bed.

Minutes later, she was awakened by a loud knocking on

the door. She called out, "One minute, please," and hurriedly put her clothes back on.

When she opened the door and stepped into the hall, she saw a man who looked just like Custer at the last stand.

Well, if he looked like Custer, then she looked like Calamity Jane. She was again dressed in her western outfit, fringed to the teeth.

The man introduced himself as Colonel Russell. He said he owned the hotel, and they did not allow animals. She would have to move.

Cynthia told him she loved horses and dogs, and this dog was all she had left in the world. "Besides," she said, "if you kick me out before I can find a job, I won't be able to pay for this room."

He shook his head in disbelief.

"You mean you checked into this hotel without the money to pay for your room?"

She admitted that she had. He said, "You are really unbelievable. Well, you said you loved horses, so let's see if you can earn your keep. I'll see that you get a job somewhere. In the meantime, I just lost my stable man, so maybe you can exercise my horse."

She readily agreed, and he drove her out to a little unpainted barn and small corral located out on the desert. He brought out a large mare named Bonnie Mae, and they saddled her up.

Cyntha knew she was being tested. Colonel Russell offered to help her mount, but she declined. Putting her foot in the stirrup, she swung her leg over Bonnie Mae's back. She was no more in the saddle when they were off like the wind. It was unlike any horse she had ever ridden. It felt more like she had been shot out of a catapult! She mentally thanked the rodeo rider who had taught her to use her leg muscles to hang on.

This horse never bothered to avoid the sagebrush, but simply jumped right over the tops. Cynthia had let the horse have her head, but now she saw a train coming in the distance. Fearing that the horse would spook if the train whistled, she turned her heel into Bonnie Mae's side and pulled her around with the reins. This slowed her, and she cantered around in a curve.

Heading back, she put Bonnie Mae in a full gallop until they reached the barn, then asked the horse for a full stop. Bonnie Mae responded instantly, and dramatically skidded to a halt.

Cynthia was bolstered by the Colonel's compliments. He told her she had done very well. He said it was too bad the race tracks did not allow women riders, because Bonnie Mae was a race horse and he sure would like to use Cynthia for a jockey.

They rubbed Bonnie Mae down, blanketed her, and drove back to the hotel.

Before Cynthia returned to her room, she went out for ointment and bandages. Western riding skirts offer no protection for the legs, and hers were in bad shape. She took a shower, tended her sores, and lay on the bed to nap.

The phone rang and it made her jump. Her first thought was that Turk had found her, and she timidly answered. But it was the desk clerk, saying that it was all right to answer a knock on the door because a package was being delivered. It came, and to her astonishment the package contained a pair of western whipcord riding pants with leather inserts. She found a note from Colonel Russell: "I am sure these will fit you. Take tomorrow off to heal up. Here is a letter you can take to the manager of the restaurant. You can order anything you want to eat for two weeks."

She had made her first friend in Las Vegas, and she was filled with gratitude over his thoughtfulness.

Chapter 24

A week later Colonel Russell called her and said she was to go to the Last Frontier Hotel and ask for Evelyn Harris in the dining room. He was sure Evelyn would be able to fix her up with work.

Cynthia did have one outfit that she usually kept in the trunk of her car. She dressed with care in her suit and dress shoes, wanting to make a good impression. She had one set of underwear which, she washed nightly and wore daily. She sure did need a job.

Cynthia had been instructed to go over in the late afternoon, before they got busy. She entered the dining room and stood by the desk. The hostess approached her and said, "I'm awfully sorry, but you're here too early. We don't open up for an hour."

Cynthia asked her whether she was Evelyn Harris, and,

when the woman said yes, explained that Colonel Russell had suggested she see Evelyn about a job.

Evelyn looked her over and said, "I'm sorry, but you don't look like you've ever done a day's work in your life. I can't hire you because I really don't have the time to train an inexperienced girl."

Cynthia spoke right up. "How do you know if I can handle it or not without giving me a chance? I've had a great deal of experience, and I know you would be pleased."

This seemed reasonable and Evelyn agreed to try her out the next day in the coffee shop. Cynthia breathed a sigh of relief. She could not continue living on the Colonel's largesse forever!

Evelyn told Cynthia to go to the housekeeper and get a uniform. Evelyn asked her whether she had western riding boots and was pleased when Cynthia said she did.

Cynthia found that the "uniform" actually was a whipcord skirt with a western blouse. The housekeeper helped her find the right size and also told her what the other help wore in the hotel.

She showed her the different-colored satin cancan dresses and black lace hose the cocktail waitresses wore, with matching hats adorned with colored ostrich feathers. The dealers and bartenders wore western frontier outfits, in keeping with the theme of the hotel.

The hotel itself was mostly a one-story structure, except above the lobby where stairs led up to a balcony. There the guests could sit and write postcards to their friends

Cynthia needed this job desperately and was determined that Evelyn was going to be happy with her performance. She reported early the next morning so as to acquaint herself with where everything was kept and to find out her exact duties.

The coffee shop was called The Canary Room, and she thought it was beautiful. The walls were decorated with yellow wallpaper on one side, and on the other side were windows looking out over the desert. The floor was covered with grass-green carpeting. Crystal prisms hung from the chandeliers, and white birdcages held real singing canaries!

The room was tastefully done and very cheerful. A special, family-style long table in the rear was designated for the help and entertainers.

The coffee shop did not serve liquor and closed at ten at night.

Cynthia had had the job only four days when a handsome fellow in uniform came up to her and said, "Hi, Cynthia."

She looked up. "I don't remember you. Where did we ever meet?"

He smiled. "My name's Bill Neary, I'm a first lieutenant in the Air Force. I remember you from The Mission in Phoenix." Cynthia had met many men when she was there and did not recall him. This surprised her, as she thought he was very handsome and possessed lovely manners. They chatted for a while, then she excused herself because she was at work.

Bill started to see her often, coming back repeatedly to pester her for dates. She was reluctant to accept, as she was really still married and had no intention of becoming involved with anyone. Finally, when he kept following her and begging her to go out, Evelyn Harris interceded. She said, "For heaven's sake, Cynthia, tell him you'll go out with him and get him out from under my feet." She finally agreed to go dancing with him when she got off work.

She had fun with him that night and learned about his background. He told her he was a bombardier. He said he was divorced, and she told him she was still married. Every moment he had away from the air base was spent with her, for the next six weeks. He spent money like water coming out of a tap. He told her that he was from New York and that his parents were dead. She thought it must be lonely to be in the service without parents who would write you. He said his father had been a well-to-do funeral director. He told her about the years when he was growing up. Their house was the first one in New York City to have an elevator installed. He said that, although he frequently saw bakery trucks at their establishment, they never ate baker's bread. This confused him for years until he found out that the trucks actually held bodies brought back from World War I to be prepared for burial.

Bill introduced her to his squadron. They had become known as the Marrying Squadron, as the fliers often married after a brief acquaintance so that someone would write, and wait for them.

Bill proposed, and suggested she obtain one of the quick divorces you could get in Las Vegas. But Cynthia feared that, once free, she might make another mistake, and she hesitated. As a further inducement he added, "If you marry me and I get killed, you will not only get the money from Uncle Sam but also everything my father left me." Now, even though she had been in Las Vegas the thirty days necessary to obtain a quick divorce, she declined. "Bill, I must tell you, I am still in love with my husband. Yes, you and I know that he has wronged me, but I carry a torch for him as big as the as the one on the Statue of Liberty."

Bill was obviously terribly disappointed but asked whether she would at least wait for him. She agreed, and within a few weeks he was shipped out. Before he left, he pinned his Air Force wings to her blouse. She was touched, and had her picture taken wearing them.

Cynthia was working alone one night near closing time. A door leading to the lobby opened, and as she looked up she saw a white-haired man come stumbling in. He was dressed in tan frontier-style clothing and cowboy boots. He came unsteadily down the aisle between the tables and she rushed forward to help him. He had a real package on, and she was afraid he would fall. Cynthia asked him to let her help him. Guiding him to a table, she helped him into a chair.

She said, "I've got just what the doctor ordered for a case like yours." She rushed off to the kitchen and brought him black coffee, toast, and a bowl of hot vegetable soup.

Cynthia placed a whole pot of coffee on the table and watched while he ate. He requested another bowl of soup, and she quickly complied.

When he was finished, he signed the check and politely thanked her. She walked with him to the door.

The next day, Miss Harris took her aside and said she wanted to talk to her.

Cynthia was concerned, and wondered whether she was in trouble. Evelyn asked her, "Do you know who that man was you helped out late last night?"

Cynthia said, "No, I have no idea."

Evelyn smiled.

"He just happens to be W. R. Griffith."

Cynthia looked perplexed, and Evelyn smiled, saying, "He owns all the movie theaters in Texas. He has a hotel in Gallup, New Mexico, and he also owns this hotel. His brother is the big movie director, D. W. Griffith." Evelyn enjoyed seeing the surprise on Cynthia's face.

Evelyn continued. "He was so pleased with the way you treated him that he wants me to have you replace one of the waitresses in the main dining room!"

Cynthia said regretfully, "Oh I'd love to work in there, but I don't want to take away anyone's job."

"Well," said Miss Harris, "that's one more gold star for you. Your stock has shot up with me even higher. One of the girls will be leaving anyway in about three weeks, so why don't you plan on taking her place."

Cynthia was very pleased. She would not only be in the main dining room, where the tips were bigger, but she would also be provided housing.

Mr. Griffith had built an entire subdivision for his employees. The houses were ranch-style with good-sized rooms, and they were all furnished. He also provided housekeepers and a yard man. The rent was, Cynthia had heard, quite reasonable. Each house had two bedrooms and was shared by either two couples or four girls.

Just as Evelyn had said, the waitress left, and Cynthia replaced her and was assigned one of the houses.

One of Cynthia's roommates was a girl who said her nationality was "Georgian," because she came from that state. The other girls were cocktail waitresses. One was a pretty blonde who talked baby talk. She came home one day with a black eye, looking as if she had been involved in a brawl. Cynthia thought the bruise and the baby talk were terribly inconsistent, but awfully funny.

One day, Cynthia had just reported for work when Evelyn flew to her side. "Cynthia," she warned, "get out of here quick—your house is on fire!"

It was spring, and Cynthia noticed as she flew out the door that the mountain winds were up. She arrived at the house and saw that it was gone. She was sick. She had only recently received the furs that she had left in Detroit and had finally sent for. Turk had bought her a leopard coat, a mink scarf, and three fox coats of different shades. All gone.

Cynthia had also just purchased a complete set of white Samsonite luggage. She stood looking at the last of the fire. She was soon joined by her roommates, and they circled the remains. Much to her surprise, when she came to the area where her closet was, she found that it had not burned with the rest of the house! True, one side of her new luggage was scorched, but, miraculously, not one hair of her furs was damaged!

Relieved, she returned to the hotel and her duties. When she told Evelyn that her house was gone, the hostess was sympathetic. She said she thought she knew of another house which Cynthia might be able to rent. Evelyn said the local prosecuting attorney had been called into the service, and his house was located right across the street. She would see whether he would rent it to Cynthia.

True to her word, Evelyn went to the attorney and got his consent. Cynthia could move into the house in just one week, when he would be gone.

Cynthia and Pancho shared a couch in another subdivision house while they waited. The week passed quickly, and she moved with her few things that had not burned. The other employees had kindly taken up a collection for the girls when they had gotten burned out, and Cynthia began to purchase a few necessities with the money.

The house was perfect. It was close to work, yet it offered

her privacy. She had liked living with the other girls, but she liked this even better.

One bit of news, however, spoiled her pleasure. She heard from some of the fellows at the base that Bill Neary's plane had been shot down over Germany on the second raid. Later she found he had listed her as next of kin, and she received a message from the war department stating that he was officially dead. She was stunned. Only a few weeks ago, they had been together and she had promised to wait for him. This new, terrible loss would remind her of the other tragedies in her life. Again, she would ask herself whether her association with those she cared about actually did bestow on them the kiss of death. She would speak their names aloud: "Denelda. Durwood. Bill." She would then respond in a soft whisper, "Please, God, no more deaths. No more deaths, please." She kept repeating their names and her entreaty until it became a haunting litany.

Chapter 25

When Cynthia was not working or keeping up her house, she spent a good deal of time riding. Colonel Russell had found a new stable man and no longer needed her, so she would ride one of the horses owned by the hotel. They kept about two hundred of the animals for the guests to rent. This was a very popular form of recreation, and often every horse would be taken. It was a common sight to see fifty horses and riders setting off for the El Rancho Vegas, where they would be served an English hunt breakfast.

At the stable, Cynthia met an old man named Bud Simpson, who had once been a world-champion rodeo rider. He had also worked as a stunt rider in the movies and had been used as a double for Tom Mix, the popular Western movie star. Now he was in his seventies, and unable to take that rough life.

Bud worked around the stable, helping all he could, and

the hotel allowed him to stay in the bunkhouse.

Cynthia liked the old man and loved to listen to his stories. He admired her ability to ride tough horses and thought she should be given the opportunity to ride W. R. Griffith's stallion, King. King was a seventeen-hand, blue-ribbon-winning, palomino stallion. He was so famous that his picture was displayed on the Santa Fe railroad brochure.

Bud thought it was a shame that the animal never got any exercise. They only took him out of the small corral to have his picture taken or to breed a mare.

Bud and Cynthia approached Mr. Griffith about letting her ride and exercise his horse. He listened to them and, much to her delight, gave his consent. He did say, however, that she must not let anyone else ride him.

Cynthia was more than a little apprehensive before she got on King the first time. It had been several months since he had been ridden, and she was concerned that he might be a handful.

Bud thought she looked good on King, because they were both blondes.

Cynthia got on King's back, and he was a perfect gentleman. Whoever had trained him had done a good job, and she seemed to never have a speck of trouble.

Every day, she would take him out on the desert and gallop him, but she could never curry or brush him down afterwards, because Bud loved the horse and reserved that right for himself.

Cynthia wanted to tip Bud, but felt it would hurt his pride. Instead she would bring him treats of cigars and cookies.

One day when out riding, she was overtaken by a man riding another palomino. He told her he had just gotten his horse out of a trailer and wanted to give him a run. He asked her whether she would mind joining him in a quick gallop, and she readily agreed. Who would ever turn down the chance to join in a ride with Roy Rogers!

Roy was wearing a blue frontier suit with white boots and a white Stetson. They took the horses on a fast gallop along the railroad track, then turned back toward the stables. He then asked whether she would ride further with him, into town. She was absolutely thrilled. They entered the town and saw a U.S.O. bus full of entertainers who waved at the horseback riders. She proudly joined Roy in waving back.

King was bigger than Trigger, and Roy was very impressed with him. Cynthia thought Roy quite amusing when he spoke to Trigger and told him not to be jealous.

Later that night, many of the servicemen came to the Frontier to see the show. The tables had been moved to allow for a wider aisle. Roy rode into the lobby on Trigger, who wore felt boots to keep from slipping on the floor. They reached the stage and performed for the crowd. It was a great act and very popular. Cynthia thought Roy was a wonderful gentleman and great fun. She was sorry when he had to leave town for another engagement.

Another day, after Cynthia had been out riding on the desert, she returned to town and realized she was very thirsty. She saw a place to get a drink, tied her horse to the hitching post, and entered.

Cynthia had seen this place and wondered about it, but had never been inside. She had heard the place was owned by an eccentric man named Frank Dio. Frank had first built it as a home, then later converted the front bedroom into what he called the Piccadilly Circus Bar. She remembered hearing that he used to let people into his living room to gamble, until he caught the dealer taking a card from the bottom of the deck. He kicked the man out and never allowed gambling again.

Cynthia had just settled herself on a bar stool when the owner came in. He was carrying a pit bull in his arms, and tears were running down his face. His voice choked as he said his dog had just been bitten by a rattlesnake.

Cynthia rushed around to get behind the bar. She grabbed a towel, filled it with ice, and placed this ice pack on the dog's lip where he had been bitten. She asked the owner, "Do you have a car?"

"Yes," he replied, "but I'm too shook up to drive."

"Do you know where we can find a vet?"

He said, "Sure."

"O.K.," she commanded. "I'll drive and you give me directions."

Frank would never get over her swift response. He often told people about her efforts and the fact that his dog had been saved.

This chance encounter and rescue gave her a friend that would last for many years.

The little town of Las Vegas was beginning to gain in popularity. The gambling was, of course, a draw. But the fact that you could come and see the stars of the movies in person brought in many tourists, too.

Inside the Frontier on one side of the lobby, W. R. Griffith's two sisters had set up a shop where you could purchase cigarettes, flowers, and lovely, Indian silver-and-turquoise jewelry.

One day Cynthia approached Mr. Griffith and asked him whether she could work in the gift shop. Mr. Griffith suggested she drive out and meet his sisters to discuss the request. Cynthia found they were two lovely and gracious women. One was a widow; the other had never married. They took an immediate liking to Cynthia and discussed how best to work out the arrangement. It was finally agreed that she would work in the gift shop from eleven in the morning until three in the afternoon. She would receive a salary and a percentage of any frontier suits and jewelry she sold. At night, she would walk about selling cigarettes and flowers. The women admitted that Cynthia's help would greatly lessen their hours, leaving them free during the day to do other things.

Later, Cynthia learned from her friend Evelyn Harris that she had been given hotel privileges just as if she were a paying guest. These permitted her to eat in the dining room and use the swimming pool.

With this change in jobs, Cynthia decided that she was through being a waitress and also through with dull uniforms. She went out shopping for the most glamorous clothes she could find. As the first cigarette girl in this town, she was going to make her own rules and dress the way she wanted.

Cynthia bought a black, fringed skirt and a long-sleeved, black blouse with a low neckline, which made a perfect backdrop for a squash-blossom Indian necklace which she borrowed from the gift shop. She also wore some of the shop's turquoise rings. She knew she would get compliments on the jewelry, and then she could offer it up for sale. She would then get a commission on these sales from the gift shop.

What a great change this made in her life. Gone was the rush of serving dinners and cleaning tables. She was now her own boss and could make far more money. Immediately she thought of all the clothes she could buy!

Cynthia was beginning to realize that she had inherited her mother's beauty. She had an hourglass figure topped by lovely blonde hair and beautiful blue eyes. She could not ignore the many heads that turned her way when she passed by. This realization did not swell her head or make her egotistical; she thought of her looks only as an asset, helping her make sales.

Without waitress duties, she could now enjoy the patrons, who were often from the world of films. One evening, she was stopped at the bar by a dark-complexioned man who introduced himself as a Hollywood director, telling her he had just finished making a picture outside of town, in the desert. He said the picture starred John Wayne, who was coming into town for the wrap up party that they always had after the completion of a film. He asked whether she would like to join them. Her date would be John Wayne.

Cynthia could hardly believe her good fortune. She jumped at the opportunity. She had always loved to watch his movies and thought he looked kind, yet very rugged.

A bit later that night, she met other movie stars, Andy Devine and Joey of the Dead End Kids. They had ridden into town on their motorcycles and were clowning and cutting up. Cynthia thought they were very funny, teasing the director and making jokes.

When they found that he had proposed Cynthia be John Wayne's blind date, they turned to the director and chastised him for making these arrangements.

Andy said, "How could you ask this nice young lady to be his dinner partner? You know he's just been recently divorced. His wife found out he really doesn't like girls. John Wayne prefers men!"

Cynthia excused herself and fled back to the gift shop, where she turned in her cigarettes and flowers. She told the manager, "I'm afraid that I can't stay. I feel sick and I've got to go home." She could hardly wait to get out of the place.

The next day, when she went back to the hotel, she ran into Andy and Joey. They apologized to her about what they had told her.

Andy said, "We were only kidding you. John Wayne is all man, and he's been out on the desert so long acting in this film, he would have turned you every way but loose. You might have been the next Mrs. John Wayne!"

Cynthia realized she had missed the boat. Too late now, for her blind date had already left for California. She could not be really angry with Andy and Joey; they were such good fun. She blamed herself for not picking up on the fact that they were always teasing and kidding, and that their description of the actor's tastes had been just more of the same.

Cynthia had been working as a cigarette girl for only a couple of months when she saw her sister-in-law, Sarah, sitting in the dining room with her husband, Jack. They had spotted her, so she could hardly avoid them. She had never liked Sarah, who looked down on her because she was not Jewish. Nevertheless, Cynthia gritted her teeth and went over to their table to say hello. Sarah wasted no time in going for the jugular. "Well, Cynthia, I wonder if you've heard that Turk is living with Martha Raye out in California."

Cynthia didn't answer. She raised her chin and, with her head held high in feigned indifference, she left the dining room. She was not going to let that bitch know how badly her words had hurt her.

She went into the gift shop, feeling as if her insides had been torn apart. The pain was terrible and she started to cry.

She tried to stop, but could not. "Well, Turk," she said through
her tears, "I hope you're happy with her." But even as she said
this, she knew it was a lie. She did not want Turk to be happy
with anyone but herself. She mopped her eyes and blew her
nose, then got up and went into the ladies' room. She wet a
towel with witch hazel and pressed the cool compress to her
eyes. She did not want Sarah and Jack to see the telltale
redness and know that she had been crying.

Cynthia had to return to the dining room. She was determined not to let that dreadful Sarah have the satisfaction of
knowing she was upset. She checked her face in the mirror. It
looked all right, and she went back.

Cynthia carefully avoided looking at Sarah and Jack's
table. There were so many questions she wanted to ask, but she
would not give them the satisfaction of knowing she cared.

She wondered whether Turk had filed for divorce. He
could claim that she had deserted him. She imagined he had
probably sold The Mission. He had probably also sold his
interest in the nightclub to Andy Womack. She wondered
whether Andy felt any guilt about insisting that Turk take him
out to California. She doubted it. She felt lower than she had
in a long time. But she was not going to let it show. With a fixed
smile on her face, she wandered around the tables and sold her
cigarettes.

One day as she was passing through the dining room, she
ran smack into Tony from Phoenix! This was a shock, as she
had tried to put Phoenix out of her mind. Cynthia was not only
surprised—she was scared. Tony was part of the Greenbaum
gang, the one that had arranged to loan her the money to pay
off Turk's gambling debt. She figured Turk had left for
California and never repaid the money.

Tony said, "What are you doing here? I heard you had run
away to Michigan. What time do you leave here?"

She told him, and he said he would meet her at the El
Rancho. His last words to her were, "Be there!"

She was frightened. You never cross the mob. Not if you
wanted to stay alive.

When Cynthia arrived that evening, Tony led her to a table and introduced her to the crowd. It was there that she first met Bugsy Siegel, who was described to her as being in "real estate."

Tony said, "This is the kid I was telling you about." He turned to Cynthia, "O.K., Baby, the truth now, what happened in Phoenix?"

She said, "You want me to tell it in front of everybody?"

He said yes, so she proceeded to tell the whole story about Turk and Martha, and why she had run away.

She finished, and Tony said, "O.K., Baby, you're off the hook. You only made one mistake. You didn't ask for enough money. The way you looked that day, in that sweater, you could have had ten thousand dollars." The group at the table laughed. He continued.

"I'm going to tell you something else. Any woman who would go out on the limb for her old man like you did is a winner. The debt is cancelled."

Bugsy spoke up. "The man had to be a jerk to have thrown her over for that tomato Martha."

Cynthia felt instant relief, and rapidly her tension eased. Suddenly she decided it was a swell party.

Chapter 26

Cynthia tried to keep busy and forget what Sarah had told her about Turk living with Martha, but it was impossible. She tortured herself with mental images. She saw them kissing, and imagined them in bed together. She would try to dismiss them from her mind, but they would keep reappearing.

Cynthia went back over her life with Turk, trying to find any area where she thought she had failed him. She really had tried to be a good wife and helpmate. Eventually she had even won over her mother-in-law. Clearly this was not enough for Turk, or he would not have taken this path.

She wondered what Martha could offer him that she could not. She finally concluded that Martha could offer him money, and the glamor and excitement of Hollywood and all the stars. Is that what had drawn him out there? Was that so wonderful that he was willing to put his marriage in jeopardy? She decided, unhappily, that it was.

Gradually, time, that great healer, started to work, and she thought about Turk and Martha less and less. Of course there were the nights that she lay in her bed and missed his arms around her, and she would feel wounded until sleep finally came to rescue her from her torment.

She did keep busy. She had her job, a house to keep up, and new friends to visit. She often saw Frank Dio because he was a close neighbor and a good friend. Frank had introduced jazz to Europe, and had many stories to tell. He had been the conductor of his band and had also played the piano. He had been, at one time, so famous that he was asked to give a command performance for the Prince of Wales.

When he had returned to the United States, he had stopped overnight in Las Vegas on his way to the West Coast. A faithful follower of astrology, Frank had happened to read his horoscope in the local paper. It had advised him to buy land. That was enough for Frank and he never left town. He had settled right down, built a house, and proceeded to buy up land piece by piece.

Frank was a good deal older than Cynthia and their friendship verged on a father-daughter relationship. He knew many Hollywood stars and he always included Cynthia when they visited, asking her to play hostess. She also was introduced to many movie stars when working at the Frontier.

Cynthia was impressed with the glamor and high life of Frank's friends. He introduced her to a style of fine living which until this time she had known only from magazines. Frank's home was filled with priceless treasures which he had accumulated in his travels. Cynthia fell in love especially with the six-hundred-year-old Italian tapestries that hung from his walls.

Frank composed songs, and was greatly admired by Jerry Colonna, Jack Haley, and Bob Hope, whom Cynthia met during their frequent visits. She had seen Wallace Beery in the movies and had always thought he would be like the roles he played—warm and natural. Much to her disappointment, she found he was actually a very crotchety person and extremely hard to please. When Cynthia had worked as a waitress, she, like the other waitresses, had relied on her tips and had worked hard to earn them. But, despite her normally winning ways, she had found there was just no way she could please this unpleasant man.

In contrast, she had found Errol Flynn most charming. The newspapers at the time were being very tough on him about his new marriage to a nineteen-year-old girl. Perhaps he felt an affinity between his Irish soul and this Irish waitress. At any rate, she found him not only handsome but also very polite and amusing.

He smiled when she approached the table and asked, "I heard they actually serve steak here at the Frontier—is that true?"

She confirmed this, and he said, "Well, in Hollywood we can't find steak. It's so bad that we've started to eat producers."

Cynthia answered, "Well, with the kind of pictures that you've been in lately, I don't blame you."

Errol threw back his head and laughed. The crowd joined him in the fun and laughed, too.

He had asked Cynthia her name, and now said, "Cynthia, you are serving my wedding dinner. This is the new Mrs. Flynn, and we want this to be special. I will leave it all up to you. The sky's the limit."

Cynthia brought them cocktails after telling the kitchen what she wanted prepared. When it was ready, she brought out a planked Chateaubriand and the best red burgundy the Frontier offered. The chef came out to pour the brandy around the steak and light it. The flames burned dramatically around the platter, and heads turned. Cynthia placed the Flynns' plates in front of them and served the dishes that she had carefully chosen to accompany the meat dish. The meal concluded with a very fine brandy.

When it was over, Errol said, with a gorgeous smile, "We want to thank you, Cynthia, for making everything so lovely. Please don't believe what you read in the papers about me. My wife is a good deal younger than I am, and the papers are making me out to be a rogue."

Cynthia replied, "I never believe Hollywood gossip. I only judge what I see for myself, and I like you and your wife."

She presented the bill, and he was visibly shocked. It came to one hundred and sixty dollars. He looked up at her. "Cynthia, you have bled me."

She spoke up.

"Mr. Flynn, if you didn't want to go first class, you should have stayed in Hollywood."

Again, Errol threw back his head and roared with laughter. He said, "I asked for that, and you only gave me what I asked for."

He reached into his wallet and drew out his card. "I want you to take this card. Our home address is on it, and also our unlisted telephone number. You have really made our evening a lot of fun, and we would love you to visit us. Remember, if you're ever in Los Angeles, you aren't to stay in a hotel." He signed the check, and the couple left.

Much to Cynthia's astonishment, she found that he had failed to leave her a tip. She wondered then whether his profuse thanks were just empty words. Maybe the gossip columnists were right after all.

Two days later, Evelyn Harris stopped her and said, "Cynthia, you must have really captivated Errol Flynn, because when he checked out, he left this, saying it was for Irish." Cynthia took the envelope and opened it. Inside were five one-hundred-dollar bills and a note restating his invitation to have her visit them at their home. The note was signed, "Your friends, Mr. and Mrs. Errol Flynn." When she got over her shock, Cynthia felt bad that she had so misjudged him. She offered to share the tip with her friend, but Evelyn responded, "Of course not, Cynthia. I am pleased you handled Mr. Flynn so well, and you deserve all the money."

As much fun as waitressing had been, Cynthia was glad that she had left the dining room and become a cigarette girl. Her sales were terrific and she also had an income from the flowers she sold to the guests.

She loved adorning herself with pieces of Indian jewelry and earning money when guests purchased them. She also bought some of these pieces for herself. Her prize possession was an especially beautiful squash-blossom necklace. One day she was approached by a man in uniform. This in itself was certainly not unusual, but this time, it was none other than General Dwight D. Eisenhower. He introduced himself and his pregnant daughter-in-law, who admired Cynthia's necklace. At that, General Eisenhower asked Cynthia to sell it to him. She was reluctant, since she had never found one so beautiful, but her intense patriotism finally won out. Silently, she thought of General Eisenhower's courage and wondered whether he would be returning from the war. If buying the necklace for this girl would make him happy, surely she should comply. She agreed to sell it to him and asked only for the one hundred and fifty dollars that she herself had paid. She wouldn't think of making a profit from this great man. Little did she ever imagine that she was facing a soldier who would one day be president of the country.

I now had a new man enter my life. His name was Erwin Ashley, and he was an artist from New York. He had designed the label used at that time for StarKist tuna. It showed a lovely scalloped sea shell with a single pearl inside. The label read, "StarKist, Pearl of the Sea."

Erwin was very good to me. He loaned me a blue Cadillac and gave me an open account at a gas station. We dated for some time and eventually he proposed. I was in love with him, but the condition he insisted on was harsh. He said he didn't want children, and I would have to sign a contract agreeing to this. He explained that he had been born with clubfeet, which sometimes is inheritable. He had gone through painful operations when he was young and would never want any child of his to have to go through this. I was sympathetic but turned him down. I wanted children and had always hoped that I would become pregnant when I lived with Turk. It had never happened, but I always hoped someday it would. Erwin was disappointed but adamant. This was the end for both of us.

During this period I heard from my old friend Josephine. She was on her way to California to visit her sister and wanted to stop in Vegas to visit me. She wrote, "Now, Sin, I want you to meet me with a big brass band." I laughingly promised. Actually, I knew the members of a local band quite well, and they agreed to help me out. Josephine was incredulous to find her silly request granted. The band played "Yankee Doodle Dandy," and we all had a big laugh with her. I then drove her to town in the blue Cadillac. We had a grand time together, laughing over things we had done years ago.

One day I answered my door, and there stood a stranger. He had flowers in his hand and a box of candy under his arm. He introduced himself. "My name is Leonard Goodyear. I make tires for a living. My wife and I are across the street at the Frontier swimming pool, and we could hear you and your friend laughing and having fun. My wife said to ask if you would join us so we could have some laughs ourselves." I introduced Mr. Goodyear to Josephine, and we agreed to join them as soon as we could change into our bathing suits.

When he was gone, we laughed some more but held it down so he wouldn't think we were laughing at him. I said, "Josephine, can you believe him? 'My name is Leonard Goodyear and I make tires for a living.' That's like a man coming here and saying, 'My name is Henry Ford and I make cars for a living.' Leonard Goodyear is a household name, for goodness sake." Josephine agreed, and we cheerfully changed into our suits to join these people. They wanted to be amused, and it wasn't difficult. Josephine had a million funny stories to tell, including her brass-band welcome into town. Later the Goodyears took us to dinner. They stayed two weeks, and we joined them each day at the pool and had lunch with them. They were a pleasure to be with, and it provided a diversion for Josephine and me. Great people and great fun!

After a couple of years of this life, Frank Dio encouraged

Cynthia to invest in some land for herself. When she found she could buy the house she was renting, Frank told her it would be a good move and predicted that as Las Vegas grew, her land would become more valuable. Gratefully, she took his advice.

This was a real departure from Cynthia's previous approach to life. She had always lived to earn and spend. Her admiration, however, for her good friend was such that she willingly went along with his suggestions.

Cynthia's winning charm and good humor at the Frontier helped her make friends with many of the customers. She met a young starlet and was immediately taken with her innocence and sweet personality. The young girl's name was Shelley Winters, and they struck up a friendship. One night Shelley came up to Cynthia while she was selling cigarettes and asked her in her natural little Shelley voice, "Why are you always being chased by the most handsome and richest men?"

Cynthia did not have the heart to tell Shelley that the heavy makeup she had to wear and the brutal bright lights on the Hollywood sets were giving her a bad case of acne. This certainly was hardly attractive, but Cynthia hesitated to hurt Shelley's feelings

Cynthia had just finished reading a story about a boss and his secretary, and she decided to tell part of the plot to Shelley as if it was the truth about herself.

The book involved a secretary who was trying to get her conservative boss to make a pass at her, but was having no success. Finally, in desperation, she reached out and grabbed him, saying, "You're going to have my body if I have to ruin yours in the struggle."

Cynthia told Shelley, "I'll let you in on my secret for attracting men if you'll pay me twenty-five dollars."

Shelley immediately went up to her room and returned with the money.

Cynthia proceeded to explain in exactly those words how you had to grab the man and threaten him. Shelley was shocked and said, "Oh, Sinny, I just don't think I could do such a thing."

Cynthia told her, "Well, I won't take your money now, but if you ever want a man and you win him this way, then you'll owe me the money. One thing about it, Shelley, I can guarantee this method really works."

Hollywood was trying to present Shelley as a new sexy starlet, not realizing that they really had missed her true personality. Cynthia believed Shelley was about eighteen years old at this time, and she thought Shelley innocent, adorable, and quite shy. She was very sweet and pretty, but hardly the material for a provocative siren.

Cynthia met another starlet and was struck by her impressive beauty. Her name was Ava Gardner, and she was in Las Vegas seeking a divorce from her husband, Mickey Rooney.

Ava walked into the lobby one day with Bugsy Siegel and the original Nick the Greek. They came up to the gift shop, and Ava looked over the western outfits for sale. She told Cynthia she wanted to buy one to wear that night, but she knew she was hard to fit.

Ava tried on an outfit, and Cynthia could immediately see the problem. Ava's waist was incredibly small, and the outfit needed to have a large amount of material taken in.

Cynthia told Ava that she knew a dressmaker in town who could make the necessary alterations. She thought the woman might be able to do it right away, so Ava could wear the outfit that night.

Bugsy invited Ava to pick out something in the jewelry case for him to buy for her. While Ava considered the articles made by the local Indians, Bugsy turned to Cynthia and offered to buy her something also.

Cynthia had long admired a lovely large ring that held a big turquoise stone with a rattlesnake twined around it. She showed it to Bugsy, and he agreed that it was a good choice.

Ava picked out a silver cigarette case decorated with turquoise and coral. Bugsy paid for the gifts, and the girls thanked him for his generosity.

Cynthia still was unaware of Bugsy's ties to the mob, and continued to believe he was in real estate. He was so handsome and conservatively dressed that he looked like anything but a gangster. Only years later did she discover how he actually made his money. She doubts very much that Ava was aware of his true occupation, either.

Nick the Greek she knew somewhat better, as he would come in to gamble and stay for two or three days and nights, standing up only to go to the mens's room.

Cynthia wrote down for Ava the address of her dress-maker, but Ava said, "I don't know this town and I'll never find it. Why don't you come with me in my car and tell me how to get there?"

Cynthia agreed to meet her when she came off duty at three o'clock. At the appointed time, she was met by Ava in a white Cadillac convertible with a rumble seat. On their way Cynthia was convinced that Ava was driving at ninety-five miles per hour through town. She was thoroughly frightened, but held on and kept it to herself.

They met with the dressmaker, who said the alterations would take several hours, so the girls decided to "do the town."

Initially they talked about Bugsy. He was, after all, the one who had first brought them together. Cynthia told Ava about his generosity and how the waitresses vied with each other to wait on him. He left enormous tips and never expected anything in return.

Cynthia and Ava went from one gambling club to another and wound up having coffee in the Apache Hotel. Cynthia thought Ava was one of the most beautiful women she had ever met. She needed no make-up, and wore only a little lipstick.

That night, both women had plans to attend a big cookout at the ranch of Ballard Baron. He was in charge of one of the gambling casinos, and it was his job to keep the guests happy.

When the casino closed at midnight, in those early days of Las Vegas, the guests were invited to Ballard's ranch. He had a big swimming pool and a wonderful wife, who served as hostess.

The guests either rode horseback or were driven in

stagecoaches and covered wagons. These were authentic vehicles that had been purchased by W. R. Griffith.

The entertainers were also invited, and everyone gathered around a huge bonfire to sing. The string band played old western songs and everyone joined in.

Cynthia said these parties were greatly enjoyed, and undoubtedly kept the gamblers in town long after they had planned to leave.

Cynthia found it amusing that the bandleader at the El Rancho, Hal Grayson, had fallen in love with Ava. When she entered the hotel, the bandleader would signal the players and lead them in a song that contained the lyrics, "Put a three-cent stamp on me and send me back to Tennessee." The bandleader thought she was from that state. He was really torched over her, but she was just getting out of one mess and was reluctant to get involved. Besides, he was much older than Ava. She did enjoy his music, though, so she continued to go to his club, but she never gave him any encouragement.

For the next three years, whenever Ava came back to town and Hal saw her, he would play the same song.

There was a false story at this time that was widely believed and circulated. It involved the use of monkey glands that could be implanted in a man and—the claim was—restore his youth. Hal confided in Cynthia that it would be like finding Ponce de Leon's fountain. He said he was going to find a doctor to do this for him, to help him win Ava.

Cynthia found this terribly funny. She listened to him, finding it difficult to keep her laughter under control. She had never believed the story.

Ava had her sister Bea with her, and they were wild about dancing. They would dance until they dropped. They never felt the need for partners, but would dance for its own sake. Hitting top speed in Ava's car, the three would arrive in a cloud of dust and dance to exhaustion. They were having a wonderful time.

All too soon, Ava's stay ended. Cynthia had never questioned her about her divorce, feeling it was none of her business. Cynthia, caught up in Ava's joie de vivre, had simply joined her in living for the moment; she was awed by Ava's stamina.

Years later, Cynthia would look back and think of how parallel their lives had been over the years, with their many marriages and the resulting heartache that would go with each breakup.

Certainly, great beauty can have its rewards, but it also can be a great detriment to happiness. Possibly that is what this book is ultimately all about.

When Ava was gone, Cynthia had an opportunity to see just whom Ava had divorced. Mickey Rooney came to town, and Cynthia was able to make her own judgment. She found him dreadfully short. There had always been a lot written about his height, but it still came as a shock when she found herself towering over him.

Mickey loved to gamble, and would insist on having a bar stool provided for him so that he sat up taller. This helped make up for his deficiency and allowed him to become more relaxed.

Cynthia waited on Mickey in the gift shop and they had conversations and shared jokes. But she never mentioned the divorce or any involvement she had had with his ex-wife.

Cynthia thought his face had great expression when he rolled the dice, displaying the intensity of the true gambler looking eagerly for the big win. He always drew a crowd, and was so interesting to watch that Cynthia was sorry when at last he, too, left town.

Chapter 27

One night Cynthia rode King to the El Rancho. After leaving King in the stable, she learned that they were having a big barbecue out by the corral. She walked over and was watching the activity when, suddenly, she felt someone put his arms around her, and she was lifted off the ground. She yelled, "Put me down at once!" When she had regained her balance, she turned around to face the man who had treated her with such rudeness, and she shouted in anger, "Look, but don't touch." With that she hit him over the head with her riding crop.

The man apologized.

"I'm sorry, I never meant to offend you. I'd like to be friends. My name is Hal Wallis." He did not add that he was a big Hollywood producer. She walked away.

Cynthia went to the gift shop the next day to pick up her flowers. and was told that there was an orchid there for her.

The card was signed "Hal Wallis." He began wooing her in earnest, and each day there would be a new orchid waiting for her. Often the orchid would be black, which Cynthia knew was dreadfully expensive. These flowers were flown in from Los Angeles.

Cynthia gradually began to soften toward this man who was so eager to prove he could be a gentleman, and she began to date him. For his part, he was, in the terms of the day, smitten with her.

About once a month Hal would invite Cynthia to join him in Los Angeles for an evening out on the town. When she accepted, they would make the rounds of the famous night-clubs. Besides having a pretty face, Cynthia also had a dazzling figure. Now that Turk was no longer around to criticize her, she could dress to emphasize her impressive bustline. Hal loved to show her off.

One evening, he suggested they go to the Brown Derby. "All the stars hang out there, and you sure are star material yourself." She laughed. They arrived at the restaurant in a big, black limousine, and as she got out of the vehicle, she caught her heel. It broke off and she pitched forward, landing in the arms of the doorman. Hal took her arm so she could balance herself. He said, "Take off your slippers and give them to the doorman." He then slipped a bill to the man and said, "Will you please go out and get this lady a new pair?" The doorman agreed.

"Now, Honey," Hal said to her, "we will just go in as though nothing had happened. Hold your pretty face high, and no one will be looking at your feet."

One evening Hal told her they were going to a party given by a movie star. Cynthia paused and said, "Who is it, Hal?"

He said, "Martha Raye."

She pleaded, "Hal, I can't go there. She took my husband away from me, and he's living with her. I just couldn't bear to see them together." He readily understood, and they went out to dinner instead.

Going to Los Angeles also gave Cynthia a chance to shop. Her closets at home were already swollen, but this did not stop her from acquiring more clothes. Some of the dresses were really more appropriate for Los Angeles than for the "cow town" where she worked, but that did not stop her, either. She also ordered blouses and had them embroidered with the word "SIN" in contrasting colors. If someone laughed and pointed this out, she would say, "Yes, that's me: sin personified."

She did have to be a bit more careful about her spending now, as she had house payments to make. Still, the clothes were lovely, and she bought and bought.

Hal was in love and wanted to marry her. She explained to him that she was still in love with her husband and would not think of marrying again. He understood, but continued to date her. Perhaps he thought she or the situation might change.

So all was not work and home to bed. She enjoyed her days in Los Angeles, and also loved her job. As time went on, memories of Turk and their idyllic moments together began to fade, though not quite into oblivion. Only occasionally would she glimpse someone from the back whose straight spine and beautiful hair would make her heart jump. Could it be? Then back would flood the feelings of tenderness and longing. When, upon further inspection, her hopes proved groundless, the feelings of bitterness returned. Had it been so much to ask that he be faithful to her? And Martha, who had all the glamour and stardom anyone could wish for. Did she have to have Turk, too? But living was not to be done in the past; Cynthia's life had to go on, and she would make the best she could of it.

Cynthia loved to tease Bugsy Siegel when he was in town. Years later, after she had learned that he was really a mobster, she found out how he had gotten his nickname. It seems he first made money by bootlegging liquor. Once, while he was driving a truck loaded with liquor, a rival mob forced him over. He stopped his truck, jumped out with a machine gun, and mowed them down. Then, he practically fell apart in his nervousness, shaking and acting—in the words of his partner in the truck, "bugsy."

His real name was Benjamin, or Benny, and he hated to be called Bugsy. How Cynthia got away with calling him this is anyone's guess, but he took it without any anger, and even laughed. Perhaps he admired her gutsiness.

She also naively made fun of his walk. Approaching his table, she would swagger in imitation of him. Ironically, she thought that Bugsy was imitating George Raft, who was famous at that time for his gangster roles in the movies. George would have a cigarette hanging out of his mouth, and would swagger and talk tough. Cynthia thought that Bugsy felt this was smart. He would send for her to bring him his favorite Omar cigars, and she would affect this gangster walk as she approached his table. He would only laugh.

As a young girl, Cynthia had easily passed for someone several years older. Now, pushing thirty, she had retained that beauty of youth remarkably, and Bugsy and his friends treated her like a kid sister, protecting her at every turn.

One day, the sheriff came into the hotel. His eyes were wide as he reported that a large, three-winged plane had crashed into the mountains. Cynthia asked just where, and found that it was behind her house, though some distance away. The sheriff said he doubted that there would be any survivors.

When the crash was reported, it was learned that one of the passengers had been Carole Lombard, the beautiful actress and wife of Clark Gable. She had been on the plane to attend war bond drives, and had been going around the country to raise money for the war effort.

The town was stunned, and Cynthia felt terrible. Clark came to town and made two trips up the mountains to try to find her body and recover it. Both trips failed to find the wreckage. He was despondent and crying.

Mr. Griffith suggested to Cynthia that she take Clark either to Frank Dio's place or to her own house. She elected to take him to Frank's house and bar, because there was liquor available.

Cynthia and Mr. Griffith went up to the room where Clark had holed up. Mr. Griffith talked to him and suggested he go with Cynthia to Frank's house. "Mr. Gable, we think you will need something to eat and drink. You need to be in a place where you can have some privacy. You're too well-known to go into our public rooms where people might bother you."

Mr. Griffith and Cynthia each took one of his arms and led him out.

It was a short walk to Frank's place, and they sat him down on an ice cream chair. They produced a bottle of whiskey and a glass, and Cynthia poured him a drink. Clark drank it and stared at the glass. She poured him another.

Cynthia sat beside him for three days and nights. Neither one of them slept. He drank steadily, but never seemed drunk. He sat in a stupor.

She tried to interest him in food, but he never ate a bite. She would fix him hors d'oeuvres, fussing to make them attractive. She made deviled eggs and even broiled up a steak one night for his dinner. He ate nothing and said nothing.

On the third day, the searchers came into town with Carole's body in an ambulance. Cynthia and Frank helped the weakened Clark into the ambulance beside the driver. Clark, without having spoken a word, then left town.

After the war Clark came back to Las Vegas in his Air Force uniform. His old director was giving a party for him. Cynthia was seated beside Clark, and they had eaten dinner and were watching the floor show. Cynthia says she was laughing and she turned to him, saying something "corny." Without a word, he rose from the table and left.

When he did not reappear, she asked her table companions if she had offended him, and was told, "No, just that you look so much like Carole, and your remark was just the sort of thing she would say. He just couldn't take it."

Chapter 28

Cynthia still considered herself married, although she knew Turk could have gotten a divorce on the grounds of desertion. She didn't confide any of this to anyone for a long time, and, except for those brief interludes with Bill Neary and Erwin Ashley, and the recent one with Hal Wallis, she never dated. It soon became known that she always refused to do so, and after a time no one asked her out anymore.

One of her acquaintances was Leon Schwab, the man who owned the drugstore where Lana Turner supposedly had been discovered. She found him a very fun-loving and friendly man. One day, as she was about to pass by him with her cigarettes, he stopped her. He had been gambling and losing badly, but the moment she stood near him, his luck changed.

Gamblers are, as a rule, very superstitious, and he felt she had brought him luck. He said to her, "Don't move; stay right here."

As if her presence really did bring him luck, he won back all he had lost, and much more. He trusted in this, and whenever he came in to gamble, he would seek her out to stand by him.

He called her Lucky, and when he won, he would pick up a stack of silver dollars and place them on her tray, out of gratitude.

Of course it was still wartime, and many of the Hollywood stars had husbands stationed near Las Vegas. Cynthia particularly remembers Rosalind Russel and Dorothy Lamour, because they were such ladies. They stood out in a town where other movie stars were so obviously promiscuous. Prostitutes were barred from the town during wartime, so they were not a problem. These movie stars, however—the townspeople called them The Tramps, and their behavior was outrageous. Some got so drunk, they had to be carried up to bed. You saw all kinds in this town, whose numbers kept swelling.

Cynthia's dear friend Frank Dio kept her busy playing hostess when he entertained the stars. Of course she felt privileged to be asked.

This dear man would eventually own miles of land in and around Las Vegas. Years later, after the war, she would learn that all the property Frank had invested in had been taken away from him by mobsters. They first had killed his dog, then had threatened to put him in a copper casket and dump him into Lake Meade if he did not sign his properties over. He had signed.

She also learned that he had wound up playing rinky-dink piano on a street of prostitution. It would break her heart to think of all his success, and how he had been brought down so low.

A friend of Turk's came through Las Vegas, and Cynthia remembered him from when she had lived in Detroit. His girlfriend had once made a play for Turk in Phoenix, and Cynthia, under the pretext of being friendly, had driven the girl to the top of Lookout Mountain. Cynthia had then threatened to jump out of the car and let it go over the mountain cliff if the girl did not leave her husband alone. The girl agreed: she would be on the next train out of town.

Turk's friend was Lenny Marks, and he and his girlfriend were just checking into the Frontier. When they saw Cynthia, the girlfriend turned and said something to Lenny.

The next thing Cynthia knew, Lenny had seized her hand and was crushing it behind her back.

Bugsy Siegel and his right-hand man had spotted the trouble, and Lenny suddenly found a gun in his back. Lenny hurriedly let go. Bugsy warned him, "Go get your luggage and get out of town fast, or you'll be food for the vultures out in the desert."

Bugsy told Cynthia to come outside, and she hurried after him. When the threatened couple also came out and were passing her, she stuck out her tongue at them. Bugsy laughingly said to his right-hand man, "See, I told you she was nothing but a kid." Lenny and the girl sped off in a cab, and Bugsy turned to Cynthia and asked, "Now, what was that all about inside?" She explained that this girlfriend had tried to break up her marriage, and told what she had done to the girl. Bugsy understood, and after this incident he seemed to always be around her. She counted him as a true friend and was grateful for his protection.

Cynthia was still riding King nearly every day. The town was often used for a movie location, and Arlene Judge came in to work on a segment of the musical film *Take It Big*. The film starred Jack Haley, Ozzie Nelson, and Harriet Hilliard. Arlene turned up drunk on the first day, and was instantly relieved of her job. Hal Wallis replaced her with an actress who had been given a bit part, Jeanne Crain. It was now necessary to fill Jeanne's place. Unwilling to wait for a replacement from Hollywood, the producer looked anxiously around for a substitute. He knew Cynthia well, and he also knew she was very good on a horse.

The solution was quickly found. Suddenly, Cynthia was to be an actress in a movie. Pretty heady stuff for a cigarette girl! She was to be paid one hundred twenty-five dollars a day, which at that time was big money.

This segment of the film was about twelve cowgirls who were competing against twelve cowboys at a rodeo. No special costumes were required for her, because the film called for western attire, and with her full closets, she had plenty to wear.

The film proceeded. Cynthia was learning to take direction, and was finding out how scenes were shot with aids that the theatergoers would never see. What they would see was two women racing in a wagon. The camera was held in such a position that, on film, you could not see the man crouched near the women's feet and actually handling the reins.

She also learned the hard way about what went on in the cutting room. She had spent many days of hard work on the set, but when the film was released, her appearance was so brief that a mis-timed blink would mean missing it entirely.

As if this opportunity were not enough excitement for Cynthia, out of the blue came a man to see her at her home. He identified himself as an FBI agent and told her that they needed her help once more. She was shocked, and wondered how in the world they had found her. Many years later, she realized that when she had first come to Vegas and worked as a waitress she had had to show her Social Security card. The FBI could have easily traced her.

The agent had a nineteen-page document in his hands. It was a list of all the Nazis that Cynthia had uncovered in Detroit. He wanted to go over the names with her, to find out just what each one's role had been in the Bund. It took them a long time to go over all the names and discuss each individual. Finally, they reached the end. Then the agent told Cynthia that her memory was remarkable and that she would not be needed again for this project.

There was, however, another matter that concerned them. Once again, the FBI needed her help.

It seemed there was an Italian countess in town. She had been seen being squired by the commander of Nellis Air Force Base. She had a son, and the FBI had every reason to believe that the countess was getting information on troop movements from this commander, then passing it on to her son, who in turn was alerting the enemy. While they often saw the countess, the FBI had yet to see her son.

The Countess Francisco was an older woman with very dark eyes and black hair, graying at the temples. Despite her title, Cynthia had noted, she wore very inexpensive clothes. Cynthia also knew that her husband was an American admiral. He was out to sea, serving his country, while she apparently was trying to sink it. Frank Dio had once tossed the countess out of his bar, saying, "She was throwing that Countess stuff all over, just showing off." At the time, Cynthia had been sorry. She thought she could open a conversation with the woman by telling her of Frank's lovely Italian vases and tapestries.

The FBI agent said that Cynthia was to watch for the countess and the son, and report to him. Again, she was offered money for her help, and, again, she indignantly turned it down. She explained once more to this new agent how she had been partly brought up by an extremely patriotic grandfather, and how she would not feel right about taking money for doing what she considered her duty.

Now she frowned and said, "I don't know how I can help you. I see the countess quite often, too, but never with anyone but the commander. I don't even know what the son looks like."

The agent spoke up, "He is fair-haired and about six feet tall."

Cynthia still looked doubtful. "I can't think of anything I can possibly do for you. If you have never seen the son, she probably meets him in private."

"Well," he said, "just do the best you can." He gave her the new post office phone number assigned to her, and left.

Cynthia, try as she would, just had no idea how to find this lady's son. This assignment made the work she'd done on the Bund look simple. All she had had to do there was join the Bund and collect names and facts. This was much more difficult. How could you find someone who was never seen? She shook her head in frustration.

One night when Cynthia was working in the dining room, she saw the countess and the commander at a nearby booth. She had neither an idea nor a plan, but she edged closer, hoping something would come to her.

As if by divine providence, she overheard the countess say, "Oh, how I wish I had a place where I could cook for you."

Cynthia's mind raced. She turned to the couple and said, "Excuse me, but I couldn't help overhearing you. I have a house right across the street, and you are welcome to go there any evening you like and cook. I wouldn't be in your way because I would be in here, working."

The countess was thrilled. "Oh, you are an answer to my prayers. What a nice lady you are to be so generous."

They made the arrangements, and Cynthia excused herself. She was careful to keep a look of triumph off her face. This just might be the big break for her.

She worked, but she also kept an eye out for anyone entering her house. The Frontier was brightly lit outside, and the light reflected on her house.

One night, Cynthia saw the countess enter. She kept her eye on the house and, after some time, saw a tall young man enter. She ran for the phone and called her post office number. She ran back to the window and waited. After a time, she saw the front door open. The countess appeared in the doorway, saying good-bye to the emerging young man. Just then, two agents converged on the man and led him away. The countess hurriedly closed the door.

Cynthia heard the next day that the countess had just fled, boarding the train to California

Days later, she also learned that the countess's body had been found slumped forward in its seat. She had been strangled to death.

Cynthia would always wonder which government was responsible.

Chapter 29

The excitement of playing a role in a movie was over, and it had sparked no desire to make further moves into this arena. Though Cynthia now began to receive calls from the studio, asking her to come to Hollywood for a screen test, her answer remained firm: "I'm not interested." The woman from Hollywood began to call every day, but Cynthia's response never wavered. Finally, the woman was almost pleading, telling Cynthia what an opportunity this was, and how very many women would give their eyeteeth for this chance. Eventually, to Cynthia's relief, the calls ceased. She knew that the woman was perplexed. But she also knew that Hollywood was a small town and that there was not enough room there for her and Martha Raye.

Cynthia's life and routine had now become fairly predictable, so it was a shock when, out of the blue, came a phone call:

It was Turk! Oh, how wonderful to hear his voice! She had tried hard to get him out of her mind, always, in the end, failing, and always, deep down, longing for him. Her bed was so very empty, his arms so far away.

A friend who had known them both in Detroit had seen Cynthia in Las Vegas, had told Turk where to find her. Turk's call was a plea . . . he missed her . . . still loved her. She was wrong about Martha; Martha was only a friend, an employer. When Cynthia had left Phoenix, he had sold out, and he was now Martha's manager. That was all there was to it. Nothing personal, just a business arrangement.

The fact that he was living in Martha's house, he wisely did not mention. But Cynthia knew this from the words that Sarah had thrown out at her. Words that had caused her such anguish.

Now, at the sound of Turk's voice, Cynthia's misgivings went out the window, and all the old yearning returned. Maybe he was telling the truth this time. Yes, she would see him. He would come to Vegas, soon.

The rush of excitement, of pent-up love, of terrible anticipation was so great that Cynthia could scarcely attend to her daily routine. Her most effective therapy was riding. The pounding hoofbeats and the wind across her face helped relieve the hammering in her heart.

One day she was returning with King when they passed a corral of other horses. Without warning, King suddenly became unmanageable. One of the mares was in heat, and the smell drove King wild. He was going to get to her any way he could. Reining him in was useless, but it never occurred to Cynthia to bail out. She hung on, and using her crop, she repeatedly beat him, trying for control. The battle seemed interminable, but at last King gave in to the harsh punishment. Cynthia was exhausted.

Turning the horse, she headed for the barn. A car drove up beside her and stopped, and a man got out. It was Turk! With him was Jack Dempsey's manager, and Bud Abbott and Lou Costello.

Turk approached her with his gorgeous smile and said, "Get off that horse and kiss your old man."

She wanted to leap off the horse and into his arms, but she was too frightened of King. The horse was trembling and his chest heaved with every breath.

Cynthia pleaded to Turk, "I don't dare get off. He and I have just had a battle, and if I get off he'll get away on me. Meet me at the Frontier, will you? I'll be there as soon as I've put him away." Turk agreed.

She nudged King into a walk, and they approached the barn, where they were met by Bud Simpson. Bud shook his head in disbelief at the condition of the horse. "What in the world happened to you?"

Cynthia answered, "Oh, Mr. Simpson, I had a terrible time with King. He tried to get rid of me and get at a mare in the corral."

Bud was aghast. "You never stay on a stallion when there's a mare in heat. He could have killed you!"

Cynthia was shaking as she returned to her house to clean up and change her clothes. She wasn't sure how much of this was due to her close call with the horse, and how much to the anticipation of meeting Turk again after their years of separation. At last she was as ready as she could be. She took a last critical look in the mirror, and, satisfied, crossed the street to meet Turk.

He was in the dining room, and he stood up when she came in. God, she was glad to see him.

They had a lot of catching up to do, as they talked and ordered dinner. She learned she was still married, which surprised her, after all this time and after his long association with Martha. Later, they visited the gambling spots together.

Turk was in town for two days. He tried hard to persuade Cynthia to come back to him, but her head managed to subdue her heart. She knew he was still Martha's manager and, despite his protestations to the contrary, she was sure he was also Martha's bed partner She would not share him, and that was that. She did, however, agree to return with him to Los Angeles for a few days.

While they were there, Turk took Cynthia to the Brown Derby. As they entered, the doorman said to her, "Hal just left."

Turk swung around in surprise and asked, "Who's Hal?"

Cynthia forced innocence on her face and said, "Turk, I have no idea."

Inside she seethed at the ignorance of the doorman. If Turk knew she had been seeing Hal Wallis, he would assume they had been sleeping together. This assumption was not true, but it would have led to a fight. It would also have given him justification for living with Martha.

In Las Vegas, Turk had stayed at Cynthia's house; now, in Los Angeles, they shared a hotel room. They made love often, as if to make up for the lost years.

Now Turk told her he had to go to Detroit. He suggested that she go for a visit at the same time. She had not seen her family in eight years, and this would be a perfect opportunity.

Cynthia returned to Las Vegas and made traveling plans. Before leaving, she saw her physician, because she had been missing her periods for some time. The doctor prescribed a medication, saying that it was far too early for her to go through "the change." He warned her, however, to take careful precautions, because the medication would increase her chances of becoming pregnant.

She knew she had no worry on that score. Just look at all the years she had lived with Turk, never taking precautions and never getting pregnant.

She made arrangements to be gone from her job, and left by train for Detroit.

Chapter 30

I arrived in Detroit, and Turk and I went to Tawas to see my people, where we stayed for several days. My mother had started another family, and it was fun to meet the new children. We then went back to Detroit and stayed together at the Detroiter. I planned to stay for the summer.

Turk was still begging me to go back to him. He tried to convince me he had changed. He said I was his life, that what had gone on in Hollywood was all past.

This sounded good until some of his friends told me he was on the phone with Martha every day. I never accused him, just told him we were now too far apart, and that Las Vegas was now my way and my home. He soon had to go to New York to manage Martha's affairs, and eventually I returned to Vegas.

I had been back several weeks and realized I had now missed four of my periods. This really surprised me because

I had been careful to take the medication the doctor had prescribed. I was also sick to my stomach, turning myself inside out over the toilet each morning. I made an appointment with the doctor and was utterly shocked when he told me I was pregnant. What the hell was I going to do now? There was only one realistic answer.

Turk had given me his phone number. That night I called Martha's residence in New York and asked for Turk. When he came to the phone, I told him I was pregnant and needed money for an abortion.

He was terribly upset, and his voice rose. "You're not going to kill my baby. Cynthia, maybe this is God's way of getting us back together. I'll quit my job with Martha and meet you in Detroit. Let me know when you are at the Detroiter."
I agreed. Surely now with a family on the way, he would give up Martha and be true to me.

Cynthia was utterly happy at this totally unexpected turn in her life. She had always wanted children, and now, miraculously, she was going to have one. Best of all, her precious Turk was leaving Martha!

She worked at assembling all her clothes and the other things she had accumulated. Just finding boxes for her clothes was a headache. Finally she finished and headed back to Detroit. She and Turk met and stayed at the hotel until they could find a flat to rent.

Life was better than she ever imagined it could be. Her morning sickness passed, and Cynthia was content. Turk was so loving and solicitous, it almost seemed like a second honeymoon. Whenever Turk came through the door, they fell into each other's arms, hungering for each other, as if trying to make up for all the lost years.

For the first time in her life, Cynthia did not seek work, but busied herself making and embroidering baby clothes. It was fun to work on these little garments and wonder what the baby would look like. She hoped it would be a boy and look like Turk. He was so damned handsome.

The months slipped by. Turk formed a partnership with the Bernstein boys and opened what he called Turk's Music Bar.

When the baby was born it indeed had Turk's features. Cynthia named him Patrick because of her Irish heritage.

It was common in those days to stay in the hospital for a fairly long period following a birth. Cynthia stayed two weeks. On the seventh day, according to Jewish tradition, the baby was scheduled for circumcision by a rabbi in the hospital. Turk's parents were now living in Detroit again and joined their son in attending this important religious event. The rabbi made the incision, but the sight of his son being cut, and the resulting blood and cries from the infant, proved too much for Turk. He passed out on the floor. He soon regained consciousness, but then had to endure the kidding from Cynthia, who thought it was hilarious for a big man such as Turk to faint over such a small, routine operation.

When Cynthia and Patrick were finally released from the hospital, she returned to find that Turk had arranged a homecoming party for her and their son. As Turk circulated around the room, showing off his newborn, Cynthia sat at her in-laws' food-laden table, chatting excitedly, happy to be home at last. But as she began to eat, she was horrified to find that she was hemorrhaging badly. She had had difficulty with this in the past and was known as a "bleeder." It was a familial problem. Cynthia's whole family had suffered from being bleeders. Eunice had almost died when Cynthia had been born, and Cynthia in turn almost died when Patrick was born. Her sister, Gladys, had also had a few bouts in which she almost bled to death. Even a tooth extraction posed a threat. So this spelled real trouble.

Cynthia was rushed to the hospital where she would remain for two months, receiving a total of forty-five pints of blood. Turk visited every day and showered her with flowers and tender concern. Finally she was released, and could return home to her husband and darling baby. Turk hired a nurse to help her while she regained her strength.

Cynthia and Turk were absolutely enthralled with their

son, and their lives revolved around him. After all these years and after all their heartbreak, perhaps at last they could lead relatively "normal" lives as a real family. Turk was proud of his new role and enjoyed showing off their new addition.

Time passed, and Patrick turned one. By the baby's second birthday, Cynthia's new-found happiness had begun to erode when Martha had started calling Turk again.

One evening, Cynthia was at his new nightclub. Turk was busy counting out the cash drawer, so when the phone rang, Cynthia answered it. It was Martha, calling person-to-person. She turned to Turk and said, "All right, Turk, this is Martha, and I want to hear you tell her she is to stop badgering you for once and for all." He took the phone from her, but instead of repeating the words she had insisted he say, he simply hung the phone up.

Cynthia now began to snoop in Turk's drawers. One day she came across a letter It said:

> *Darling,*
> *I have had your picture enlarged and enlarged again. You have such a pensive look on your face. I have it in the mirrored frame of my vanity in our bedroom.*
> *Love,*
> *Martha*

Cynthia lost no time in confronting Turk with the letter. He denied involvement with Martha, and said that the letter had been written by Martha's mother. This made no sense to Cynthia at all, and she remained suspicious.

Cynthia also knew that Martha was sending Turk person-to-person letters which required his signature for delivery. Cynthia searched their apartment repeatedly, but failed to find even one of those letters.

Cynthia now had a daily cleaning woman. She took the woman into her confidence, and they formed a plan.

The next time one of the letters arrived, the cleaning

woman started a flirtation with the mailman, then informed
him that Turk was in bed with strep throat. He was unable to
come to the door, she said. Would it be all right if she took the
letter to the bedroom for his signature? The mailman agreed,
and she took the letter to Cynthia, who forged Turk's name on
the slip and sent it back.

Cynthia read the letter.

> *Darling,*
> *When are you going to get rid of Cynthia and that*
> *kid and come home to me?*
> *Love,*
> *Martha*

Again, Cynthia confronted Turk and, again, he denied any
involvement. Clearly, she was getting nowhere.

Two weeks later, the cleaning woman managed to talk the
mailman out of still another letter. Again, she brought it to
Cynthia.

Cynthia tore the envelope open, and when she had read the
letter, she felt herself reeling. The cleaning woman caught her
and helped her into a chair. She took the letter from Cynthia
and read Martha's words for herself. They said:

> *Darling,*
> *Our daughter has arrived. Come home to me and*
> *Melodye.*
> *Love,*
> *Martha*

The cleaning woman was shocked, and said in a whisper,
"What are you going to do?"

Cynthia looked up. "I'm going to get a divorce, that's what
I'm going to do. He swore he hasn't seen her since he left New
York. Well, it's pretty obvious to me now, he certainly has
been with her!"

She confronted Turk and he again denied that he had been

with Martha. He swore he never saw her. Cynthia sneered,"Then explain this letter!" His explanation made no sense. These letters, he claimed, were all from Martha's mother.

She packed, left the flat, and found a place to stay. Turk would have to help support her and the baby.

Turk called repeatedly, proclaiming his innocence and calling Martha a tuchos (ass). Cynthia would rail at him. Once more she reminded him of her words on their wedding night. "Turk, I told you I would never share you with either liquor or other women. If you really loved me, you wouldn't have strayed. Well, you couldn't keep away from Martha, and now you can have her for good, because I am through!" She hung up.

She was devastated. She loved Turk so much. Why could he not be faithful to her? She had had many opportunities herself, and had never even considered an affair or a hop into bed. She felt she should be able to expect the same from him. Her bitterness returned, and she became adamant about ending their marriage.

All the joy seemed to have been drained out of Cynthia. The days dragged by. Patrick was the only ray of sunshine in her life now, yet he looked so much like Turk that even he was a constant reminder of Turk's final betrayal.

One day, Cynthia's spirits were revived when she heard from Bill Neary. He had not been killed, after all, when his plane had been shot down over Germany! He had survived the crash, but had been held in prison camps and had only just returned. He had remembered where Cynthia's sister lived and, through her, had found Cynthia's phone number. She was delighted to hear from him and told him where she was living. He came right over.

I felt so bad for Bill. He had gone through hell and depredation in those cruel Stalag camps. He was six-feet-two, and when he was released he weighed only eighty-nine pounds! The Red Cross was dispensing coffee and doughnuts to these newly released, starved inmates, and Bill stood in line with the rest. When he managed to reach the front of the line, they had run out of doughnuts and he had to do without. This turned out to be a lucky break, because the suddenness of the food killed some of those men. When he did eat, he could only manage an egg, his stomach was so shrunken. For years Bill would crave doughnuts. He would go to the bakery and buy four dozen. He only managed to eat one or two, but the sight of all those tempting treats would continue to bring him immense satisfaction, and he would continue to buy.

Now that Cynthia was separated from Turk, she began to see Bill again. Turk was furious and filed for a divorce.

Cynthia went to Jerome Rothenberg, a lawyer she knew, and cross-filed. She took Martha's letters with her. Jerry read them, and his eyebrows raised. He was sympathetic when she told him her story, calling Turk a fool. He made out the necessary papers, and they waited for a court date. Within a month, Jerry called to inform her that he was getting threatening phone calls, saying that if he did not drop the cross-suit, he would be killed. The caller said Cynthia would be killed, too.

The lawyer was livid. "I didn't work hard to be a lawyer only to be pushed around. I'm not going to drop the case over a bunch of little punks."

Cynthia said, "Jerry, I want you to drop this cross-suit. It just isn't worth getting killed over." They argued, but he would not budge.

While she waited, Cynthia also had another concern. Her dear friend Ann became terribly ill. She was found to have a tumor on the brain. It was well-advanced, and there was nothing the doctors could do. She was not ill long before she died. Cynthia was saddened by this new tragedy in her life. Divorce, death threats, and now death itself. Life was so hard!

Chapter 31

The court date arrived, and Cynthia dressed with care. She presumed that photographers would be there, and she was right.

Martha's lawyers were there also, of course, but not Martha.

The Detroit Times had Martha's and Cynthia's pictures on the front page under this caption:

THE MOUTH—THE WIFE

The Detroit Free Press ran this article:

DIVORCE JUDGE OK'S WRIT
FOR MARTHA RAYE

DETROIT—Martha Raye, Hollywood singer and actress, was ordered to show cause why she should not be cited for contempt for failure to appear as a witness in a divorce case between a Detroit night club owner and his wife.

Miss Raye was accused before Circuit Judge Chester P. O'Hare of ignoring a subpoena. The actress appeared recently at the Downtown Theater.

Herman Prujansky, 35, proprietor of Turk's Music Bar, 1239 Griswold, brought the divorce suit against his wife, Cynthia.

* * *

In answer and cross-petition for separate maintenance, Mrs. Prujansky accused her husband of staying away from home several nights at a time. She also charged that he associated with a Hollywood movie star, designated as "Miss X."

"Martha Raye doesn't mean any more to me than Joe Zilch. If she ever comes back to Detroit I'll have her brought in," Judge O'Hara said.

Jerome Rothenberg, attorney for Mrs. Prujansky, said that he and his law partner, George Kratchman, twice served Miss Raye with a subpoena.

To escape a contempt citation, Miss Raye must appear before Judge O'Hara at 2 P.M. Oct. 12.

Another account was in *The Detroit News:*

MARTHA RAYE'S ACT
LEAVES JUDGE COLD

DETROIT - Asserting that "Martha Raye can't ignore a summons of this court," Judge Chester P. O'Hara in Circuit Court has signed an order to show cause, returnable Oct. 12, why the movie star and night club entertainer should not be cited for contempt of court.

However, as the order was signed, Miss Raye, otherwise known as Martha Raye Condos, was a long way from Detroit, being reported variously in Chicago and Philadelphia.

Judge O'Hara cited her for failing to appear at 10 A.M. Saturday as a witness in a divorce case in which the principals are Herman Prujansky, operator of Turk's Bar, and Cynthia Prujansky.

Prujansky charges that his wife has an ungovernable temper, and Mrs. Prujansky, in turn, accuses him of associating with other women, including "Miss X and Mrs. X, a Hollywood movie star and her mother."

Miss Raye was served with a subpoena at the Book-Cadillac Hotel last Thursday—in fact she was served twice. Jerome A. Rothenberg, attorney for Mrs. Prujansky, decided to take no chance on Miss Raye's leaving the city without testifying.

Rothenberg said Saturday: "And if she isn't in on the 12th, we'll get a bench warrant for her arrest whenever she returns to Michigan."

At this hearing, Cynthia's lawyer advised her to come in with her little boy in order to win sympathy for herself from the judge. One of the Purple Gang was in the courtroom, and Cynthia overheard him say, "What a mouthpiece. Too bad that he has to go."

Jerry was still getting death threats. Cynthia and his friend were having lunch with him and pleading with him to drop the cross-suit. His friend was Paul Zuckerman, who owned the Peter Pan peanut butter company. When Cynthia could not persuade him, she hoped that Paul might have more influence. This was not to be, and Jerry firmly refused.

Jerry had worked as a "dollar-a-year man." In other words, this was his agreement with the government: he would accept only a dollar as compensation for going after some of these gangs. He had broken up a number of them and sent many members to jail. The Masonic organization, in gratitude, was making him an honorary thirty-two degree Mason.

The Masons held a dinner in Jerry's honor and made the presentation. He was on his way home, when a car began to chase him. He drove faster and faster but could not lose it. Finally, the speeding car drew up beside him, and forced him off the road and into a tree. Jerome Rothenberg was dead.

By now Cynthia had a bodyguard, and he was at her door in the morning to report the bad news to her. She burst into tears. Why had Jerry been so stubborn? He should have dropped the suit. She wondered what more she could have done to prevent this tragedy. She was sick.

Cynthia needed money and found a job. Leaving work one night, she crossed the street to go to an all-night restaurant for a bite to eat. She heard a car approach at high speed, and when it jumped over the curb, she dived for the restaurant door. It was close, and she was shaking all over. She found a seat, trying to regain control over herself. Now she was thoroughly terrified.

Cynthia called George Kratchman, Jerry's law partner, the next morning, to report the incident. He was very upset. They discussed who could be behind the attempt on her life.

Detroit was full of gangs. There was the Purple Gang made up of Russian Jews. There were gangs that were Polish, and then there was the Mafia, headed by Dutch Schultz. Given the Mafia's close ties to the movie industry, they finally decided that Schultz was behind this. In those days, divorce was considered a scandal. It would hurt Martha's career and, in turn, hurt Martha's studio.

George Kratchman now agreed to handle her case. He met with her, and they arranged to have Cynthia drop her cross-suit. Otherwise, he said, she would have to find another attorney. He said he was not about to end his life as Jerry had. She agreed with him: the risk to them both was just too great.

Chapter 32

This was a poor time for Turk to be embroiled in a divorce suit. He was in trouble, and *The Detroit Times* headlines confirmed it:

STATE PROBES UNDERWORLD BAR OWNERS

> LANSING, OCT. 24—*The State Liquor Control commission today combined a probe of rumors that politicians are soliciting and receiving "shakedown" money from applicants for liquor licenses, with their investigation of reports that hoodlums have muscled in on Detroit bar ownership.*
> *John P. Aaron, commission chairman, said that politicians receiving money for purported influence with the commission would face prosecution.*

210
CYNTHIA

PROBE OWNERSHIPS

He added that exhaustive investigation would be made by the commission into bar ownership as the result of recent disclosure of known police characters in Detroit operating liquor businesses through "fronts" or partners.

He cited yesterday's surprise license suspension of Turk's Bar on Grisworld and Leon 'n' Eddie's Supper Club on Woodward for alleged hoodlum ownership.

Turk's Bar closed immediately yesterday on receipt of the suspension order. Herman Prujansky, the registered owner, is to appear tomorrow before the commission in Detroit for a hearing on charges of selling to a minor.

BAR CLOSES

The bar at Leon 'n' Eddie's in which [Sam] Bernstein is also allegedly interested, was closed last night but the establishment remained open for serving food and presenting scheduled floor shows.

License holders of both establishments were cited to appear tomorrow before the commission in Lansing Tuesday to prove that "unscrupulous" characters are not joint owners.

Commissioner Theodore L. Fry revealed that Sam Bernstein held a chattel mortgage on Turk's Bar for $29,000, representing an investment in the establishment.

He declared that Bernstein was a known police character and had been refused a license because he had not been recommended by the Detroit Police Department.

Cynthia did feel sorry for Turk. She figured he would be

forced to sell his bar. She also thought that when this was over, he would go to California and move back in with Martha. Sadly, she was right on both counts.

TURK'S BAR ORDERED SOLD

LANSING, OCT. 30 - *The State Liquor Control commission today gave Herman (Turk) Prujansky until Dec. 15 to dispose of Turk's Bar, his drinking establishment at 1239 Griswold.*

In the meantime, Prujansky was ordered to sever all connections with [Sam] Bernstein, whose brother, Lou, holds a chattel mortgage on the property. Prujansky's liquor license had been indefinitely suspended because of his alliance with Sam Bernstein, whom the commission had twice barred from the liquor business.

Prujansky admitted he paid Sam Bernstein $85 a week for "checking the cash register" in Turk's Bar, and acknowledged the mortgage held by his brother. He denied there was any further tie-up.

ACTION JUSTIFIED

At a public hearing today, police and liquor commission investigators furnished testimony which was the basis for the commissioner's decision that the establishment was conducted "unsatisfactorily."

Police Inspector Miles Furlong of Detroit testified that during the summer months members of the "Twelfth Street Gang" had been in the habit of loitering on the sidewalk outside of Turk's and "people were constantly being insulted" as they passed by.

"I went over there myself," the inspector testified, "and found this was true. And who should be with them but Turk himself!"

"These gentlemen certainly weren't planning an

ice cream social, as they hung around this bar, were they?" Commission Chairman John P. (Pat) Aaron asked the inspector.

"Obviously no," Furlong replied. "These gentlemen don't traffic in ice cream."

Cynthia read these accusations with disgust. The story about men standing outside of Turk's Bar insulting people was not only false but ludicrous. In the first place, the gangsters who patronized the place were always courteous. Far from being insulting, they had lovely manners, would always be well-dressed, and would tip their hats to the ladies. Also, on the face of it, Turk would hardly be involved in standing in front of his bar insulting people. He was, after all, in business and would not have wanted to chase away prospective customers.

GUN CHARGES DENIED

Prujansky denied a charge that gangsters carrying machine guns had been seen frequenting his bar.

The charge was voiced by Jerome A. Rothenberg, attorney for Prujansky's wife, Cynthia. In a suit for separate maintenance which listed screen actress Martha Raye as a witness.

Rothenberg since was killed in an automobile accident.

Prujansky pleaded to be permitted to sell his bar, declaring he was "sick and tired" of the business and wanted to get a fresh start in California. He said orchestra leader Sammy Kaye, the Marx brothers and other movie people were trying to interest him in a place in Hollywood.

Nor was this the only trouble that he would face. A year later, Cynthia read these further accounts, one from *The Detroit Times* and then one from *The Detroit News*. Under his picture it said:

Herman Prujansky, former proprietor of Turk's Bar, was arrested by the FBI in Los Angeles Friday charged with fleeing Judge George B. Murphy's rackets grand jury. Arraigned in Los Angeles before a U.S. Commissioner, he was held under $20,000 bond.

TRIO'S EXAMINATION TO START
MONDAY, MINUS PRUJANSKY

DETROIT—*Though Herman (Turk) Prujansky, key witness in a labor rackets grand jury conspiracy action, will not be in Detroit until later this week, examination of three defendants will start as scheduled Monday in Recorder's Court.*

The three are James R. Hoffa, Teamsters Union (AFL) boss; Orrin A. DeMass, former chairman of the State Liquor Control Commission, and James J. Stewart, suspended chief investigator for Prosecutor O.Brien.

Prujansky, arrested Friday in Los Angeles, will be arraigned here Thursday before Federal Judge Theodore Levin. He was seized there on a Federal indictment similar to the one which brought Charles F. Hemans back from Washington.

Prujansky is the former proprietor of Turk's Bar, 1239 Griswold St.

The three defendants were named Sept. 7 in a warrant charging them with attempting to obtain $3,000 from Prujansky and two others in return for assurances of a "fix" of the Liquor Control action against Turk's Bar.

Louis and Sam Bernstein, the pair mentioned with Prujansky, are being returned from Arizona to be state witnesses in the examination before Judge Gerald W. Groat, in Recorders court.

A liquor commission showed the Bernsteins to be part owners of Turk's Bar.

Cynthia was not surprised that Turk had tried to get his license back. After all, without it he was completely cut out of business.

This turn of events caused Cynthia to think back on the many men she had met through Turk. It had never really occurred to her that Turk might have been actively involved with the criminal world. Nevertheless, she and Turk certainly knew a good many questionable types from their days and nights working in bars, which the gangs would use as places to hang out. Cynthia often went with Turk to the gambling dens. She would go for the free lunch that was offered, but Turk of course went for the gambling itself. It offered everything that Las Vegas gambling did. There were card games, roulette wheels, blackjack tables, and dice. Above the players would be a balcony with a man stationed there holding a machine gun in case a law officer came in. The Purple Gang were well-known hoodlums. You learned to know them well and kept your mouth shut if you became aware of any rumors about their activities.

Cynthia met many of these men through Turk. He had grown up with many of the men who became gangsters. They thought he was a sap to work hard for his money, but they remained friends. She met the Licavolis and the Bommaritos who ran the juke box businesses. This might sound innocent, until you learned of the force that was used to make the business owners use their machines. She met the Millmans, the Coopers, and Sam Finazzo, who they thought were running the numbers racket. She and Turk were invited one year for Christmas dinner with Sam and his wife. Young Patrick was taken from them at the door and tended by a hired woman while they ate. The dinner was served on a long table with real gold dinner places and flatware. They sat for eight hours, as course after course came out. Cynthia thought there were about twelve courses served, and with each there would appear another wine. Each plate had a gift beside it. Cynthia's was a pair of slippers from Saks Fifth Avenue, and Turk received a gold watch. The party ended at midnight.

Cynthia also remembered Hymie Cooper, who she had

learned was a hit man. He went to war and flew so many missions over Germany that he was grounded and sent home with war fatigue. Later, he signed up again to fight the Japanese. Whenever he killed one, he would inspect his victim's teeth for gold. If he found gold teeth, he would knock them out and send them to his mother, hidden in tiny match boxes.

One of the Millman brothers stuck up a bank at the corner of Woodward and West Grand Boulevard. He was crossing Woodward carrying a bag with the money when he was caught. There were big pictures in the paper, but that was the last thing heard of the incident. Obviously someone had been paid off. This was in the thirties, and the city was run by the mobs.

Joey Cousins was a member of the Purple Gang and was mixing things up with the Italians. He was taken out to Huntington Woods, and eleven bullets were pumped into his body. That night was very cold. When he was found, the cold had slowed his circulation and saved his life. You were only killed once by the mob. They did not try again, feeling that he had paid his debt.

Now, it appeared, the chickens were coming home to roost. The papers continued to be filled with accounts of the upcoming trials. Cynthia watched as Jimmy Hoffa's parents came into Detroit. They had all their belongings inside a tablecloth with a broomstick under the knot, so two people could carry it. They rode in on a flatcar.

COURT READY FOR PRUJANSKY

Turk Flying Back in time To Testify

By Robert S. Hall

DETROIT—*With dates to appear before judges in two courts, Herman (Turk) Prujansky, much sought racket jury witness, was to reach Detroit today.*
Prujansky will be taken before Judge Gerald W. Groat, in the Recorders Court, Wednesday, as a witness

*in the examination of James R. Hoffa, head of the AFL
Teamsters Union; Orrin A. DeMass, former chairman of
the State Liquor Control Commission, and James J.
Stewart, chief investigator for the prosecuting attorney.*

*On Thursday he will be arraigned before Federal
Judge Theodore Levin for violation of the Federal
fugitive law.*

*Prujansky left Los Angeles by air late Monday,
after he was freed on bond of $20,000 by a Federal
Judge. The Federal hearing will be continued here.*

*Prujansky is the principal witness against Hoffa,
DeMass and Stewart, who are charged with attempting to collect $3,000 from Prujansky while he and
Louis and Sam Bernstein operated Turk's Music Bar,
at 1239 Griswold Street. It is charged that they promised to fix violation charges against Turk's Bar with
the commission.*

*The examination, which heard testimony from half
a dozen witnesses at Monday's opening session, was
adjourned until Wednesday morning to await
Prujansky's return to the city.*

*John P. Aaron, who resigned as chairman of the
Liquor Commission last August, and Theodore Fry,
commission member, testified that they received telephone calls from DeMass a few hours before a hearing
last Oct. 29 at which charges of hidden ownership of
Turk's Bar were to be aired.*

The Detroit News ran this article on October 23:

DETROIT—*New legal entanglements threatened
to engulf Herman (Turk) Prujansky today as the former
Detroit bar proprietor left his cell in the Wayne
County Jail to appear as the key state's witness in a
conspiracy examination before Recorder's Judge
Gerald W. Groat. There were strong indications that
he would refuse to testify.*

Just seven hours after returning from California on a Federal fugitive witness warrant Tuesday, Mr. Prujansky was sentenced to 60 days for contempt of the labor rackets grand jury. He refused to testify.

HURRIED TO JURY

Arriving at Detroit City Airport at 3:30 P.M., he was escorted immediately to the grand jury chambers. At 10:30 P.M. Judge George B. Murphy, grand juror, ordered Prujansky to jail on the contempt charge.

The witness had been questioned at length by Special Prosecutor Lester C. Moll and members of the staff, presumably in connection with matters affecting the conspiracy charges against James R. Hoffa, AFL Teamsters Union boss; Orrin A. DeMass, former Liquor Commission chairman, and James J. Stewart, suspended chief investigator for the prosecutor's office.

HAS NO ANSWERS

Asked by Judge Murphy if he had anything to say before hearing sentence pronounced, Prujansky replied: "I refuse to answer any questions."

Complaining that he was sleepy and fatigued from his long flight from Los Angeles, Prujansky picked up two suitcases and left the chamber for the County Jail.

Regardless of the outcome of today's court appearance, Prujansky is scheduled to appear Thursday at 1 P.M. before Judge Theodore Levin for arraignment on the fugitive warrant. He faces a maximum sentence of five years if convicted.

FEARFUL OF VIOLENCE

Prujansky is charged with fleeing from the labor rackets grand jury after giving testimony three months

*ago which was the basis for the indictment accusing
Hoffa, DeMass and Stewart of attempting to obtain
$3,000 from Mr. Prujansky in return for a promised
"fix" of charges pending against Turk's Music Bar
before the Liquor Control Commission.*

*When arrested by FBI agents in Los Angeles last
week, Prujansky said he was afraid to testify further
before the grand jury and was afraid to appear as a
witness in the conspiracy examination.*

Again in *The Detroit News* another article appeared on October 25:

TURK SILENT, CASE DELAYED

Moll to Fight Ruling, Upholding Prujansky

*DETROIT—Examination of three defendants
named by the grand jury in a conspiracy case was
adjourned for 90 days Thursday after Herman (Turk)
Prujansky, the key witness, was upheld in his refusal
to testify.*

*Recorder's judge Gerald W. Groat took the Charles
F. Hemans case as a precedent in ruling that Prujansky
was not required to answer questions which might
incriminate him.*

*Lester S. Moll, special grand jury prosecutor, was
allowed to put Prujansky on the stand for the record,
but the witness refused to answer questions.*

*Moll then announced he would appeal Judge
Groat's ruling to the Michigan Supreme Court and
asked for a six month adjournment during which, he
said, the Federal case against Prujansky would be
disposed of, but Judge Groat permitted a delay of only
90 days.*

*The balking witness is accused under a Federal
fugitive warrant and has insisted he would incrimi-*

*nate himself by testifying in the Recorder's Court
examination of James Hoffa, Teamsters Union (AFL)
official; Orrin A. DeMass, former chairman of the
State Liquor Control Commission, and James J.
Stewart, suspended chief investigator for Prosecutor
O'Brian.*

*Samuel L. Travis, assistant special prosecutor for
the grand jury, argued that Prujansky went to California while the grand jury was seeking him for questioning and that he could not incriminate himself by
testifying in the Hoffa-DeMass-Stewart case.*

Cynthia knew that Turk had no choice but to initiate the
protection of "taking the fifth." You just didn't rat on the mob
and hope to stay alive. His stand on this proved to hold up. He
never had to testify against these men. She breathed a sigh of
relief when she read that. She might have been angry enough
to divorce him, but still she would not want to have him put in
jeopardy. She still loved him too much.

In his book *The Enemy Within*, Robert Kennedy wrote of
the work done by the McClelland Committee, which was at
the time investigating corruption in the labor unions. Robert
Kennedy was the counsel for the Senate Permanent Subcom-
mittee on Investigations, and did the questioning. He tells of
talking to Robert Scott, who had been a top figure in the Michigan
labor movement, with many friends in political life throughout
the state. Scott had once been close to Jimmy Hoffa but had since
broken bitterly with him. Robert Kennedy writes:

"Scott told the committee that the information he had
obtained from inside the grand jury investigating Hoffa was
that a bar owner, Turk Prujanski [sic], had testified that Hoffa
had tried to shake him down for five to ten thousand dollars to
get his license restored; and that the money was to be split with
Hoffa's friend on the liquor commission, Oren DeMass. Scott
said that after Hoffa learned what Prujanski had told the grand
jury, he said he would have Prujanski run out of the state so he
would not be able to testify at the trial. Scott said Hoffa sent

two men out to the racetrack to send Prujanski on his way. Prujanski ended up in California.

"When he was brought back on a fugitive warrant, he no longer would talk about Hoffa's shakedown attempt. To the authorities he announced: 'I refuse to answer any more questions. I am entitled to my rights, am I not? Throw me in jail.'

"He was thrown in jail for sixty days for contempt of court.

"Hoffa and DeMass were cleared of the extortion charges against them. The case had to be dropped when Prujanski refused to testify."

Years later, Cynthia would learn from Turk that before he left Detroit and returned to Los Angeles he was presented with a new Buick, compliments of Jimmy Hoffa.

Chapter 33

Cynthia arrived in court on the arm of her attorney. Flashbulbs popped and reporters shouted questions. She and George did not stop, but went directly into the courtroom, where they sat and waited. Soon the judge came in and banged his gavel, and the case began.

The complaint by Herman said that Cynthia had befriended a prisoner-of-war and had gone to New York to be with him, when she had said she was going to her sister's house. He claimed that because of this divorce and her accusations, he was in a precarious position with his business: he had been accused of serving underage persons at his bar, one of whom was a Detroit Tigers player. Several police officers and a representative of the Michigan Liquor Commission were subpoenaed to testify. Herman asked for a reduction of his child support payments, as he was unable to work.

He claimed that she had a bad temper. She said that he paid no attention to their child. The judge granted Turk the divorce. She was to get a cash settlement of $3000 and $35 a week child support.

I lied about the baby. Turk loved the little boy and would come to where I lived to see him.

I did go to New York to see Bill Neary, but I thought nothing of this. After all, Turk and I were separated and seeking a divorce. Bill Neary still wanted to marry me, but he had no luck finding work in Detroit and had to return to New York. He asked me to wait for him and I agreed. I had been so glad to hear he was alive after all, and had not died when his plane was shot down.

There really was no reason to continue to live in Detroit. I also had no desire to return to Vegas. I had gotten tired of the wind and the sand blowing and had let my house go back. Frank Dio had been right about urging me to buy it. He just hadn't been with me in Detroit to tell me I was crazy to let it go.

I returned to Tawas City where my mother and stepfather lived and thought about starting an antique store. I found an old, dilapidated building for sale. I said to the place, "You look about as beat as I do."

I bought the place and worked hard fixing it up and finding antiques to sell. My stepfather was a contractor, and he built another floor above the shop for an apartment I could rent out. He also built shelves for display of the dishes in my new store. I swept sawdust and wallpapered and painted until I was satisfied with the appearance.

I called it The Wagon Wheel—I had bought an old one from a farmer and placed on the outside. Tawas is a good tourist town, located as it is right on Lake Huron. My shop was a real success. I could make a living and watch my son at the same time.

One day a man entered her shop and inquired about renting

the apartment. He struck up a conversation and asked her out for dinner. He definitely was on the chase. His name was Rex Anderson, and he and his partners owned a trailer factory. He was quite well off. They dated for a while, but when he asked her to marry him, she hesitated. She was still trying to get over her second failed marriage and the divorce. She had been deeply hurt and was unwilling to trust another man right away. Cynthia's mother, Eunice, urged her to marry Rex, and finally threatened that if she did not, she was going to turn Cynthia in as an unfit mother and have Patrick taken from her. It was easier to marry than to see her mother carry out this threat.

Rex was good to her and absolutely adored her son. He wanted to adopt him, but Turk refused, saying that his boy would never carry another man's name. Rex had daughters from an earlier marriage, and Cynthia grew to love them as her own. She kept working at her shop, but when Rex got squeezed out of the factory by his partners, she sold the shop to help him start a new factory, A.B.C. Trailers in Bay City. Things were going well.

Patrick was now four years old.

Cynthia heard from Bill Neary again when he returned from Venezuela, where he had been working putting in railroads for two years. He was disappointed to find she had remarried. He said, "One of these days I'm going to catch you between marriages."

It was Halloween, and Rex came to the door announcing with a smile that he was the baby sitter. He was dressed as a woman, with a wig, blouse, skirt, and red shoes. Patrick was not fooled. He piped up, "Don't be funny, you're my daddy." Cynthia thought Rex was quite amusing.

Rex branched out. He had gone to court over his factory in Tawas and had won a settlement, with which he started another A.B.C. Trailer factory in Pinconning. Cynthia, in turn, started a restaurant. Patrick was now going to school, and this meant time on her hands. She rented a corner building and proceeded to decorate it. She had taken the wagon wheel from her shop and had it placed outside. Planning to serve Italian

food, she bought red checkered tablecloths and placed a
candle in the center of each table. She wallpapered, and
bought a Tiffany hanging lamp. She had long admired movie
star Hedy Lamarr, who had long, dark tresses. Cynthia thought
it would be in keeping with her Italian theme to also have dark
hair, and so she had it dyed black.

Cynthia hired an Italian woman to help her with the
cooking. She introduced the town to Italian pizza and also
offered homemade ravioli, eggplant parmigiana, and Italian
pastry. She named the restaurant Cyn's Villa, decorating it
with antiques she had saved from her shop. Many Hollywood
stars came to town to entertain. They would dine at her place,
claiming they had seen nothing like it outside of New York.
She made enough profit to pay for their rent and food.

Once Rex was out of the red, he came to her at her business
and took her outside. There stood a new DeSoto. He handed
her the title: It was in her name. Handing her the keys, he said,
"It's all yours and you deserve it." She was terribly pleased.
"Now," he continued, "I want you to start looking for land to
build a house."

She elected to buy property on the bay. The house they
would erect would cost two hundred-thousand dollars. A
princely sum at that time.

Rex was an inventor with numerous patents. Like Edison
he needed little sleep. Cynthia thought he was a genius. He
claimed that once he had had a brain scan at the University
Hospital in Ann Arbor, and they had told him his brain was the
size of Einstein's and that he should will it to science. He was
constantly thinking up new inventions, and their income
became considerable.

After four years, his business was doing so well that he
asked her to give up her restaurant. He said he would sell it for
her, and he did. It was renamed Terry and Jerry's, and still
exists.

Rex himself worked on the new house at night, and
Cynthia frequently went out to the property to visit him. On
one occasion, she watched for a while and then decided to go

fishing. She was all dressed up, but she knew her husband kept some coveralls in the trunk of his car. She opened it and stepped back with a gasp.

Recently, the headlines had shouted the news of a brutal murder in Bay City. Missing from the scene was pair of red slippers. The paper predicted that when the police found the slippers, they would have the killer.

Cynthia reached into the trunk and, from the pile of clothes, picked up a pair of red slippers. She went back to the house and found Rex. Thrusting the slippers before him, she asked in a trembling voice, "Are you the murderer?"

Rex was horrified.

"My God, no. Look Cynthia, you know I had all those trunks of clothes left when my mother died. I've been burning them and just hadn't gotten around to the ones left in my car." Cynthia was relieved and they had a good laugh over it. The next day, the real murderer was found. She never gave the incident another thought.

Their life together was turning out well. They had built a sailboat when they'd lived in Tawas. Now they built a cabin cruiser. They joined the Yacht Club and went to their dances and watched the regattas. Rex continued to be loving to Patrick, which meant everything to her. The couple became very attached. Years went by and life was good.

Cynthia's love for clothing continued, and Rex loved to go with her and his daughters to pick out dresses.

She thought that, at last, her life was turning out well. They had now been married for six years, and she was very happy.

Cynthia and Rex worked hard and long hours, and they looked forward to attending a trailer convention in Chicago, where they would be able to relax and have a little fun. She had bought a new formal and had her hair styled. Cynthia was still extraordinarily beautiful, and Rex was justifiably proud to show her off at the convention dance. Afterwards, he assured her that she had been the belle of the ball.

When they returned home, she decided it was time to let him know how much her feelings had grown for him. She walked over to his armchair, kissed the tiny bald spot on his head, and said, "Rex, I always liked you, but I want you to know this has now turned into love. You are very special to me." She left the room and went into the bathroom to wash her hair and shower.

She was sitting at her dressing table brushing her hair when she heard him give a cough from the doorway. She turned to look and saw him standing there in a bright fuschia nightgown and a black wig. She felt like she had been hit by a baseball bat. She never let on how shocked she was. She thought he had suddenly gone crazy. She got dressed, found Patrick, and fled from the house. As she drove away, she recalled an odd incident that had happened in Chicago. Rex had shopped with her and had said, "You can have all the pretty clothes you want, but you must let me have all the pretty clothes that I want." She had not understood his remark at the time.

Cynthia went to her sister's and blurted out her story. Her sister worked for a doctor, and she took Cynthia to his office. Perhaps not believing her, he gave her sodium pentothal. When Cynthia came out of it, the doctor told her there were many men like Rex. He called them "transvestites" and said for her to forget this and go back home. She later found that the doctor himself was gay.

She did go home, but found that Rex had left with all his belongings.

Cynthia engaged an attorney, who advised her to see a psychiatrist to gain some understanding of the situation. Ignorantly, the doctor warned her that Rex might be a psychopath, and told her to arm herself and shoot to kill if he attacked her or her boy.

This frightened her so badly that she packed up and left for Detroit. It was a very difficult time for her. She had to face the fact that she now was a three-time loser.

Chapter 34

Cynthia contacted her attorney to file for a divorce. In those days, you had to prove your situation was impossible. When the attorney heard what she had discovered, he said the court would want proof. She thought she might know how to find it. Cynthia drove back to Rex's factory. Still having the keys to his car, she opened the trunk and took out his briefcase. Inside, she found money and negatives. She left the money but took the negatives back to Detroit with her.

Sure enough, when they were developed, they showed him posing in his dress and wig outside a trailer. Proof, indeed. She could also show by the age of the trailer windows that he had been like this well before he had married her.

Still, this would not get her a divorce. Rex had to be found in order to serve him with papers. Before they could find him, Rex put their furniture in storage and moved his factories out of state.

Cynthia grew impatient. He was sending no money. She had landed in Detroit with fifty dollars and had to pay rent. She had to have additional money for gas, and she needed a loan. The loan she got from an old friend, Berney Sakosiac, who worked in a nearby bar. She then approached the Boesky brothers for a job in their restaurant.

They hired her eagerly. She was a good worker and a valued employee.

Finding out her circumstances, the brothers asked if she needed money and how much. She told them that luckily money was not a problem, as she had gotten a loan from an old friend.

Cynthia worked and waited for her court date, but she heard nothing. It was frustrating. Gradually she repaid the loan and started to create a new life. She had left Patrick with her mother in Bay City and missed him terribly.

One day at work, she had a terrifying experience. It was Thanksgiving, and she was waiting tables. Her customers wanted cocktails, so she left the dining room to put their order in at the bar. Suddenly, she saw a man come rushing in from the street with a revolver in his hand. She and Abe Boesky saw him at the same time and fled to the walk-in freezer where they kept their pickles, corned beef, and pastrami. They heard a shot and feared to venture out, standing in the freezer shivering together. Some time passed, and finally the cold drove them to the door which they cautiously opened. When they emerged, they found the dead bodies of two of the Purple Gang, including one of the Millman boys. They were questioned by the police but were unable to identify the man with the gun. Cynthia had no idea who the gunman was, and if Abe knew he certainly was not about to tell the police. You left these gangs alone. You knew nothing, and if you did, you told nothing. Another time a gang came in threatening to bomb the place if they did not hire more Negro waitresses.

Time passed and she was no closer to a divorce. After three long years had gone by, she returned to her attorney and told him that something must be done. He threw up his hands and asked her what she would suggest.

Cynthia said, "I want you to go the the judge and have him sign an order for Rex's partner to quit hiding him and produce him for the court. I am married to Rex, so legally he is my property."

The lawyer said, "He'll never sign such a thing."

She said, "How do you know if you don't try?"

He was exasperated, but made out a statement and left for the courthouse.

She waited in his office, and soon he returned. He said in an incredulous voice, "My God, I never heard of such a thing before, but damned if the judge didn't sign."

Within days, in a closed session, she got her divorce, a settlement of almost two-hundred-thousand dollars, and her beautiful home. She remembers the judge in the case trying to hide his amusement when he found that Rex wanted possession of Cynthia's full-length sable coat.

Cynthia now found that people did not believe her story about Rex. Her neighbors even talked of getting up a petition to get her out of their area. They were finally convinced only after she showed them the photos.

Cynthia was now in her forties and still yearning for a stable family life. Poor Patrick missed Rex dreadfully. Rex had been an exceptional and loving father. He had told Patrick from the beginning that he was his daddy, and had had Pat call him that. She realized that her son was missing out on the stability she wanted, too.

Cynthia had known Berney for many years. Her girlfriend Josie had dated him for eighteen years, but she had finally broken up with him because of his terrible jealousy.

Berney not only had made Cynthia a loan when she first hit Detroit after leaving Rex, but also had helped her out when her car had broken down. He would often go to Saginaw to visit his sister and would take Cynthia with him. She was then lent the use of his new car, so she could drive a bit farther and visit her mother and son.

Berney and Josie also had trouble believing her story about Rex, until she showed them his hidden clothes and pictures. They had been guests at her home and had liked Rex very much. Josephine said, "My God, Cynthia, what more can happen to you!"

Berney often took Cynthia to dinner, and he would get tickets to see the Broadway shows that came to Detroit. He now told her that he had never married Josie because, years ago, he had fallen in love with Cynthia herself.

Cynthia thought this over and said to herself, "You'll get over it."

She planned to leave Detroit and go back to her home. She certainly could do without another marriage!

Much to her surprise, Berney quit his job, finding employment in Saginaw just to be near her.

Berney proposed again and again until gradually she began to feel sorry for him, and accepted.

Unfortunately, she had forgotten Josie's words about his jealousy when she agreed to marry him. Josie had moved to California and was not around to remind her.

She married him and swiftly found his jealousy unbelievable.

An old, male friend had only to say hello, and Berney would accuse her of cheating on him. Their phone was on a party line, and if he called and found the line was busy, he would shout at her when he next saw her, accusing her of talking with men over the phone and making dates. His accusations and screaming fits sometimes would last all night and ruin her sleep.

Then, suddenly the harangue would stop and he would want to make love. She would hardly be in the mood.

Once she threw a frying pan at him. It missed and sailed through their picture window. She was glad, for it drove him out of the house. He was absolutely unreasonable.

Again she had made a major mistake. She wondered whether she would ever learn.

This marriage had lasted only six months, and, again, she felt like a failure. She became despondent. Now she would again have to seek a divorce.

Cynthia had many witnesses to support her in the trial, and

she easily won her suit. So once again she had a failed marriage. She was devastated.

About a year later, Cynthia ran into Bill Neary. He had said he wanted to catch her between marriages, and he had! So once more she married, and once again it was destined not to work out.

She rented her home, and they bought a new Cadillac convertible and drove to Las Vegas. They had happy memories of their times together there and thought it was a good place for them to start in. Patrick was now nine years old and thought it was going to be a big adventure.

Bill was hoping for a new start. He had found his job in South America very difficult. The work itself he could handle, but the men were hampered by natives who would try to attack them with poisoned blow darts. Certainly not your usual occupational hazard! He also needed to resolve his feelings about his family. When he had been liberated from the German prison and returned home, he had found his life in a shambles. When he was thought dead, his brother, who was an attorney, had had Bill's inheritance transferred to their sister. When Bill asked for a return of his money, it was refused. His anger was fearful to see, and Cynthia was sympathetic. He had spent four years of his life in a prison camp, living in unspeakable conditions, and to have his homecoming spoiled by the greed of his family was a crowning blow.

Cynthia questioned him about the Stalag where he had been incarcerated. He told her of the conditions and putrid food. His reports to her were chilling. He described in detail the many prisoners who had died of starvation. Eventually, he and others had been marched to another Stalag camp. It had been a death march, and many of these weakened prisoners had fallen or faltered on their way. If they were not found to have already died, they would be shot and left by the roadside. Bill frequently had nightmares and would find sleep difficult, sometimes nearly impossible. Cynthia would be comforting, but clearly this was not enough.

They arrived in Las Vegas and found some real changes.

In Cynthia's absence, a giant structure had been erected: the Flamingo. She was also shocked to see another hotel, the Dunes, partially built on the grounds where her house once stood. Cynthia turned back and looked again at the Dunes. Frank Dio had been right when he had said to invest in that house and property. How foolish she had been to let this investment slip out of her hands.

Cynthia and Bill quickly settled in, renting a house and enrolling Patrick in school. Cynthia found she could not go back to the Frontier, as it had burned to the ground. The new places by now had their own cigarette girls, so that was out. She ran into some of the employees from her first years in town, including the old chef from the Frontier. He told her an amusing story about something that had happened in her absence. He said that the town was buzzing when Bugsy Siegel announced he was going to build the Flamingo. He informed all who asked that he was first going to dig the swimming pool. This sounded like putting the cart before the horse, and the town tittered. They were unaware that the hole would later be filled with bootleg whiskey and partially covered with sand. It would serve as a hidden storage area until the hotel could be built. Cynthia laughed in amusement, but at the same time, her eyebrows rose. She began to suspect for the first time that her friend and protector might have interests not entirely associated with real estate.

Cynthia soon found work waiting tables at the Dunes. Bill was not so fortunate. He tried to find a job as a bartender or waiter, but he had no union card. It was a Catch-22 situation. Without experience, he could not get a card, and without a card, he could not get a job. He was also a C.P.A. but was unable to find a job using his accounting experience. He eventually found work at the Sands—running the big dishwashing machines. This hurt his pride, but it was the only thing available. Cynthia tried to comfort him, but he hated his circumstances and became quite bitter. Life and his troubles began to gang up on Bill, and in frustration he started to drink.

Patrick also had his own troubles. Instead of being a big

adventure, his new life was difficult. Patrick was the new kid in school, and the other kids challenged him, compelling him to fight to defend himself. He was very unhappy. Cynthia soon realized this was not a town in which to rear children. Nor was it a town where Bill could be restored to his former self. She also had a couple of bad experiences that rankled. One evening, she was serving at the table occupied by Frank Sinatra. He was known as bad news, and the maitre d' would cringe when he was coming in. One of the members of Frank's party was Martha Raye. Martha looked at her with a perplexed expression on her face and said, "You look familiar. Don't I know you from somewhere?"

"No," Cynthia replied, keeping her voice even, "I've never seen you before in my life." She took their order for drinks and soon returned. She placed a martini in front of Sinatra, who, for some reason, at the same moment stuck out his hand. His hand collided with the glass, and it fell over, spilling its contents. His face contorted with rage, and he yelled at her.

"You son of a bitch." It was unfair of him to blame her, and she immediately retaliated. Doubling her fist, she smashed Frank Sinatra on the side of the head. The blow was sufficiently hard to knock him off his chair. He jumped up from where he had fallen and went after her with fists of his own. Seeing this altercation, a waiter and the maitre d' rushed over and grabbed him, holding him back from getting to Cynthia and striking her. She fled to the kitchen and hid. Meanwhile, Sinatra's party left in embarrassment, and he soon followed.

Bill and Patrick were decidedly unhappy with their lives. Things were not getting better, and finally after six months, it was agreed it had not worked out. As their money was running thin, they decided to move back to Bay City.

When they had returned, Cynthia asked Bill what he thought of her going back into the restaurant business. She told him of her success with Cyn's Villa and her ideas for a new place, and he seemed enthused. She found an old hotel called the Arlington. It was the oldest in town, and she thought it would serve her purposes. She wrote to Rex, asking for more money from their settlement, and he quickly complied. She met with the owner of the hotel, who seemed very eager to sell. She explained that she lacked enough for the down payment until she sold her house. This interested him, because he said he and his wife would need a home if the hotel sold. Once he saw her lovely place, the deal was struck, and he agreed to accept it in lieu of $250,000. Suddenly she found herself in business.

With her usual enthusiasm, she tackled the tremendous job of renovating this old structure. The building was three stories high and held an assortment of bums who were living there at low rent. It was not her intent to run a flophouse, and she soon gave them notice. She had no intention of fixing up the hotel portion. The building was too old and lacked bathrooms. People now wanted more convenience and more privacy. She did, however, make a suite on the second floor for their own living quarters, and they soon settled in.

Bill found a job working for the railroad, which enabled him to help out at the restaurant in the evenings. Patrick was happy to be back and overjoyed to be reunited with his grandparents. This solved two of their problems right away.

Cynthia had formed a picture of what she wanted, and she proceeded to carry it out. This was a more ambitious venture, and she worked hard to make the place sophisticated and attractive. She started with the walls, putting red flocked wallpaper in the area above the wainscoting. She had dark-red carpeting laid, and the place began to look like her dream. Her theme was Victorian and, she ordered a sign made with the name she had chosen: Diamond Jim's. Again, she brought in her antique plates for decoration.

One day while she was working to complete the renovations, a salesman came in and talked to her. He told her about a place in Chicago that had just gone out of business. He said a grand piano surrounded by a circular bar was for sale. She dropped everything and hurriedly made a trip to obtain this unique combination. She was excited, knowing she was going to have the first piano bar in Bay City.

Cynthia had the bar installed in the lobby, turning it into

a sing-along music hall. She hired a piano player and a drummer. The bar where the actual drinks were prepared was separate, and became an old-time saloon. The word "Saloon" appeared over the entrance to the room. She found an antique sideboard in an anteroom off the barroom. It was left over from the days when women were not allowed in bars, and they sat together, waiting for their husbands. She now had this sideboard placed on the back wall. Next to the restrooms she had a hat-check room. An aisle ran from the barroom to the dining room. Across the big front window she put up a brass rod and hung deep-red drapes. She bought tall bar stools, so people could rest their feet on the old brass railing at the base of the bar.

Her ideas about what food to offer took planning. Gone were the days of spaghetti, pizza, and other Italian dishes. This time, she would offer more elegant fare. They would have, among other choices, oysters Rockefeller, steaks, trout, and lobster.

Years before in that town, there had been a certain Dr. Brown, who had attended to the medical needs of the girls in a house of prostitution. He had greatly admired a painting on the wall of a nude standing by a spring. He had asked the madam whether some day she would leave it to him. The madam had died and, as promised, left it to him. When he in turn died, it went to his daughter, whom Cynthia knew. The woman asked Cynthia whether she would like the painting. She and her husband were schoolteachers, and the community would be shocked if they displayed such a thing. Cynthia was pleased to accept the lovely painting and had it hung prominently above the bar. This put the finishing touch on the place, and when her liquor license came through, she felt that all was ready.

She opened up on New Year's Eve, and so many people came that some had to park as far as four blocks away. She dressed in her most glamorous outfit and acted as hostess. Bill tended bar and acted as host, ushering people to the tables. The evening was everything she had dreamed about: a complete success.

The business went well. Word soon spread about the originality of the place and how much fun it was, and about the excellent food. It soon became very popular, and they attracted more and more customers away from their competitors. These owners eventually got together and raised a complaint with the authorities. They said she should be cited for a misdemeanor because she used the word "saloon" instead of "cocktail lounge." Cynthia fought back and won. It was true that once this would have been against the law, but prohibition was long past, and all the laws in effect at that time were now invalid.

Cynthia jumped up each morning, making sure all was in readiness for the new day. She would get Patrick fed and off to school. He was now settled into a routine and doing well. When he was gone, she worked hard to assure herself that all would go smoothly. Certainly she had the background to know how to run such as operation, but it was new to Bill. She found she could count on him only to make out a list when liquor was needed.

Bill came home from work each night, but more and more often he seemed disturbed and moody. The drinking that had started in Las Vegas continued, and she began to worry. He continued to be despondent about losing his inheritance, and would dwell on the unfairness of it. Cynthia told him it was gone and there was nothing he could do about it. She told him to forget it, but it continued to bother him. Getting fired from his job certainly did nothing to help. He had gotten into a terrific fight with the office secretary, who had accused him of stealing her papers. He told Cynthia that the woman was careless and often sat on the very papers she was looking for. The accusations and fighting continued until the boss finally took the side of the secretary, who had a great deal of seniority. Bill was now without a job. This hardly helped him with his drinking problem, which again escalated. He now filled in more at the bar and restaurant. He had a marvelous singing voice and was in great demand at the music bar. They would clamor for him to join them, but all too often he was rewarded with even more of the drinks that were ruining his life. The drinking continued, and even worsened. Bill would get very drunk, and if he fell, he would let out with a scream. Cynthia could feel sympathy for him, but his drinking was a terrible embarrassment to her. He was often drunk in front of customers, and she feared it would drive them away.

Pat was now another problem. He had grown to love Rex and to think of him as his father, and he greatly missed him. He also resented Bill's strict discipline. Bill would demand military correctness and insist upon being answered with "Yes, sir" and "No, sir." Bill monitored Pat's every waking hour and enforced a tight timetable. But Pat was now in his teens and felt he was being treated as a child. Worst of all, he witnessed Bill's bouts with the bottle and was greatly disgusted.

Cynthia absolutely hated the drinking and tried to talk to Bill about it, but he would brush her aside. She had so wanted this marriage to work, but she felt she was fighting a losing battle. She contemplated divorce, but kept rejecting it. She wanted a home for Pat and some kind of family life. She had four failures to her credit and was reluctant to add another. Now, in her late forties, she needed continuity in her life. The years went by.

When Pat turned fourteen, he was secretly contacted by Rex, who wanted Pat to have his name changed to Anderson. Rex had always considered Pat his son and wanted him to share his name. Surprisingly, Pat went along with this without telling his mother. At the appointed time, he was met by an attorney who took him to court, and the legal change was made. When Cynthia learned of this, she was stunned but managed to take it in her stride. She could hardly offer resistance when the change was already made.

The years continued to pass, and even though Pat had turned into a very responsible young man, Bill kept him on a tight rein.

Cynthia now had another worry. While her restaurant and bar had been doing well, she often found the cash register short. Sometimes there were only small shortages, but more and more often the amounts reached proportions that threatened the existence of the business. Finally, the point came when she was no longer able to meet her payments to the former owner.

Cynthia began to watch the help carefully. It was not unusual to find employees who thought they could augment their pay with a little on the take. She was never able to catch anybody, and eventually the employees themselves reported to her that it was Bill who was the culprit. This was truly alarming, and she worried about how she could stop this. She also wondered just what happened to the money he took. But before she could resolve this, something else came up.

Cynthia had a step-brother named Floyd. He and his wife had twins, and they had called Pat and asked him to babysit for them. Pat was always supposed to be home by nine o'clock. He sat with the children, and when the parents came home, he decided to take his earnings and get a haircut. He stopped at a phone booth to leave word with the barmaid that he would be late. The barmaid forgot to pass on the message. Nine o'clock came and went, and no Pat. This sent Bill into a towering rage. He had, as usual, been drinking, and he stormed to Cynthia, his voice rising into screams. He threatened to give Pat a beating when he returned, and she believed him. He had obviously had a great deal to drink that night, and she was unable to calm him. His raving continued unabated and his threats mounted, becoming increasingly frightening. She finally had had enough. She raised their heavy phone and repeatedly brought it down on his head until he dropped. He was bleeding and begging her to call an ambulance, but she refused, saying, "I wouldn't lift a finger to help you, you bastard." She discarded the phone, which was broken into pieces, and left. Bill crawled down the stairs to find another phone with which to get help. Shortly, an ambulance took him away. He remained in the hospital for two weeks, recovering from a severe concussion, and when he returned, she made him clear out.

This was absolutely the end, and she sought a divorce. She went to the law offices of Bill Hellerman and Bob Traxler. Bob would later become a United States Congressman and would help her when she had a difficult problem, but these were his early days, before he entered the political arena. Bill Hellerman took the case, as he had when she had divorced

Rex. He became sympathetic over her troubles. She told him she faced losing her business because her husband had stolen from her. Even her certificates showing investments in a Canadian gold mine had been taken. She wondered how she could manage, with a boy to support and see through school. Bill offered to lend her the money to keep going, and she eagerly accepted his help.

Armed with this money, she felt renewed hope that she could make a go of it. It was a struggle; her payments were huge, and she was far behind. Cynthia worked hard, trying to manage on her own and to regain the lost ground. The former owner had at first been understanding, but as time went by he began to press her for money. She was making headway, but it was slow going. She struggled on for three more years but could never see more than a glimmer of light at the end of the tunnel.

Pat had turned seventeen and suddenly announced that he was getting married. Cynthia was opposed and, in vain, used every argument she could think of. She was not unhappy with his choice, but she thought him far too young. She cited her own mistakes in taking such a major step while still in her teens. She even dragged up his grandmother's similar mistake, but Pat remained firm. He was in love and could see no sense in waiting. His urgency made her unhappy, but she eventually gave in. Pat got married and, suddenly, she found herself alone once more.

Cynthia stood before a judge and listened as she was granted yet another divorce. It would be many years before she found out the whole story about her failed fifth marriage. She was sorting through some old papers, throwing out the ones that were no longer important or useful. Bill was an accountant, so she had always had him fill out their income tax statement. She came upon one of these forms and began reading through it. She had felt only casual interest until she saw the line indicating the name of the spouse, and the name was not hers! Dear God, he was a bigamist! She also found that he had returned to this woman, and that the money he had stolen from the business he had been sending to New York, to an account of his own. Cynthia now suspected that he had also stolen the lovely ring given to her by Bugsy Siegel. She had thought previously that it had been taken by a housekeeper.

Cynthia talked to her mother one day about all her failures, and Eunice brought up the fact that both Turk and Bill had had wonderful singing voices. Her mother commented, "Well, Cynthia, I hope that's the end of your songbirds."

Chapter 35

Cynthia had spent many of her early years in Bay City. Over the years she had kept in touch with her old friend Dorothy Avis, and she was able to watch the rise to success of Dorothy's brother Warren.

Warren started his career when he returned a hero from the Second World War. He had flown into Bay City and found no transportation—not even buses. The seed of an idea formed in his mind. Over the next few years it would eventually sprout and blossom.

He and his mother were very close. They had rented a building and started a short-order lunch counter, where Warren cooked the hamburgers and his mother made the pies. Once that business was making money, he started buying used cars and repairing them behind his mother's house. With these cars he started the Avis Rent-A-Car company in Bay City. His success was phenomenal, and eventually he was able to buy new cars to rent out. He then branched out to Flint and Detroit, and over the years, he acquired car rentals in all the major cities. Not content with just rentals, he started a Ford dealership in Detroit, with a used-car lot that covered two city blocks!

I went to his dealership one day to have my car repaired. I talked to the mechanic, and he asked me if I knew Mr. Avis. I told him I had grown up knowing the whole family and that his sister Dorothy was my best friend.

He said, "Well I can tell you he is one grand man. My wife was in the hospital last Christmas. She was very sick, and we had big hospital and doctor bills. Believe me, there was going to be no Christmas for my kids. It would not be a special time for us, just me working here in the garage, trying to earn enough to pay those bills off.

"Well, much to my surprise, Mr. Avis went and paid all those bills for me. Not only that, but he sent food to the house and gifts for our children! Can you believe that? I can't begin to tell you what it meant to me. Here I had this sick wife and no money to buy the kids a stinkin' thing, and Christmas coming."

While he worked on my car, I stood listening to him as he continued. He told me about all the young people Warren had put through college, kids who would have never been able to pay the tuition. He said this was not the end of those kids either. "He has a farm up near Ann Arbor. On Sundays you should see all those kids show up for a big barbecue. Some were all grown up, and Warren would tell them to bring all their wives and kids if they had them, too. I can tell you he is the most generous man I have ever known."

I wasn't surprised. Warren had always stood for kindness and generosity.

The mechanic did tell me something new about Warren. He had a guest house at the farm, and would have about a dozen people at a time, with opposing views, stay there for seminars. The purpose was to give them a perspective other than their own.

Typical was the meeting between the New York City Chief of Police and a group of prisoners, who would spend their days comparing viewpoints. He said Warren had even had someone come from Russia, and, in turn, had sent someone there for this same purpose.

He said Mr. Avis thought there was some good in everyone, and if we could just hear them out, we could all live in peace.

I told the mechanic a story I had heard. During the war his captain had his plane shot down. The captain miraculously survived, and when he returned home, Warren invited the captain and his family to his hotel in Bimini, at Warren's own expense.

We agreed he was a great man. The mechanic was finished, and I left.

Dorothy Avis came to see Cynthia. She found her friend very depressed over her latest divorce and her financial worries. Try as she would, Cynthia still continued to be far behind in her payments. It was a constant worry, and she was unable to figure out how she could finally recover. Knowing that Warren bought real estate, she asked Dorothy whether she thought he might be interested in buying her business. She knew it had been very profitable, and still was. It was just that Bill had stolen so much from her, she could never hope to make it all up. Dorothy said she would ask him, and thought it very likely he would be quite interested.

Dorothy came again, telling her that Warren did indeed want to buy her business and in the meantime wanted to treat her to a vacation. Dorothy asked whether Cynthia would drive her and her mother to Fort Lauderdale, Florida. Her brother owned two hotels on Bimini in the Bahamas. They could all then take a plane from Florida and have a vacation with Warren. All expenses would be paid by her brother.

Cynthia lost no time in accepting. A vacation? Just what she needed. She had no one to run the business while she was gone, so she gave her employees notice, had her antiques stored, and packed her bags. She felt nothing but relief when she turned the key in the lock and left.

Cynthia picked up the women and they proceeded on to Bimini.

They stayed in a suite at one of the two hotels that Warren owned. The island had lovely beaches, or you could swim in the big indoor swimming pool.

Days passed, and Cynthia wondered why Warren never said anything about purchasing her property. Twice she started to ask him, only to have Dorothy interrupt her by asking her brother a question and then taking him off somewhere. Finally came the realization that Dorothy had never brought the matter up with Warren at all. She had wanted Cynthia to drive them on this trip, and had lied to make sure it was possible. This conclusion Cynthia felt was obvious, and she was appalled. Cynthia knew the last due date for the money would soon come, and the former owner would foreclose. Warren was always so darn busy, but she was determined to seek him out. If Dorothy tried to interrupt or interfere, she would object and force Warren to listen.

She woke up the next morning and hurriedly dressed. She swiftly searched for him, but he didn't seem to be in his usual places. Her heels tapping in the halls were matched by the beating of her heart. Finally, upon inquiry she was shocked to find he was out of the country. It must have been a sudden decision, because she had heard nothing about a proposed trip. She found out from his mother that he had gone to France, but the woman didn't seem to know when he would return or how to get hold of him.

Cynthia worried about what to do and kept hoping he would come back. The dreaded deadline eventually came and passed, and she now knew that her place was lost.

Cynthia brooded over this, and her anger at Dorothy was difficult to conceal. Warren returned at last, and she found it hard to keep her mouth shut. It was tempting to confront Dorothy in front of her brother, but she realized that this would not do her any good. It was too late to save her building, and telling on Dorothy would only cause an ugly scene. After all, she was a guest. She found it hard to accept that, after their long friendship, Dorothy could do this to her. All she had worked so hard for and all the money she had invested would go down the drain. She had lost her home, her restaurant, and her settlement from Rex, altogether eight hundred and fifty thousand dollars. She thought again about exposing Dorothy, and finally rejected it. She loved their mother too much. This woman had been extraordinarily kind to Cynthia, telling her to call her "Mama" when her own mother had been so cruel. How could Cynthia hurt her by telling on Dorothy? She unhappily concluded that she would just have to forget it, and get on with her life.

I never brought it up, and somehow managed to put a good face on it. It did help to be in such lovely surroundings with "Mama" and Warren. I lived in this heaven for four months, playing the part of Warren's hostess, meeting his guests, and seeing to their comforts.

I met so many people. Some I found interesting and some I didn't care for. I was never keen on the fake ones who would try to put on the dog. All in all, however, I enjoyed my visit there very much.

I met the fabulously wealthy Princess Satilis from Greece. She had homes in Athens, Paris, Milan, New York, Geneva, and Alexandria. The Princess was very clever and talented, and she designed beautiful and costly jewelry. The pieces were gorgeous. I still have her catalogue and marvel to this day at her creativity.

We struck up such a friendship that she gave me all her addresses and phone numbers and asked me to come and visit her. A wonderful offer, but I never had the money for passage over there.

Warren loved his sister, but his money had gone to her head. She went on spending sprees that made my own habits seem tame. I watched her one day buy twenty-seven watches so she could have leather straps in that many colors to match her outfits.

She would go to the stores and shop for her daughter, completely furnishing her home. She bought her everything she would need. She ordered custom-made drapes, picked out carpeting and bought all her furniture—even a sewing machine, and charged it all to her brother.

Cynthia also helped Warren with his mother, Lottie, who was suffering after cutting her leg on a conch shell. Lottie was in pain and could not get around. Cynthia tended her just as if she were a nurse, helping Lottie out and running errands for her.

Warren was appreciative and generous. He was always asking Cynthia whether she needed money. He would hand her his wallet and tell her to take out what she wanted. She would always refuse, and then he would extract some bills himself and hand them to her. It was nothing for her to find five hundred dollars in her hand. She would object, telling him it was too much, but he would shake his head and insist she take it. He would do the same for his mother, who in turn would give the money to Dorothy. Cynthia privately thought that her mother had taught her to be greedy.

When they returned to Michigan, Warren and his mother asked Cynthia to stay with them permanently. He had an apartment near the Ambassador Bridge and a lovely dark-red brick home at what they called simply The Farm. The house was really a chateau designed by a French architect. The property had stables for the horses, tennis courts, and a helicopter landing pad.

They alternated among living at his Detroit apartment, Bimini, and The Farm. It was a good life, and Cynthia was grateful to be with these good friends and have it so easy. Once, at the chateau, she was introduced to the king of Denmark, King Christian X. He had bowed to her and kissed her hand. Quite a thrill for a gal who grew up in the boonies of northern Michigan.

Once, in Bimini, she and Warren had gotten in a small argument. He said to her, "If you don't shut that pretty mouth of yours, I'll never marry you."

She answered, "What makes you think I would ever marry you?"

He said, "Oh, you'll come around."

I never answered him, and he never mentioned marriage again. The truth was that I was scared. I had made many mistakes in the past, and found it hard to trust my own judgment anymore. Coupled with this was the fact that Warren was constantly being chased by women. This was not surprising, as he was very rich, extremely intelligent, and very handsome—certainly an unbeatable combination. I honestly felt I would not be able to handle this, because I was certain that his being married would not stop the women from seeking him and trying to push me out. The price was just too great.

One year, Warren announced that he wanted to give his mother and Cynthia a very generous Christmas present. he was going to pay their way to Hawaii! This was truly exciting. They were going to drive to the West Coast, then sail to the islands. It was wonderful of Warren to include Cynthia, but also a necessity, as his mother had come to depend on Cynthia for help. She had some time earlier fallen down the basement steps and broken both hips. She now walked with two canes, and needed a competent companion to help her.

They set off in Cynthia's Cadillac for the long trip. On their way, news came over the radio about a huge tidal wave that had hit the Hawaiian Islands, causing much destruction and loss of life. This shook Lottie up so badly that she said she would not feel safe going over there. So they changed their plans, canceled the ship reservations, and decided to just sightsee in California.

Lottie had Warren's expense money and was extremely tight with it. The only food she bought was cookies and orange juice, sold cheaply at roadside stands, to eat on the way. She could not see why Cynthia would want anything more than this to eat. Clearly she should be satisfied, and Lottie told her so. Cynthia hated to make a fuss, so she called Dorothy and asked her what to do. Dorothy told her to spend her own money, that Warren would repay her when they returned.

They drove to San Diego to visit with the Arnolds, whom they knew from Bay City and who now owned Arnolds Bakery. Cynthia and Lottie stayed with them for a month. During their stay, they all went up a glass elevator that ran on the outside of a building to a nightclub that offered a view of the city. They found it hard not to panic when the elevator got stuck, stranding them inside for three hours. Eventually the mechanism returned to working order, and they escaped. It was not a good beginning for the fun-filled evening they had planned.

The two women traveled around California, and eventually Cynthia ran out of her own money. She knew she could expect no help from Lottie. If there was any money left from the trip, she knew it would wind up in Dorothy's pocket.

Cynthia knew that Rex lived in California, and he still owed her some money from the divorce settlement. She called him, telling him of her plight. He invited her over, saying he would help her out. She left Lottie in the car, and Rex greeted her with real feeling, telling her he missed her and sure missed Patrick. He was dressed in slacks and a silk shirt. He invited her to sit down, and she did, explaining that she could only stay a minute as she had left someone waiting in the car. She noted that his shirt was well filled-out and asked him whether he was wearing falsies. He smiled and denied this, telling her to come over and feel them, because he had had silicone implants. Cynthia got up and felt his chest. Sure enough, they felt like the real thing. She noted that he had gotten them made unusually large and wondered what would drive him to take such drastic measures.

After three months, the women decided to go home. They had seen all the sights and were getting a bit tired of traveling. Lottie wanted to see President Truman's birthplace, so they decided to take this in on the way home. Much to their horror as they were driving through Kansas, they saw the funnel of a tornado. They paused only long enough to see in which direction it was going, then Cynthia stepped on the gas, driving furiously in the opposite direction. They were terrified as they sped down the highway, and they sighed with relief when the funnel disappeared.

Soon after they got back, Warren called from France. He asked them to drive to Newport, Rhode Island, to join him while he attended the ceremony for Warren Jr., who was graduating from Brown University. They were in Bay City, and Cynthia drove straight through, going without sleep. When Warren met them and learned of this, he became quite angry and told Cynthia how foolish this was, and what a chance she had taken.

They took in the graduation and were then to stop and see friends of Lottie's who lived in Wilkes Barre, Pennsylvania. They arrived, only to find that the people had gone to Florida. They drove on for a short distance and stopped at a motel. For some reason, neither of them could sleep. Cynthia was nervous about the long drive back, and soon they packed up and left. Later they learned that a terrible flood had swept through the town that night. They also learned that the very motel where they stayed had completely disappeared.

The women agreed that there were just too many close calls in this one trip. First was the fright of the elevator, then the tornado, and now a flood. It was time to get home.

Patrick was now living in St. Petersburg, Florida. Cynthia missed him very much and decided to move south to be near him. Patrick and Darby were expecting their first child, and Cynthia was eager for it to be born, so she could see it and hold it. Patrick was going to school, and he worked part-time at a restaurant called the Careless Navigator. It was built like a sailing ship and was very elegant.

Cynthia quickly found work herself at another restaurant, the Lighthouse. The owner had conceived the idea of building it out over the water, on pilings.

Soon Darby had her baby—a boy. They named him Rex, and Cynthia was delighted that she had moved so she could hold her grandchild. She was now close to fifty and enjoying her new role. When Darby wanted to take the baby back to Michigan for a visit with her people, Cynthia offered to drive her there. She also wanted to see her people. The trip was uneventful but satisfying. On their way back, they drove through Pennsylvania. Cynthia decided to look up Rex's business paartner, Wayne Miller, and his wife. She especially liked the wife and did not want to lose touch with these people. They had a pleasant visit and drove on to Florida.

Months later, Wayne and his wife visited Florida and invited her to go out to dinner with them. They had decided to go to the Five O'clock Club, because Lena Horne was featured. The evening went well and they were enjoying themselves when, suddenly, Wayne excused himself. Cynthia thought nothing of this, as she had also excused herself earlier to go to the ladies' room. What a shock, then, to see Wayne returning with Martha Raye on his arm. Smiling, he said, "Here's an old friend who wants to see you." Cynthia rose with a face of stone and abruptly left. She returned to her apartment and stamped out her anger. How dare he pull such a stunt! Why in hell would he think she would want to see Martha? Did he think they would all sit around and have a nice chat? Did he think she would smile and ask Martha-dear how she was doing, and how her daughter Melodye, that she had had by Turk, was doing? Cynthia was outraged. Later, she found out that Martha was the owner of the club. Cynthia wondered whether Wayne had deliberately chosen that place to eat, hoping for a confrontation between the two women.

Cynthia stayed in Florida for three years and continued to work at the Lighthouse, until the place was lost forever. A hurricane came with such force that it broke the pilings supporting the structure. The chef swiftly anticipated what was going to happen and grabbed Cynthia. He thrust her up and out of the building, seconds before it collapsed into the sea. She was thoroughly frightened, but uninjured. She struggled the half-mile to her apartment, which fortunately had suffered little damage. Still shaking over her close call, she decided then and there that she had had enough of Florida. She was lonely, living by herself. Patrick and Darby had their own lives to live, and she missed her old friends and Michigan's changing seasons. It was time to make a change.

Back in Michigan, she immediately found work and an apartment. Her landlady's name was Jane, and they became good friends. Jane's father was a well-known attorney in Tawas City, so they had a common background. After work each day, they would get together and chat.

It was a surprise, then, one day to have Jane pound on her apartment door and enter in hysterics. Cynthia tried to calm her down and make sense of her wild story. Jane was shaking so hard and was obviously so frightened that it took some time for anything she said to make sense. Gradually Cynthia began to grasp the facts. Jane owned a company on Main Street in the community of Del Ray. Her company dealt in the repair of garbage trucks.

She had been in her office, when several of her workmen appeared before her, white-faced and shaking. Their outburst over what they had discovered quickly transferred their shock to her. They had taken a truck in for repair, because the driver said the grinding mechanism had gotten stuck and he had had to discontinue his route. They opened up the truck to see what had cause the difficulty, only to be confronted by the sight of a human head.

Jane's first reaction was to distance herself immediately from this horror. In a strangled voice, she told the men she would handle it and not to say a word until she got back. She flew to the arms of her sensible friend, knowing that Cynthia would tell her what to do. Cynthia quickly assessed the situation.

Jane was raving on and on, and finally Cynthia shouted at her to get her attention. She told Jane that it was common knowledge that trucking companies were mob-controlled. She reminded Jan about the barmaid down-river who had disappeared after she had run her mouth about union money being spent by Jimmy Hoffa. Hoffa had been having a causeway built over to Florida's Paradise Island, to provide easy access to a new luxury motel. Hoffa had planned to use union money to build a subdivision there, and the causeway was crucial. The barmaid had overheard some of the mobsters talking about Hoffa in a restaurant, saying that when the Teamsters learned about his use of their money, his life "wouldn't be worth a nickel!" The girl had made the mistake of repeating what she had heard, and the union men had been furious when this story had gotten out. The barmaid had later been found murdered, her body burned in a bonfire.

Cynthia reminded Jane that she had two small children to worry about. She said, "You don't know anything, and those men at your factory don't want to know anything, either. If they value their lives and the lives of their families, they will forget this whole thing."

She told Jane to bathe her face in cold water, try to get control over herself, return as quickly as possible to those men, and forcefully get the message across. They were to proceed normally: open up the garbage truck, bag up the garbage—including the head and body—and send it to Slag Island to be burned.

This was at a time when fear of the mob in the Detroit area was at its height.

Jane's reaction was not just repulsion at the sight of the grisly chewed remains, but also total fear over what the discovery really meant.

She took her friend's advice. When her shaking had somewhat abated, she returned to her shop and asked the men to come to her office. She carefully looked each one in the face and warned them against talking about the incident. She told them about the barmaid who had been murdered for running her mouth. She felt sure that this was mob-related and that they had better quickly forget everything about what had occurred that day. The men readily agreed with her, and that was the end of it.

She now started dating Bill Kofender, the manager of the Detroit Race Track.

One day I saw in the newspaper that Turk was back in Detroit and appearing in one of the clubs. Bill told me not to see him, and I said, "Why, I wouldn't go across the street to ever see him again." With that, I left him and rushed right to the phone to call Turk. The paper said he was appearing at the Hourglass on Seven Mile Road. He was back working as an emcee and singing. That sounded as if he was no longer working as Martha's manager.

I called him at work. He sounded very excited and said, "Baby, come right over." I agreed to meet him at his club. I was working in Wyandotte at the time, as a night hostess at Sibley Gardens. I called the day hostess and asked her if she would also work my shift. She was delighted to earn the extra money and said she would take my place.

I lost no time getting to the Hourglass. Turk rushed to the door when he saw me, and hugged and kissed me. We were obviously glad to see each other. I had tried hard to get him out of my mind, but hidden away was my old love for him, and it returned in full force. Obviously, he, too, hadn't forgotten what we had meant to one another, and he told me he still loved me. I knew Turk had married again after our divorce, and I asked him if they were still married. Turk said he had found out too late that she was an alcoholic. She became mentally ill, and he had filed for divorce, but a judge in Detroit refused to grant it because of her condition. Turk said she was confined to an institution but was dying, and that he wanted me to go back with him to California. I refused, but said when she actually did die, I would return to him.

I went after work each night to his club for the entire two weeks that he worked. I would sit and listen to him work as an emcee. Then he would sing a song he had written years before for me, called, "I Love You." It was his "sign-off" song, and he would look directly at me the entire time he was singing.

I hated to see our time together end. When his job was

finished, I went with him to the train station to say good-bye.
He promised to call me as soon as the funeral was over. We
kissed good-bye, but somehow a terrible premonition came
over me that this was not going to happen.

I had told Turk I would be eager to get his call, but when
it came, it was not what I had expected. He had returned to
California and, as expected, his wife died. Then, Turk's
mother died a short time later. He was faced with two funerals,
and it all proved just too much for him—he had a massive
stroke. Turk called me from the hospital and said he needed
money for the doctor and hospital. I went to a bank in
Wyandotte and borrowed the money he needed. I sent him a
thousand dollars and waited to hear from him again. My wait
was in vain, and I finally called the hospital. He had been
discharged but had left no forwarding address. I couldn't
understand why he hadn't called to thank me for the money
and to tell me to come out. I wondered if he had had a change
of heart about me, and I was devastated. I knew he didn't have
my address, but I kept hoping the phone would ring. It never
did.

I worked and gradually paid off the bank, but then devel-
oped severe bronchitis. I had been plagued with lung prob-
lems for years, but this time it was so serious I knew I needed
help. My sister, Gladys, was living up north, and I called her.
She told me to pack up my belongings, quit my job, and move
up north where she could take care of me. I was a long time
clearing up my bronchial tubes; my illness kept recurring and
I was unable to work. I was now well in my sixties, anyway, and
probably would have found it difficult to even get a job.

Six years passed. One day the phone rang and, unbeliev-
ably, it was Turk! I was stunned when I heard his story. When
he was discharged from the hospital, his secretary, Shirley,
took him to her apartment to take care of him. She nursed him
back to health, and he continued to live there. I found she took
care of his mail, and that she had never told him about the one
thousand dollars I had sent him! When he was discharged, she
didn't give her address to the hospital, thus neatly cutting me

out of his life. He was shocked to find I had sent the money and that she had taken it.

I asked him how in the world he had found me, and he said, "Your sister, Gladys, has an unusual last name. D'Arcy is far from common. I simply got out a map of Michigan and started calling information, giving town after town until I found her. Just now I called her, and she gave me your phone number."

I was so damned glad to hear from him. I wondered why he still stayed with the secretary, and he said she had been so good to him that he just couldn't walk away. He said Shirley was in love with the glamour of his career, and that was why she had made him so indebted to her. I sadly realized she was thoroughly entrenched, so once more Turk was lost from my life.

Chapter 36

I look back over the events of my life and relive them over and over. Grandfather would have been proud of me if he had known of my courage in working with the F.B.I. He had instilled in me a real sense of pride in flag and country.

Some of my memories are still terribly painful. I still think of my dreadful childhood, and of Denelda and Durwood. I still think of the tragedy of Jerry Rothenberg. The recent death from leukemia of my darling child, Patrick, breaks my heart. But my mind dwells most often on Turk.

I loved Turk so very much. I still love him. How could I possibly have left him? Why did I foolishly ever give him up? Why didn't I fight harder to hold onto him? Why didn't I do absolutely anything to keep him in my life? Why? Why?

We would have been such a comfort to each other as we grew older. We would have shared such happy times and memories. Oh, we would have fought at times, too. I would probably remind him about Martha, and there would be bitter words. But then I would have had the warmth of his body and the joy of his arms embracing me in our bed, and I would be comforted, knowing I was loved.

Epilogue

In preparing this book, I contacted Durwood's relatives in Kentucky, hoping for a picture of him. Much to my amazement, I found that Durwood was not the man who had hanged himself. Perhaps the police reporter mistook his notes, and Durwood was only one of the policeman who arrived at the scene. Apparently, Durwood gave up on Cynthia and left the police force at the same time that she was told of his death. Durwood did divorce Mary, and got married again, happily.

He was hauling lumber for a living. One night, in a motel in Oklahoma, he was preparing for bed. Taking off his shoe, he suddenly lost his balance. He fell backwards, hitting the headboard of the bed with his head and shoulders. The force was so great that it made an imprint on his body. The shock proved too much for his system, and he had a heart attack and died.

Turk came to Michigan three times to see Cynthia. He came

the last time to have me start his own biography. His life was well worth recording. You will remember that he had grown up with the Purple Gang and Jimmy Hoffa as neighbors. His friendship with Jimmy lasted throughout Hoffa's life. Turk knew most of the well-known gangsters through his position as a nightclub owner, because that is where these men would hang out.

Turk would write, and I would pick up his material and work on it. Cynthia, fortunately, lives only twenty miles from my home. I would return with questions, and he would go into more detail for me. This went on for the better part of two weeks. I was disturbed to find his health precarious at best. Each day that he was here, he became increasingly ill.

Finally he decided to return to Los Angeles. He never flew, and planned to take the Pullman back. Cynthia and I could see his weakened condition, and we begged him to go to the hospital first and get "built up" for the trip. No amount of persuasion did any good, and he refused. The day before he left, I drove down to say good-bye. I found him lying on Cynthia's couch having chest pains. A nurse was with him. He was still insisting on returning the next day to Los Angeles. The nurse, in desperation, got the name of Turk's doctor in Los Angeles and called him, to describe Turk's condition. She also told him of Turk's determination to return to California. The doctor knew Turk well. He had found him extremely stubborn and said to forget about trying to talk him into a hospital stay. After this call the nurse gave up, and eventually, so did Cynthia and I.

He left the next morning and boarded the train in Detroit. He made it as far as Chicago, where he suffered a massive heart attack. They rushed him off the train, and an ambulance rushed him to the nearest hospital, but it was too late. He was dead on arrival.

Cynthia was devastated. Within the same year, she had already had to face the loss of her only child. Now she had to accept the final loss of her precious Turk.

Despite all this, she would go on. She would simply have to tough it out, as she had always done in the past. Cynthia was, after all, a survivor.